Walking Man

THE ELECTRONIC PILGRIM

Joe Randazzo

A Sprezzatura Book

from New Renaissance Press

Sprezzatura Books
New Renaissance Press
8 Woodside Drive
South Burlington, VT 05403

ISBN 9780970827975
Library of Congress Control Number   2010905487

Front and back covers and author's photograph: Chris Koch

Dedicated to:

Rita Randazzo
My traveling companion

Also by Joe Randazzo

ADVANCE COMMENTS ABOUT *WALKING MAN*

Mr. Randazzo has captured the very essence of the people who made this country great.
Thomas Jefferson

Walking Man has given people a sane alternative to the madness that passes for daily life.
Sigmund Freud

To read Randazzo's *Walking Man* is to enter the bizarre and disgusting world of a depraved lunatic.
Benito Mussolini

Mr. Randazzo's people are not my people.
William H. Vanderbilt

David Hall is as real to me as Prince Myshkin.
Fyodor Dostoyevsky

Why is it that every mediocre writer tries to pen a coming-of-age story that is but a thinly disguised autobiography? Perhaps you should live your own life before you write poorly about someone else's, Mr. Randazzo.
Ernest Hemingway

David Hall is very sexy. His creator, Joe Randazzo, must also be very sexy.
Marilyn Monroe

I don't want people to get the wrong idea. A little bit of freedom is fine, but if the average American begins to feel empowered, like David Hall does in this book, it could cause an upheaval that threatens our very democracy.
Joe McCarthy

I just love the nude debate between Sarah Palin and Hillary Clinton in chapter three. David Hall was in the right place, at the right time, to hear that. This is political commentary the way it should be written.
Eleanor Roosevelt

The author's motivations are obfuscating. His didactic diatribes are immature and counterintuitive to the main points he was trying to make. I was left confused, not knowing what the author really believes.
William F. Buckley

Another beautiful riff by a soul brother. This is the real America.
Dizzy Gillespie

PROLOGUE

Who in his right mind would want to walk from Burlington, Vermont to Aberdeen, Washington? My name is David Hall, and this book is the story of my journey across the United States. I leave tomorrow morning, April 15th, and will arrive on the West Coast God knows when. My father also made this trip, his father made it, and my great-grandfather made it. Madness must run in the family. Last month my father challenged me on his deathbed to repeat their journey, and gave me a damned map.

I'm 29 years old and sometime on this walk-a-thon, September 11th, to be exact, I will turn thirty, and it has totally bummed me out. Yeah, I know, my birthday falls on the same day the Saudi Arabians bombed the World Trade Center. Fuck them, it's also my birthday, and turning 30 will be like a bomb going off inside my head. Thirty is right on the edge of middle age. I'm still young, strong, with incredible endurance, but I'm old enough to have had experiences that no nineteen-year-old could ever dream of. My adolescence was painful (isn't everybody's; I don't expect sympathy from you on this point), and I'm not even going to guess what I will feel like at 59.

David Hall is such a simple name. My ancestors came from England, Scotland, Germany, Italy, Russia, French Canada, and Jamaica in the West Indies. In my high school, here in South Burlington, Vermont, I was always the one with the most countries represented in his lineage. Since I am of "mixed blood," as the morons would define me, I am

1

darker than the average Anglo. Fellow students called me Heinz 57. Screw them in their ethnic purity. I went to the University of Vermont on a track scholarship, and for three years I ran NCAA cross-country. To my father's dismay, I majored in art, English, and music. I didn't minor in anything and had enough credits in all three fields to earn a BA in each.

I'm six feet two, one hundred and eighty-five pounds, and to be perfectly honest, my ears are too large for my face, and my legs are too long for my body. I have a size fourteen foot and blue eyes, which are rare for someone of my dark complexion. No more descriptive personal details are necessary at this time. You will learn more as time goes by.

There are five children in my family. Age-wise, I'm in the middle, and I'm also the darkest. My two brothers and two sisters can all easily pass for white. I can't. My mother's grandfather was from Jamaica. Looks like the gene skipped a generation before choosing me. My father met my mother in Euclid, Ohio during *his* cross-country walk. He continued on to Washington State, but later came back for her by train and carried her off to Vermont.

After they were married she told him about her mixed-race ancestry. He never seemed too upset about it, at least not outwardly. He treated all his children with the same contempt, very balanced and fair mistreatment. Everyone called my father Papa Jack. His father was known as Grandpapa Bill. Grandpapa Bill's father, my great-grandfather, was named Sam Hall. Nothing too difficult to spell here: Jack Hall, Bill Hall, Sam Hall. (There's a great song titled *Sam Hall* that I'll tell you about later.)

YEAR OF WALK	AGE	BORN	RELATIONSHIP	DIED	AGE AT DEATH
1933	39	1894	Great-grandfather Sam Hall	1957	63

CAUSE OF DEATH: motorcycle accident

YEAR OF WALK	AGE	BORN	RELATIONSHIP	DIED	AGE AT DEATH
1955	31	1924	Grandfather Bill Hall	1998	74

CAUSE OF DEATH: hit by delivery truck

YEAR OF WALK	AGE	BORN	RELATIONSHIP	DIED	AGE AT DEATH
1974	30	1944	Papa Jack Hall	2009	65

CAUSE OF DEATH: auto wreck

YEAR OF WALK	AGE	BORN	RELATIONSHIP
2009	29	1980	David Hall

CAUSE OF DEATH: hopefully we won't know that anytime soon

The above chart shows the year that each patriarch of my family walked across the United States, their age at the time, plus some other stats. Notice something interesting about the men in my family. None of them died of natural causes. They were all killed in some kind of road mishap, and they were all drunk at the time. I must admit that I feel strange walking alongside the road under these circumstances. I don't want you to read at the end of the fourth line, David Hall, died 2009, hit by a slow-reacting dullard driving a Toyota Camry. A pea-green Toyota Camry. A guy with thick glasses who was blabbing on his cellphone, as he rounded a corner in Smugsburg, Ohio. At least I have something going for me that they didn't have. I don't drink alcohol to excess or use drugs, never have and never will.

I bought a Korg MR-1 digital recorder and will be giving you an ongoing narrative. I will also record whoever interests me on my journey. I bought two (one as a spare) super-sensitive lapel microphones, the kind broadcasters and performers use. I run the wire under my shirt and into the pack where the recorder is. It's completely invisible and leaves both hands free. All I have to do is reach into the pack and turn on the recorder. It's an omni-directional mike that will pick up any sounds in a normal room. I decided not to tell the people I'm talking to that it's on, unless it's a formal interview, in which case I'll just unplug the lapel mike and use the built-in recorder mike. Yes, it is sneaky, but I'll get much better stuff with the mike hidden.

At the end of each day I will make an entry into my blog, which for those of you who have been locked away for a decade or two, means *web log*. Since this book will be written after the trip, there's no sense in giving you the URL. The blog itself will be reproduced on these pages.

It's now 9:00 p.m. on Sunday night, and tomorrow morning the trip begins. There are so many reasons why I'm making this journey, and I'll tell you all about them as we go. On his deathbed, my father told me he loved me. I was very upset because if you had observed our family for the last 29 years, you would have reached the exact opposite conclusion. I asked my mother why he didn't leave me one dime, even though he left tidy sums to her and to my brothers and sisters. It seems that most of his fortune is still unaccounted for, and wasn't mentioned in the legal documents the attorneys read after his death. My mother insists she knows nothing.

Instead Papa Jack gave me a map. There are specific instructions I am to carry out in each of ten places. I have no idea when he created this list, but it must have been fairly recently. It was done on a modern laser computer printer. My oldest sister said that I will look like an idiot going on an Easter egg hunt. She never misses an opportunity to say something nasty. So, here's what's going down.

Papa Jack died one month ago, and he dared me to walk across the country like he had done in 1974. "That's the only way you are going to learn anything about yourself," he said. "Travel with whatever you can carry on your back. Go from one side of the country to the other. You don't have a hair on your ass if you accept a ride from anybody. That is forbidden. I don't care if you have a blister the size of a golf ball on your foot, you keep going." Three minutes after he said, "You keep going," my father was dead. Quite frankly, I think he was nuts. I miss him, but he was certifiable.

He didn't talk much about his travels, but there is some lasting evidence of his journey. He had a beautifully made miniature 35mm camera called a Tessar, with a fixed lens. It was made in Switzerland. My grandfather carried a Kodak plastic camera on his trip, and my great-grandfather carried an old Brownie camera made of cardboard. I've been looking at these photos all my life. They are of Depression America in 1933, the age of conformity in 1955, and a nation torn by the Vietnam war in 1974. There are almost five hundred photos in total. I've scanned and downloaded them all into my computer. Perhaps I can find some of the same places, inns or hotels still standing, restaurants still serving, who knows what I'll find? Now it's my turn, and I'm bringing my digital zoom camera with me. It's not an SLR, because they're too heavy, but it's a great Sony Cyber-shot with 14.1 mega-pixels and 10x optical zoom. That's all I will need. It's got very high storage capacity and a 720p movie mode.

I never had my father's approval for anything I did. He put himself through school, founded his own company, held twelve unique patents in the communications and computer industry, and made a small fortune. When I told him I wanted to be a writer, he threw his dessert at me.

Seriously, the entire family, all seven of us were at the table, and we also had my aunt and uncle with us at that meal. The day before, he had given me one of his grand lectures about opportunities in the information age. So at the dinner table, when I mentioned wanting to write books instead, he picked up his favorite dessert, baba au rhum, and hit me in the forehead. He wasn't totally drunk, at least not yet. Naturally my mother threw a fit. She yelled at *me* for upsetting my father.

Hey, we live in a mansion. This house is so big you could get lost in the basement. She knows where her best interests lie. Her side of the family didn't have the ethnic purity that was generally required in South Burlington. She didn't ever upset Papa Jack, because she had an irrational fear that if she displeased him, he would return her to her origins. Nothing I ever did pleased either of them, except when I married Joan. She was the daughter of a family friend, a good family friend. Unfortunately, we lasted only two months. After our divorce, it was three years before either of my parents would speak to me.

I admit it's childish, and quite frankly impossible, to seek approval from your dead father. Maybe this is my way of one-upping him. If he could walk across the country in seven months, I can do it in six, and my accomplishment will be that much greater. As I write this down, I must admit that it *does* sound childish. What if I fail? I simply don't have that word in my vocabulary. I learned that much from the old bastard.

Here's a list of what I'm taking with me:

Bright orange backpack with special reflective tape so I don't get hit from behind by some motorist. I don't intend to walk much at night, but it is possible as the days get shorter.

Three pairs of socks, undershirts, and underpants. I will wash the ones I'm wearing wherever I am staying. I've experimented, and with bar soap and hot water, they clean up fine. I will wring them out really well so they will dry by morning.

One pair of New Balance walking shoes with air-spring heels. I will probably wear these out along the way, so I will simply buy another pair. I will also buy whatever else wears out. There's no way I can carry everything I need. I will always have two meals in reserve, and some energy bars in case I end the day far from a restaurant.

Two credit cards and one thousand dollars in cash. I have only seven thousand dollars in the bank, but that should be enough for this trip. I'll make sure I have airfare back from Aberdeen. Maybe I can sell this book when I get back to Vermont.

Guitar fingerpicks and flat picks, in the event someone has an instrument available.

One Korg digital recorder with 36 hours recording time.

One small Sony computer with a 12-inch screen. The small lightweight units are more expensive than the 15-inch screens, and this one cost me a fortune. It's the heaviest item in my bag. I will download my digital sound and photos into the computer each night. I also have a SanDisk to back up the downloads in case anything happens to the computer.

Let me tell you about my Blackberry. This is not a fruit. It's a two-by-four-inch wonder that has a cellphone, Wi-Fi, Bluetooth, a video camera, 3G technology, and a multimedia player. I can send text messages, get wireless e-mail, and it has a GPS navigation system. Hey, I'm a technical geek, and I'm taking every neat gadget that will help me along the way. I like being able to call 911 from anywhere, and have the orbiting satellite plan my route. Even my wristwatch is run by the atomic clock, and keeps perfect time to the exact second.

I'm bringing one tube of insect repellent and a tube of sunscreen, also to be renewed as I go.

One-quart-capacity lightweight canteen. I don't like the taste of water that's been sitting in plastic, but the metal ones are too heavy. I have to pare every possible ounce, even a fraction of an ounce.

One can of mace. I don't want to become a victim of some Nebraska farmer's Rottweiler. This is anti-doggie protection. My father carried a Smith & Wesson snub-nosed detective special. He said every man should carry one. I hate guns. If you have peace in your heart, you don't need one. The mace, along with my wallet, Blackberry, and Korg recorder, is in my fanny pack which is turned around so it's in the front. All three are easily accessible.

One straw hat with two extra sweatbands.

One extra pair of stone-washed blue jeans.

One bright yellow rain slicker with hood.

One lightweight mountain tent with two space blankets and a sleeping bag.

One razor, a toothbrush and toothpaste, and a small can of deodorant powder.

I carry a miniature bronze Green Tara in my pocket. I bought her online from an antiques dealer. She is beautifully detailed, was made in 1700s Tibet, and is 1 and 1/8 inches high. I'm never without her, and I'm sure she will offer protection from semis; at least I hope so.

I don't intend to do much camping. I want to mix with people, so inns and bed and breakfast joints are my first choice. But I might find myself at the end of the day miles from such a place, so I need primitive camping equipment.

Everyone needs a mentor or a hero. For this journey mine are Henry David Thoreau and Kurt Vonnegut, Jr. With Thoreau I share the name David. His journals are my inspiration. They are over two million words. I wonder how long mine will be, and if it will be as interesting.

Breakfast of Champions was my favorite book in high school. When Vonnegut wrote it in 1973, I wasn't in grammar school yet. My English teacher got in big trouble for suggesting that his students read it. I love Vonnegut's drawing of an asshole.

I'm going to borrow Vonnegut's idea for this book and create a drawing to illustrate my encounters with people of low quality. I thought of many ideas. I thought of dickweed, dickhead, Democrat, shithead, slimeball, slimehole, gargoyle, virus, cesspool, cockroach, Republican, hemorrhoid, ghoul, vampire, and vomit to name but a few. I realize that this search is anal retentive and a blatant exhibition of my immaturity, but there you have it. But try as I might, I couldn't come up with a better word or drawing to depict undesirable humans, than *asshole*. Here's my version of Vonnegut's drawing.

I have fifty books in my computer that I haven't read yet. I will be reading these at night after I transcribe my recordings and write my thoughts about what I have seen that day. I will also bring my small SONY AM/FM shortwave radio with headphones so I can hear human voices on long, lonely stretches. It fits in my shirt pocket.

I am allowing myself one other modern navigational aid. Since I have my computer with me, I will consult Map Quest at each stage of my journey to select the best routes. I will use this in tandem with the Blackberry GPS. I won't need to print out any details because I'm going to cover only twenty miles per day. Wherever possible I will choose the old routes that my predecessors walked. Modern interstate highways are unfriendly places to walk, and in most states it's against the law for pedestrians to use them.

The total distance is 3,350 miles. At 20 miles per day average, that's 2,000 miles in 100 days, 3,350 miles in 168 days. I didn't pick Aberdeen, Washington; it was chosen for me. All three of my ancestors ended up in that city. All used the same route to get there. I have to use the same route for reasons that I suppose will become clear later on. My father did it in seven months and covered about 17 miles a day. Knowing him, he never deviated from his schedule. He did take some interesting photos, but if he learned anything on his journey it sure didn't show, or at least he was unable to communicate it. He did share something with me on his deathbed that I will tell you about when the trip begins.

I'm allowing extra time because I know I'll see interesting and compelling sights along the way. Who knows, I might do what my father did and find a wife. I plan on leaving tomorrow, April 15th, and arriving in Aberdeen sometime near the end of October. This will keep me out of the winter snows and cold that begin in November. I'm glad to be using the northern route because the summer heat would be too oppressive walking through the South, say along the old Route 66. It can still get hot during the day in the northern latitudes, but it cools down at night, and usually stays cool until 11 a.m.

You often read about a group doing something for charity, such as bike-a-thon for muscular dystrophy, or walk-a-thon to combat diabetes. I decided to name my journey also. It took me a while to think of the right title. Walking to fulfill my destiny, walking for sanity, walking for recognition, walking to one-up my overbearing father, walking for the fuck of it, walking across America, walking through America, walking from the present into the past, walking into the future, etc.

I finally decided on Walking Man. That's all. Simple, has no baggage, and doesn't give anything away. All you know by the title is some man is walking. Who, what, why, when, where, and how are unknown. You have to read the book to find out. You've gotten this far. I've gone through all the pain, trouble, and sorrow to live this; the least you can do is read it.

Have you ever known a person who made promise after promise that he or she didn't keep? They say, I'll do this or I'll do that, but it never happens. We see it everywhere, friends, politicians, and entire corporations who over-promise and under-deliver. I'll make you a promise that I will deliver on. If you travel with me in this book, you will be richer. You will be out a few bucks, but you will be glad you've turned these pages.

I'm not some lawyer who decided to write poetry. I'm a professional writer. I've written two novels, as yet unpublished. My articles have appeared in many national magazines, however, and I was a sports reporter for the *Burlington Free Press* for several years. My observations will be backed by my insights, and my verbal power to decipher complex motivations. I will wade through all the shit and get to the heart of what is true. We will both really discover America by the time we're finished.

There's no omniscient narrator at work in this book to tell you what I'm thinking or feeling. An omniscient narrator is a device that a fiction writer uses to bridge the gap between the dialogue and action sequences in his novel. These are the facts that he tells about his characters that they can't show us by their behavior.

Here's an example:

"I don't care if you go out with him," Zelda said to her sister Zinnia as they sat on the porch swing. Little did Zinnia know that Zelda was heartbroken and felt totally betrayed by her, and abandoned by Bradford Hornsby.

Yeah, right. The writer doesn't have the skill to *show* us that Zelda is unhappy, so he or she has to *tell* us. This is lazy writing, and the reader will soon tire of all the third-rate omniscient descriptions. A better line would have been, *"I don't care if you go out with him,"* Zelda said, *teary-eyed with her mouth quivering.* The writing still sucks, but at least Zelda is showing and not telling you how she feels.

To hell with Zelda and Zinnia. I don't care about fiction. There is no narrator to tell you that David is sad, or that David has a pensive look on his face. *I'm* going to have to tell you, if I can summon enough courage. Everything in my book is the actual dialogue I've recorded and transcribed from my blog, or my own thoughts that I've written down. I am the omniscient narrator for everyone else. There is no tense problem, attribution problem, or any other confusion. What you read is what you get. Just pretend you're paging through Thoreau's journal. There is a fat, pink worm squirming under yonder hickory leaf. I lifted up the leaf and a centipede crawled onto my right hand and bit my index finger.

I live in an apartment on South Union Street in Burlington, Vermont. My younger brother Jonathan is going to look after the place. He will stay here while I'm away. He's a resident at the hospital, specializing in pediatrics, and my place is convenient. His home is in Stowe, which is too far to drive. He will be here at seven a.m., we will say our goodbyes, and I'll be on my way. I'm going to get a good night's rest. This is the last time I'll be sleeping in my own bed for almost seven months.

CHAPTER ONE
Burlington, Vermont to Ferrisburg, Vermont

I left my apartment, walked down South Union Street, and turned toward Route 7. Only my brother Jonathan was there to see me off. My other siblings are too busy, and my mother is afraid of Papa Jack's ghost. I weighed my backpack and fanny pack, and both of them combined are almost exactly thirty-nine pounds. That does not include a full canteen of water, or whatever food I am carrying with me. After awhile I hardly feel the weight. I'm strong and can lift 175 pounds over my head.

I had breakfast at home and plan to have lunch at the Shelburne Café, ten miles away. I'll be spending the night at Club Lucy in Ferrisburg. Lucy is a combination inn and nightclub, twenty-three miles from my apartment. I used to play in a grunge band; we called ourselves Hall's Mentals. I got all the gigs, played lead guitar, and wrote most of the songs. We had a good local following and played at Lucy's for over a year. We were there every Wednesday and Friday night, until our band broke up. Wow, that was almost eight years ago.

I have a very long stride and can cover a lot of ground quickly. I'm so elated that I feel like running, but pacing is very important. If I go out too fast, I will tire quickly. Too slowly and I will know that I could have covered more ground. This will be a learning experience. In time, I will know exactly what to expect. But then there are the mountains to cross, and I'm sure new lessons will be learned there. The weather is cloudy and the temperature is fifty-eight degrees. I decided to walk with the traffic. It feels weird walking on the left side of the road against the cars. It seems more dangerous, although I can see the cars approaching. On the right side, I can hear them approaching from behind, but the sound doesn't tell me how close they will pass. I will try to buy a small mirror I can mount on my straw hat. This will alert me if someone is too close and I have to jump to the side. Route 7 is great, the shoulders are wide, and traffic is light. The trees are just starting to bud, and there are a dozen shades of green from yellowish to dark olive.

Lunch at the Shelburne Café was perfect. I'm a lapsed vegetarian who eats pork, chicken, beef, turkey, veal, lamb, and buffalo wings. The café served a delicious hot turkey platter with cranberries and mashed potatoes. I had a hot apple turnover with a scoop of vanilla ice cream on it for dessert. I waited about a half hour after eating before resuming my walk. I'm usually very impatient, so it takes discipline for me to relax and calmly digest my food.

Walking is stimulating and soothing at the same time. The repetitive cadence of one foot in front of the other frees my thoughts, and also calms my spirit. It would have been impossible for me to do this only a few years ago. You have got to like yourself and be able to stand your own company. I will be un-intruded upon for days or possibly weeks at a time. I suppose I could argue with myself and call myself names if I want to relive my past.

My final destination is in sight. Here's the Welcome to Ferrisburg sign, and there is Club Lucy. It has a huge parking lot. Reminds me of the roadhouses I saw in the Carolinas. Club Lucy started out in the seventies as a gay bar, but over the next two decades the mix of patrons changed again and again. The clientele is now a combination of affluent college students, artsy adults on either side of mid-life, and the last time I was there a few months ago, the largest group, by far, were ordinary working stiffs out to have fun.

I made great time on my first walk. I knew this would be the case. I'm fresh and know the countryside well. I averaged almost four miles per hour. I left at 8:00 a.m., took an hour for lunch in Shelburne, between 11 and 12, and got to Ferrisburgh just after 3:00 p.m. It's been awhile since I've seen Lucy, so we caught up and I told him about my journey. I checked into a room on the second floor and took a nice hot shower.

On Wednesday, Saturday, and Sunday the entertainment is jazz, blues, or folk. On Monday night there's an open mike for local musicians and poets.

Tonight, Friday night, is the most popular of all. There is usually an hour's wait to get a table and patrons are stacked three and four deep at the bar. People travel from as far away as New York, New Hampshire, and Quebec to visit this night club.

Friday night is rant night.

No poetry or music is allowed. Lucy and the waitstaff take turns manning the fire bell. This is a twelve-inch-diameter bell from an old pump house in St. Johnsbury. People are strictly limited to a five-minute rant. Lucy keeps a timer right next to him. It's a big, black Gralab darkroom timer with white numbers so the ranter can see how much time he or she has remaining. Lucy dials in five minutes. At the end of five minutes the timer buzzes. It the ranter doesn't sit down within fifteen seconds, Lucy pounds the bell with a large ball-peen hammer until the speaker sits down. It's so loud that no one can scream over the top of it. The audience also starts shouting "sit down!" if the speaker tries to continue. As a result, all rants are short and to the point.

Five minutes was Lucy's idea. "Anyone who has something to say ought to be able to get it out in under five minutes." Lucy is six feet five, in his mid fifties, has closely cropped red hair, and weighs about three hundred pounds.

No one is permitted to interrupt a rant, but sometimes a really good rant will produce a "yeah!" or a "right on!" from the audience. At the end of a rant everyone either claps, boos or hisses, catcalls, shouts "bullshit!" or some of the other usual curses. A Club Lucy tradition is to pound the tabletops with beer bottles if the patrons want the ranter to go another round. There are always a few pounds, and sometimes the whole club loves a rant and every table is pounding. The final decision of whether or not a ranter gets a second go is up to Lucy. The next rant must be on a different subject. This is a rough crowd, so the second had better be good. Nobody gets a third rant. Lucy is quick and proud to tell all his customers that his club is not a democracy. He is the tyrant and what he says goes. The waitstaff and bartenders are tough, so there's hardly ever any real violence, just a lot of shouting. A few fights have broken out in the parking lot, and last year the police had to arrest two people.

Lucy let me use my Korg recorder. Below is an unedited rant session from 9:00 to 9:30 p.m. The usual starting time is 9:00 and ending is 12:00 p.m. I give a brief physical description of each ranter, who must also tell his or her name and where they are from. No one is allowed to remain anonymous. Any unusual crowd reactions or comments by Lucy are also noted. He had the bell between 9:00 and 10:00 p.m. I sat at a table in the back by the pay phone and cigarette machine so no one would notice that I was talking into my lapel microphone. I transcribed these notes in my room, and added the physical descriptions later.

The first ranter was a young dark-haired woman who looked barely old enough to be allowed in the bar. She was very drunk and staggered up to the podium in the center of the bandstand, raised about sixteen inches off the floor. She screamed one sentence at the top of her lungs:

"I'm Peggy Nash from Milton and I hate my fucking husband!"

She then walked off. Everyone cheered wildly, and some men in the front said the predictable, "How about coming home with me baby," etc.

The second ranter, who was only half-lit, had a permanent grin on his face. He was in his early thirties and prematurely bald. He was tall and thin and stooped to speak into the microphone.

"Hi there, I'm John Ireland from Burlington. Do you know what I just did?"

Everyone said, "What?"

"Well, you know that woman who answers the phone for every corporation and says if you want to talk to so-and-so press number 2, or so-and-so press number 4, if you know your party's extension, enter it now, if you have a question on your account press 117, blah, blah, blah? Well, I found out who she is. She lived on Fourth Avenue, and her name was Loina Bytes. I shot the bitch yesterday."

Everyone cheered again and a few pounded the tables, but Lucy just laughed and motioned the next ranter on.

The next guy was short and looked totally out of place in a business suit and tie. He carried a briefcase up to the podium, carefully removed a sheet of paper, and cleared his throat. At first his speech was barely audible, but it quickly grew in intensity and volume as he went along. By the end of his rant he was shouting.

"My name is Eddie Fishburn, and I'm from Montpelier. I'm a housing inspector for the State of Vermont. It's about time to set the record straight. I just visited the Brookside Trailer Park and there is no brook. I went to Woodside Condominiums. There are no woods, just a shopping center and a parking lot, but I did find a condom in the lot. Pleasant Acres are not pleasant at all and nobody has an acre. The houses are all close together, all the trees were cut down, most people have large dogs running loose, and rusty cars are strewn in the yards. The properties are ramshackle and look like shit. I insist we redo every lying development with a proper sign. Pleasant Acres should be renamed Low-Income Blue-Collar Cluster. Instead of Brookside Trailer Park, call it Metal House Row."

Just then someone from the audience stood up and shouted, "Hey, I live in Pleasant Acres, you asshole!" Lucy, who also has a microphone by the fire bell, told the guy in the audience to be quiet and sit down. The little ranter was now on a roll.

"I just drove by Butler Farms. These aren't farms. These are three-hundred-thousand dollar homes, each on a quarter of an acre. They all live in each other's back pockets. With all the land in Vermont, who the hell would buy out there? I'll tell you who, a bunch of dumb New Yorkers who are used to Levittown or Queens. The poor slobs get nervous if they aren't standing on line or sharing the road with a thousand other slobs. This is a development for people who think it's normal to be crammed into a subway car and who aren't used to being outside, like those idiot New Yorkers living in high-rises. They drive like they eat. They won't make eye contact with you and will cut you off without warning. I'm going to ram the next guy with a New York plate that cuts me off. They are so fucking stupid that my friend who works for the Vermont Department of Wildlife actually got a call from some woman in Butler Farms, with a thick New York accent, who wanted to know if the squirrel on her front lawn would bite her if she went outside. She was afraid of rabies. I would have told her, 'No problem, ma'am, they won't eat shit.' "

The timer buzzed at the end of this sentence. The man picked up his briefcase and left the podium to an equal number of boos and cheers. New Yorkers can be tough and impatient, so I'm glad those in the audience didn't start a fight.

Next up was a fortyish, muscular woman with short hair and overalls. Lucy started the timer and she paused for ten

21

seconds before she spoke. Her first words were screamed into the microphone.

"I'm not normal!"

Everyone cheered.

"I'm Lisa Gurney from Burlington. Do you know what normal is? Did you see that movie where they are making love and she stabs the guy over and over again with an ice pick, and the other movie where they cut this woman's head off with a chainsaw? Cool, right? That's normal. Most movies have a few good bloody scenes or a combination of sex and violence. Shit, soon that will be G-rated stuff. Hey, did you see that new primetime sitcom on channel four that all American families watch? She called her roommate a dickbrain and his friend a scumbag. This was followed by the usual canned laughter. Everybody talks like that now, so it must be normal. Business people and congressman lie; everyone expects them to. Do entertainers and athletes use drugs? Hey, hey, what's all the fuss, of course they do, they're all normal."

Most of the audience sat in silence; even Lucy stopped watching the timer and listened.

"Okay folks, how many of you here tonight are cheating on your spouses? How many took a little snort in the bathroom? May I have a show of hands? Look at me, I'm abnormal. I had a root beer, a garlic bagel, and I'm not sure if I want to have sex with men or women."

"Sit down, you fat dyke!" a blonde woman at the back shouted. Lucy stood up, glared at the woman, and in a low voice said, "You are not welcome in this club, and I would prefer it if you would leave now."

"What about free speech, Lucy?" another person shouted.

"Everybody shut up and let the woman finish," said someone seated at the bar. The blonde woman sat there defiantly and Lucy sat down again.

"I'm adding one minute to her time. Please continue," Lucy said.

Lisa held up a fashion magazine and pointed to the ads featuring the junkie-chic look.

"Check out these people. This magazine is eight years old, so I see you country cousins are finally catching up to yesterday. Congratulations to some of the women I see here tonight like my dyed-blonde friend there at the back table. You've got the look. You paint dark circles around your eyes, and make your cheeks white. You diet until every rib shows, you wear fishnet stockings, wide black belts, designer jeans and smoke two packs of cigarettes a day. You are with it, you are normal. Oh, I am so sorry, I only have on overalls, a tee shirt and no bra, I must be abnormal. Thank God, I'm abnormal, oh yeah baby, abnormal, abnormal to my feminist core."

Lisa's rant reaction was mixed with an equal number of table-pounds and boos. Lucy clapped into his microphone, something he rarely does. He turned to Lisa and welcomed her back for a second rant later in the evening.

Next up was a middle-aged couple. They had all the "right" clothes with a few patches here and there, but the fancy shoes and a Rolex watch told me that if I followed them to their car in the parking lot, it would be a luxury model. The two other couples they were sitting with clapped when they walked to the podium. They introduced themselves.

"I'm Nat Havershaw from Essex." "And I'm Silvia Wiggins Havershaw from Essex."

They had broad smiles on their faces and each spoke a sentence quickly.

"He's so stupid, every time he loads the dishwasher he breaks a pot."

"She's so dumb she thinks fuel injection is illegal."

"He's so trusting, he believes the Governor."

"She's so ugly, when she was seven, they had to tie a pork chop around her neck so the family dog would play with her."

"He's so low, he has to look up to see down."

One minute into the rant Lucy hit the bell. "Okay, Mr. and Mrs. Havershaw, that's enough. I don't appreciate your carefully choreographed act. This is not a night for comedy, poetry, songs, or well-rehearsed dinner theater. This is a rant session, so if you have a legitimate beef, get on with it. If not, please sit down."

The Havershaws angrily left Club Lucy, followed by their four friends.

"Oh my, my, Lucy exclaimed, "I can't let this place get too upscale. All my no-good patrons will feel uncomfortable and go back to their vans, watch their portable TVs, drink too much beer, and go piss in the park."

Everyone cheered and pounded the tables.

At this time the club got very quiet. A cop in uniform stood at the podium. Some people were whispering, "Is he a real cop?" "Hey, I know this guy, he's a cop all right." The uniformed state police officer was as big as Lucy, but was in prime physical condition. He wore his flak vest, and a stainless-steel automatic rode high on his right hip.

"Good evening."

"Good evening, officer," one man answered sarcastically.

"I'm Corporal Hank Crayton, and I go off duty at the end of this shift, for good. Let me tell you why I'm quitting the police force. I'm not going to take a bullet because some car thief tries to steal the Havershaw's Lexus. Hey, you in the back, yo blondie with the big mouth. You're a tough bimbo all right, except when I pulled you over for speeding last week. You started crying like a baby. 'Oh boo hoo, I've never had this happen to me before.' Nice act, honey, see you in court on the 23rd.

"I also see Mrs. Wilcox here. How are you doing, dear? Her ex-husband was beating the shit out of her, so when we responded to her 911 call and tried to take him down, she turned on us. That cleaver you threw cut my upper arm and required eighteen stitches to close. Just keep on drinking, Mrs. Wilcox, soon you'll find another man just as rotten as your ex. You'll be repeat business for the Police Department for sure. See you in court on the 23rd.

"Here's the bottom line, folks; you don't respect this uniform, and I no longer care if I serve or protect you. I tried to help an old woman cross Main Street today, and she shrugged me off and told me to go away because I was embarrassing her. Take a good hit, lady. I hope a UPS truck knocks you into next Tuesday. There I was standing in the middle of the road, and by the time I got back to my patrol car my mind was made up. Fuck you, Mr. and Mrs. Havershaw. Fuck you, blonde bimbo. You too, Mrs. Wilcox. You'd better wear blaze orange and buy roller blades, old woman, whoever the hell you are; you're going to need them. By the way, my own personal 40 caliber auto is just like this service weapon. If any of you try to fuck with me, not even the police will be able to save you. Now get the hell out of my way."

No one in the entire room said a word. No one clapped or jeered. Officer Crayton was given a clear path to the door. About two minutes later Lucy spoke.

"Don't feel guilty, my pets, he's just burned out. He'll go home and abuse his wife and kids, kick the dog a couple of times, and be fine by Monday. I'm going to cut my speed on Main Street for a while; no sense provoking him. I hope he does come back. I don't know about you, but I feel safer when he's around. Oh well, enough social science. Next ranter."

An attractive young woman in her mid-twenties took her turn at the podium.

"Hello, I'm Alice Dubois from Winooski. I was a third-year medical student at the University of Vermont. This year has been tough financially, so I took a job at Almy's Department Store downtown so I could have enough for food, gas, and some spending money. Do you know what else this job did for me?"

Everyone answered, "What?"

"It made me change careers. I dropped out of medical school this year because working as a cashier at Almy's made me hate the human race. I don't care if you people live or die." Everyone started booing until Lucy quieted them down. "I'm going to buy a fast-food franchise and feed all of you red meat and fat. I'll pay some marginal brain to run it and siphon off all the profits for my own amusement. To repeat, I no longer care if you people live or die. Ta ta."

Nearly everyone booed again when Ms. Dubois finished, and Lucy shook his head before he spoke.

"Everyone is so fried. At this rate we'll have no more doctors and no more police. Now if we can just get the lawyers and politicians into the frypan we may be onto something."

Everyone cheered and pounded the tables.

"Don't worry pets, you still have each other, the bottle of beer you're holding, and old Lucy here. Ain't that right?"

Everyone shouted, "Right!"

Lucy stood up, rang the fire bell, and barked, "Friday night is rant night at Club Lucy and for our edification the ranter will be..." He looked at the patrons and made a beckoning gesture toward the podium.

I knew I couldn't stay for the entire session, so I went back to my room to write all of this down. The soundproofing is very good, and I can barely hear what's going on downstairs. Tomorrow at this time I should be in New York State. I'll tell you all about what my father said, and my first assignment. It's in Old Forge, New York. I've got a lot of explaining to do.

CHAPTER TWO
Ferrisburg, Vermont to Old Forge, New York

Papa Jack gave me a map. The route is from Burlington, Vermont to Old Forge, New York. The distance is 140 miles. I've already chopped over 23 miles off the first leg of my journey by walking to Club Lucy; that leaves 118 to go. He gave me this simple map and nothing more. On his deathbed he told me that I would have to visit ten people who are spread out from coast to coast. They are all expecting me, so he must have set this up quite a while ago. When I get to Old Forge, I am to look up the Dobbs family who own a bed and breakfast on Shore Road. They will tell me who I am to visit next. I guess this is his way of making sure that I actually walk the same route he did. I thought about using my car, parking it out of town, and casually strolling into the Dobbs Inn, but that would be extremely dishonest. I can't fly to Aberdeen, Washington and put an end to this charade. I don't know who I'm supposed to see, or what I'm supposed to do when I get there. I will have to learn all about that at my next to last stop, number nine, which I suppose is somewhere in Washington. He never did tell me what I would find in Aberdeen. He never told me that I would get anything, but I must admit I have wild dreams of much money and material abundance. His fortune has to be somewhere. I guess my curiosity is greater than my good sense. A part of me agrees with my nasty sister. Her description of a wild psychotic egg hunt may not be too far from the truth.

The rest of my siblings and my mother have pored over every record they could find. We estimate that Papa Jack was worth between fifty and seventy million dollars. He willed each of my brothers and sisters two million dollars, and my mother has the house, our vacation property on Peak's Island, Maine, and several trust funds. All I got was this damn map.

I'm a runner. I've run dozens of 26-mile marathons and usually finish in the top three. I nearly made the Olympic team. My first two novels have not yet been sold, and I am at a transitional point in my life. Quite frankly, my father's challenge came at a good time; it fits me physically and psychically. I was about to apply for a teaching position at South Burlington Middle School. They need a language arts teacher, and I know I can do a good job with the kids. The only problem is that I don't want to teach eighth graders. I don't have the calling. I don't want to drive a cab, load and unload trucks, wait tables, or be a part of junior management in any company, doing anything for any reason. I hate business. A difficult walk across the country is much more appealing than the best corporate job available. I want to write books, but my books aren't being picked up. I don't yet know what kind of book will grow from this trip, whether it will be a novel or a memoir or what. I have no hook, no theme other than the journey itself. Perhaps my family situation could be the focal point.

(Naturally, when I wrote this I didn't know how everything would end. We now know that this is a memoir and not a novel).

I have taken my first photograph. I'm about to cross the bridge into Ticonderoga, New York, and you would not believe what is in the field next to the cows. It's a camel. No, wait, it's not a camel because it only has one hump. That makes it a dromedary. The critters were real close to the barbed wire fence, so I got some good shots. Did you ever really study a cow or a camel and watch the way they chew their cud? They schlompf off a mouthful of grass or hay and then move their jaws from side to side like some gigantic vegomatic processing machine. It's this sideways chewing that reminds me of one of our politicians. Do you remember the way our former Vice President always spoke out the side of his mouth? His eyes would roll in the opposite direction and his nose and left ear would twitch when he spoke. That's because every time he spoke he was lying.

There is a connection between all life forces, even those who are alive and those who aren't. Every human being leaves a legacy. I'll bet that dromedary leaves a greater legacy than the former VP. At least his dung fertilizes the field. If dromedary dung were placed in the Vice Presidential library, it would not smell nearly as bad as the collected wit and wisdom of his royal heinousness.

I'll say one thing for Papa Jack, he hated Republicans. Even though he was rich, he had no use for them. They never asked my father for money. They knew he would throw them out. He wasn't too crazy about the Democrats either. The exceptions were our Vermont senators, Pat Leahy and Independent Bernie Sanders. He really liked Pat and Bernie. My father was hard to analyze. I am thankful for one very important bit of heredity. I inherited his hate-

Republicans-and-Democrats gene. I am constitutionally incapable of walking into a voting booth and pressing a Republican lever, or punching a Republican punch card, or filling in a black Republican fill-in space with a black Republican pencil. On rare occasions I will vote for a Democrat, but that almost never happens.

I've done a lot of research into the word Republican, and this is what I've learned.

RE*PUB*LI*CAN

This is an interesting word, and its
origins are well documented.

During the middle ages in London, there were two
classes of people who visited the ale houses or pubs.
The first group was well behaved, would visit the
pub once a week, have a meal and a pint of bitters, then
call it a night and go home to their families.

The second group was not well behaved.
They would drink until intoxicated and return
again to do the same thing every night.

This returning over and over got them
the name of REPUBS.

Since eventually most of these people fell
into dire straits and became derelicts, they

were often found in the narrow alleys
in back of the pubs licking garbage cans.

So when the police arrested the worst
offenders for vagrancy, they labeled them
RE*PUB*LI*CANS.

I remember one fiery Republican named Garlando
Parcheesy who was running for Lieutenant Governor,
Auditor of Accounts, and Republican Weed Whacker. He
was eighty-six years old and had two of those 1800s style,
long powder-horn-looking hearing aids, one sticking out of
each ear. Every time he spoke he foamed at the mouth and
went into convulsions. He always carried a carved rosewood
collection basket that was lined with green velvet. He would
pass it around no matter where he went. Whether it was the
supermarket, a ballgame, a funeral, or at church, he saw
every gathering as a potential source of income. Here's the
fiery speech that won him the last election. He was stumping
at a televised town meeting day in the Vermont city of
Doltsville.

VOTE FOR
GARLANDO PARCHEESY FOR LIEUTENANT
GOVERNOR, AUDITOR OF ACCOUNTS, AND
REPUBLICAN WEED WHACKER
A vote for Parcheesy is a vote for
    ADMINISTRATION
A vote for Parcheesy is a vote for
    MANAGEMENT

Your vote for Parcheesy will guarantee
    MOVEMENT
Your vote for Parcheesy will guarantee
    DISCUSSIONS
Trusting in Garlando Parcheesy will add
    ITEMS
Trusting in Garlando Parcheesy will add
    ISSUES
Commission Garlando Parcheesy to clean up
    COMMITTEES
Commission Garlando Parcheesy to clean up
    UTILITIES
Your mandate for Parcheesy will
    GROW
Your mandate for Parcheesy will
    PROGRESS
Parcheesy is responsive to
    DIALOGUE
Parcheesy is responsive to
    MANDATES
Parcheesy believes in
    GOVERNMENT
Parcheesy believes in
    POLICY-PROGRAMS
Parcheesy helped organize
    YOUNG WOMEN VOTERS
Parcheesy helped organize
    RIDES TO POLING PLACES
    FOR YOUNG WOMEN VOTERS IN HIS
    WINDOWLESS VAN

Garlando Parcheesy believes in
VERY YOUNG WOMEN VOTERS

VOTE FOR
GARLANDO PARCHEESY FOR LIEUTENANT
GOVERNOR, AUDITOR OF ACCOUNTS, AND
REPUBLICAN WEED WHACKER

It's easy to see why he won. According to the Associated Press and *Time* magazine, Doltsville is a weathervane for the state. After Parcheesy carried Doltsville, the Dolts, as most New Englanders call them, did their thing. They mooed, walked in a straight line to the voting booth, and voted for a Republican Governor. Unfortunately the rest of the state followed Doltsville's lead. The Vermont Governor, who is also the State Hair Stylist, is still very popular, in spite of the horrible job Republicans have done on the national level.

The weather is beautiful. Temperature is about sixty and the sun is shining. I am about twenty-five miles into New York State, walking along Highway 28. There is something I didn't anticipate. I'm very disturbed by the roadkill. Perhaps because it's early spring, the little creatures are moving about. There is a dead animal every couple of miles, and I find it very depressing. I'll be glad when I leave the mountains. I saw a dead squirrel run over about ten times. All that was left was a bushy tail. This makes me think of another Bush.

Do you remember when this man was President?

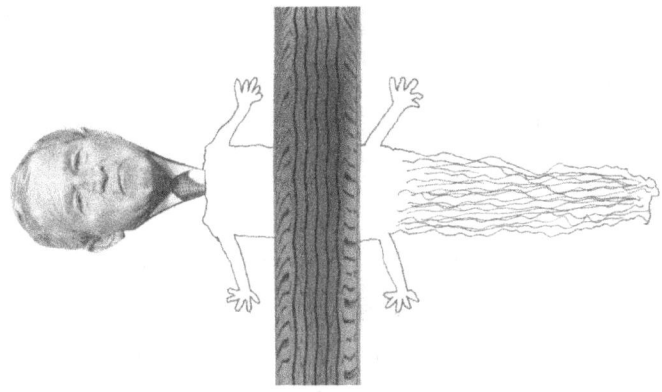

There was a dead deer in a ditch, out of sight of the road, and the smell was very rank. I remember the gross-out contests I used to have with my brothers. We would try to one-up each other with sickening stories, trying to make each other throw up.

I recall one Sunday afternoon when I was sitting in the living room with Jonathan and Seth, and I gave them my recipe for Mulligan Stew. I was fourteen years old at the time. I remember the story fondly because I would always win those contests. Words: I had an early gift. The story went like this:

Mulligan stew is a prime delicacy that is rarely offered by O'Hara's Steak House. You have to get on a waiting list, and you must be able to travel to partake of this fine meal. I was happy that they put *my* name on the list. Finally, three weeks later I got a call and rushed down to O'Hara's. They took me in their delivery van about ten miles out of town on Route Seven. There in the middle of the road was a gorgeous dead possum. This was no freshly killed dead possum. This critter had been roadkill for several days and had started to swell up. The odor was perfect, better than rotten Limburger cheese could ever hope to be. It brought tears to my eyes. The temperature was ninety-two degrees, and the hot asphalt conveniently kept my meal warm. The sous chef who drove me to the site made an X incision right on top of the possum's belly. He then gave me a small, short, plastic soda straw. I pressed down on the sides of the possum while I sucked in a whole mouthful. It was absolutely delicious.

Unfortunately, it was just after dinner when I told this story and my older sister, who was standing in the hall, heard every word. She threw up on the oriental rug and then screamed at the top of her lungs. I got in big trouble, as usual. Although Seth and Jonathan were part of the storytelling, they did not rally to my defense, and kept their heads down. Yuk, I had to get a sponge and clean up her vomit.

I'm getting ready to stop for the day. There's a small motel up ahead, and I'm cold. These higher elevations have caused the temperature to drop. I heard on my radio that the high tomorrow is supposed to be only about 37. About an hour ago I saw a rabbit that had been hit by a car. It was still alive and when I removed it from the road, it made a sound just like a baby crying. I left it under a tree. I wanted to kill it to put it out of its pain, but I couldn't bring myself to do it.

Did you ever hear of Albert Schweitzer? He was a wonderful, gifted musician, physician, and humanitarian. Schweitzer won the Nobel Peace Prize in 1952. When he was 30, about the age I am now, he decided to live the rest of his life in the service of mankind. One of his quotes that I will always remember is, "The quality of a culture is measured by its reverence for all life." That's why I will never hunt or fish. I hate cars and roads because they kill God's creatures. What would Buddha have said? Would he have ridden in a car?

I'll bet this is the first of dozens of ordeals that will test my will and resolve. After a while the sight of another dead squirrel loses its power to shock me. I wonder if that happens to soldiers in a war. Ho hum, another dead human body. I pray human life never comes to be as cheap as the lives of these small animals, but I know that it already has. Death is something I rarely think about because I'm too frightened.

Do you know what I'm really looking forward to? I was just thinking of Club Lucy and waiting for you to ask, "What are you really looking forward to, David?" I'm looking forward to a hot shower. When you endure hardships, strenuous uphill walking, bone-chilling cold, the simplest pleasures become huge. Think of how we all take a clear glass of water for granted. If, God forbid, we spent ten hours walking through the Death Valley desert at 119 degrees, think of how that same glass of water would taste.

I checked into the Indian Lake Motel. They have a nice restaurant, and my room is small and comfortable. It's really strange when the clerk asks you for your license plate number and you tell him or her that you don't have a car. I said I was on foot, and judging by her reaction, I could have said, I have leprosy, or I'm an alien from Gawonga who eats hotel clerks. If you aren't driving a car, you automatically become a non-person. But as soon as I told her that I'm a writer who is walking across the country to chronicle the people I have met, and asked if I could take her photograph, her attitude instantly changed. I then talked about my editor at Random House, who gave me specific instructions on where I was to go and who I was to see, and that's why I stopped at the Indian Lake Motel. The clerk immediately became very animated and wanted to tell me her life story. She doesn't want to be portrayed negatively, like those poor people in Doltsville, Vermont usually are.

I have a routine that I think will stay with me for my journey. The very first thing I do when I check in for the night is take off my clothes and wash my underwear and socks in the sink. If my jeans are really dirty I'll wash them too. Once every three days is fine for the jeans. Then I take a nice, long, soothing, hot shower. The next thing I do is plug in my computer and my tape recorder. The tape recorder, computer, radio, Blackberry, and camera all have

38

rechargeable batteries. The tape recorder always needs recharging. I haven't yet needed the computer's battery, and the radio and camera can go for weeks on a single charge. I have two batteries for the Blackberry, good for about 12 hours. All this gear makes me feel like an electronic pilgrim. Hey, that would have been a good title for this book: *The Electronic Pilgrim's Progress*. Of course, there would have to be a tip of the hat to John Bunyan who wrote *Pilgrim's Progress* in 1678. The next thing I do is shave. I want to look my best when I sit down for my evening meal. Tonight I'm going to look extra sharp because there is an iron and board in my room's closet. I will have freshly pressed blue jeans and red plaid flannel shirt.

By the time I got to the restaurant, word had spread of my book. I don't feel good about lying. Of course the bit about Random House is nothing but a fantasy, but I'm starting to believe it myself. I always bring my tape recorder and camera with me wherever I go. When I walked into the restaurant, the motel owners, the chef, three waitstaff, and five patrons who live nearby all greeted me at the door. They must have asked me dozens of questions. I told dozens of lies, and took dozens of photographs. I don't feel good about lying. Perhaps I can think of another reason why I'm walking across the country. I could say that I'm an electronic pilgrim and I'm walking for God. They may think I'm a nut case, but I certainly would not be a threat to anybody, and nobody questions God.

President Obama is just like me, or should I say that I'm just like him. He had both white and black parents. I could say that I'm planning to follow in his footsteps and run for

President of the United States when I turn 35. I want to personally see how our road and bridge infrastructure is holding up. It's amazing. When people see me, they don't hesitate to ask me who I am and what I'm doing. If I were a light-complexioned man in a three-piece business suit, driving a new Lexus, they wouldn't dare to ask me anything except what could they get or do for me. Never underestimate the power of power.

Don't you love people who say never do this or never do that? Here are some examples I am going to brainstorm as I walk along Route 28. By the way, I'm freezing my ass off. I wish I had a heavy coat and gloves. I can barely turn on this tape recorder because my fingers are so cold I can't feel the button.

Mmm, let's see, some Nevers.

Never ask a Republican who drives a Volvo
to back you up in a fistfight.

Never work in an office building
with a glass front.

Never trust a bleached blonde
who drives a white or red convertible.

Never read the poetry
of Ezra Pound.

Never listen to a corporate lawyer
with a degree from anywhere.

Never swim in the ocean
near New York City.

Never buy music made by anyone
who has performed in Las Vegas.

Never eat in a restaurant with fewer than

four pickup trucks in the parking lot.
   Never believe anyone
who wants to sell you self-esteem.
   Never open your car windows
along the New Jersey Turnpike.
   Never let anyone
dismiss or diminish you.
   Never listen to more than
one straight hour of German opera.
   Never eat ravioli or spaghetti
from a can.
   Never tell a Boston cab driver
that you are late.
   Never blame a squirrel
for stealing your apples.
   Never cut down a tree
unless it's already dead.
   Never believe any writer
who keeps telling you what to do.

   What about the word "Always"?   Shouldn't any scribe
worth his or her salt also have positive affirmations?
   Always play with your cat,
even if she scratched you yesterday.
   Always dream of growing something big,
whether or not it is harvested.
   Always listen to your favorite music
at a life-affirming volume.
   Always turn off the sound
during beer commercials.

Always eat at a restaurant with more than
four pickup trucks in the parking lot.

Always look at the stars
on a clear night.

Always leave work
in plenty of time to play.

Always take a walk in a late autumn rain
when all the leaves are wet.

Always watch the Boston Red Sox
against the New York Yankees.

Always learn a new word and
listen to a new kind of music.

Always try to create something
where before there was nothing.

Always give thanks and be grateful
even when you are down.

Always speak the unspeakable
and rob evil of its power to hurt.

Always face a tough problem
eyeball to eyeball.

Always speak kindly
of the image you see in your mirror.

Always live the life
that you would want your children to live.

Always challenge someone
who tries to distort reality.

Always know where
the back door is.

Always share an unpleasant task
with someone you don't like.

Always appreciate the little things
and take nothing for granted.

Always make up your own mind
and ignore bored writers who make up quotations.

If you have very young children and you've taken a long trip with them, you probably heard the now famous line, "Are we there yet, Mommy or Daddy? Are we having fun yet?" They start squirming after a while, so you give them a toy, a puzzle, a palm pilot, a chloroform-filled bear, or whatever to quiet them down. You think of games to play, such as let's all count the big blue Lexus SUVs that are burning up all our gas and ruining our planet. After a while even that doesn't work, and your child throws a full-fledged, all-out tantrum. This usually happens when you are lost and your mate is also yelling at you for being such a stupid navigator.

I'm only in the first stage of my journey and I'm already inventing games to play as I walk along. I should throw a full-fledged tantrum somewhere in the middle of Indiana.

You would not believe what is happening. (You're supposed to say, "What's happening, David?"). It's snowing. I thought it was cold, and it obviously is cold. It's actually snowing rather hard, but it's not yet sticking to the road surface. It is sticking to the grass and to the trees. This isn't good. I'm on the open road and Old Forge, my next stop, is ten miles away. Perhaps the midday sun will raise the temperature above freezing. I put on my yellow rain slicker because it obviously keeps me drier, at least the top half of me, and I'm more visible to traffic. The snow is now sticking to the road. I have on lightweight open-mesh walking shoes and I can't feel my toes or fingers. I think I'm in trouble.

"Hey mister, you need a ride, it's dangerous walking. A car might slide into you."

"No thanks, I'm fine, but I really appreciate your offer. I'm just getting some exercise."

That sometimes happens. I'll be talking into my tape recorder and it will also record someone who stops to talk to me. In this case, it was a very kind older woman in a red pickup truck. I wonder why she wasn't afraid of a perfect stranger? There are some amazing and wonderful people in this country. I feel like an idiot refusing her ride, but a quest is a quest. I wanted to leap inside her Ford and place my hands and feet under the heater. I'm putting both hands in my pockets. The snow is two inches deep now and, oh shit, a salt truck just went by. This will melt the snow on the road, which is a good thing for the cars, but since I am not walking on the road, I am walking alongside the road, I am still walking in the snow. Now the cars are splashing me as they pass, and my jeans are soaked with salty crud. It can't get much worse.

It got worse. A snowplow just went by and deposited a mound of snow on the side of the road. I crossed over to face traffic because there is now a foot of snow on the right shoulder.

It got much worse. A snowplow approached from the other direction and now both shoulders have snow piled one foot high.

It's two hours later, three in the afternoon, the snow has stopped and the sun has come out. It's also gotten very windy and the temperature is dropping. Both my feet are soaking wet and I can't feel my toes. Soon the snow will turn to ice, and I still have five miles to go before I reach Old Forge. I see some buildings up ahead; I'm going to have to stop before I get frostbite or get hit by a swerving car.

The same woman in the red Ford pickup truck is again stopped alongside me.

"David, you had better get in the truck. My name is Adele Dobbs, and you don't have to walk the rest of the way to our inn. You've done your job by making contact with me, and we only have three miles to go. I almost told you the first time, but I knew you had a chance of making it on foot. Now it's too dangerous, so please get in."

I jumped in the truck and hugged Adele Dobbs. I then put my hands and feet under the heater. She told me Papa Jack had sent her a photo of me, so she knew right away who I was. I feel stupid because I also have a photo of her and her husband Thomas from when my father visited in 1974. She is older, but looks much the same, and I should have recognized her.

CHAPTER THREE
Old Forge, New York to Euclid, Ohio

Adele and Thomas Dobbs are two fine people. They are in their late seventies and both are remarkably fit. They have a house on the farthest of the Fulton Lakes, and now that the ice has melted, they take their Boston Whaler Newport boat to their inn which is right on the lake in the middle of Old Forge. The inn has ten rooms, a beautiful living room with full library, and a roaring fireplace. They have a staff of five that does the day-to-day chores. I said a quick hello to Thomas Dobbs and went directly to my room. I was dripping wet and didn't want to ruin the rugs. Thankfully my backpack is waterproof, and the rain slicker kept the top half of me dry. I took a hot shower. I enjoyed this one more than any other I've ever taken. I was singing a Kurt Cobain song, *Something in the Way*, while I lathered up with sweet smelling soap with aloe.

Did you know that Cobain was from Aberdeen, Washington? That is a coincidence, because in many ways my band, Hall's Mentals, was a Vermont version of Nirvana. My tastes have changed over the years, and now I'm more into jazz and world music, but every once in a while I like to blast out with some grunge. So I already have an Aberdeen connection.

I looked up Aberdeen on the website encyclopedia the other day, and here are some famous people who are from that city:

Kurt Cobain, rock musician from Nirvana

Dale Crover, rock musician from The Melvins

Kurdt Vanderhoof, rock musician from heavy metal band, Metal Church

Patrick Simmons, rock musician from The Doobie Brothers

Robert Motherwell, painter

Douglas Osheroff, Nobel prize-winning physicist

Robert Arthur, actor

Violet Blue, porn star

Colin Cowherd, radio presenter

Bryan Danielson, professional wrestler

Brandon Rogers, renowned chemist

Helena Shipman, actress

Clarence E. Vammen, Jr., aviator

Mark Bruener, pro football player for the Houston Texans

Vanessa Minnillo, Miss USA 1998, MTV, "Entertainment Tonight," lived briefly in the city during 1991.

Also, according to the encyclopedia:

"On the day of May 9, 2006, the couple commonly known as 'TomKat' (Tom Cruise and Katie Holmes), came to Aberdeen for the premier of 'Mission Impossible 3,' due to a competition won by a local Aberdeen resident. Because of this celebrated day, it will always be remembered as 'Tom Cruise Day,' and will be recognized annually on the ninth of May for the rest of time."

A professional wrestler, a porn star, an aviator, and a radio presenter named Cowherd are sharing the spotlight with my favorite, Kurt Cobain. I'm sure glad that Vanessa Minnillo lived there briefly in 1991. This is certain to make Aberdeen immortal. If she didn't do it, recognizing May 9 as "Tom Cruise Day" for the rest of time should stir your heart.

In twenty years nobody will know who any of these people are.

Aberdeen used to be the most notorious city on the West Coast for whorehouses and other amusements. I wonder if that's why my ancestors always ended up there. We have a long way to go before Aberdeen is mentioned again, if I ever do get there.

I rejoined my hosts for dinner. There's no restaurant at the Dobbs Inn, it's just a bed and breakfast, but the three of us had a fine meal that Adele seemed to create magically with absolutely no notice. We didn't talk about my trip because Thomas Dobbs forcefully put the quest on hold. He said in the morning we would take the mail boat back to their home on the lake, where he had the information on the next leg of my journey. Meanwhile, we should just relax and enjoy the fireplace. I showed them the photo of the dromedary I saw in the field, and we talked about Papa Jack and his visit. I learned that my father was instrumental in insuring that the Dobbs family survived. They didn't tell me all the details, but it seems they were in trouble in the early eighties. Mr. Dobbs was ill. The doctors gave him little hope of survival, but he beat the odds. Papa Jack must have given them a gift to keep the inn open. They speak of him as if he were some kind of saint. I felt like telling them about my reality, but that would have been totally out of place and rude. I just listened to how fine a man Papa Jack was.

Adele could see that I was very tired, and she ordered me back to my room. I felt like I was in the company of family and not perfect strangers. So help me, you can have this same feeling for any people you meet by chance. You don't have to have a common background or interest, only a joyous heart and a desire to give more than you receive. Chance meetings between strangers can result in better friendships and relationships than you have with your own family, since there is usually too much baggage and dysfunctionality with your own siblings.

Thomas Dobbs showed me his collection of shotguns. He's an interesting man. He has these double-barreled English and Italian 12-gauge shotguns, most of them worth thousands of dollars. They are in glass display cases all around the living room, but he doesn't hunt. He doesn't believe in killing anything. Lots of guns, no shooting, that's my kind of arsenal.

Here's a gun that I found alongside the road. It's stamped U.S. Government Property on one side of the frame, and USA on the other side. Next to the gun was a badly dented badge in a leather wallet that said, U.S. Department of Homeland Security, #568402. I believe this was part of President George Bush's anti-terrorism campaign in Iraq.

The late April snow was melting quickly, but the mornings were still very cold in the Adirondacks. After breakfast, I went to Bauer & Sons Inc., and bought a warm, lightweight coat, Thinsulate-lined gloves, and a wool cap that I can pull down over my ears. I also bought two pair of wool socks.

We walked to the dock and boarded the *President Harrison* mail boat. This is one of the few remaining mail boats in the country. I had no idea that mail was still delivered by boat. There are dozens of homes all around the lake, and the easiest way to deliver mail is by water. This is a classic 35-footer with a glassed-in cabin. It's rated for ten passengers and has a restroom. The deckhand makes the daily mail delivery by throwing mail sacks onto the docks of the lakeshore homes. This morning we are traveling to the Dobbs home by mail boat because they thought I would find it interesting.

They were right. There were only seven people on this morning's run, which takes about three hours and covers 22 miles: Adele and Thomas, the captain, the deckhand, two tourists, and me.

I'm glad we had a light cargo. Very recently there was a tragedy in Lake George, New York, not too far from here. On October 2, 2005, *The Ethan Allen*, a forty-foot tour boat, capsized with 47 senior citizens from Michigan and Ohio. Twenty passengers died.

Let me tell you how it happened. In 1995, one of those poor senior citizens from Ohio had an extra bag of potato chips. In 1998, another from Michigan had a bottle of Coca-Cola that he or she wouldn't ordinarily have drunk. In the year 2000, still another had a McDonalds Big Mac and a large milkshake, between meals. Those poor people were killed on that Lake George boat, one potato chip and one shake at a time. It took decades for this to happen, one munch and one sip at a time. I don't know what God's divine plan is when he allowed this to happen to those poor souls. He's also allowing us to industrialize the entire Third World and drive big cars as the temperature on Earth rises. He/She is trying to tell us something, but we're not listening.

Because of this horrific accident, the State of New York made all vessels undergo tests and post new weight limits. There is a sightseeing boat on the Fulton lakes named *Clearwater*. As a result of these new tests, the capacity was reduced from 125 to 115 persons. Americans are getting fatter and fatter. By the year 2050, the capacity of the *Clearwater* will be 57, because the average person will weigh about 350 lbs.

What about jet planes? You can't make the engines bigger or the wings longer. All those potato chips and McDonald's milkshakes are sitting on those poor aircraft tires. I was in the Pittsburg airport coming back from Florida when an announcement came over the loudspeaker for my flight back to Burlington.

"We need five volunteers to give up their seats because we are overweight. If you re-book for a later flight you will get a free ticket to any city that Northwest Airlines flies to."

I freaked out completely. I thanked Northwest for their diligence, but I prayed that they had lots of kickapoo juice in that jet fuel. The weather was hot, and there's not much lift under these circumstances. A plane taking off in the summer

51

can carry less weight than a similar flight in the middle of March when the temperature is fifty degrees. We think we are so much in control of science, it serves us so well, until we become runway kill.

The formula below is what they use to calculate whether or not your aircraft can handle a plane load of wide-bodies. It accurately computes air-lift capacity:

Density altitude can be calculated from atmospheric pressure and temperature (assuming dry air).

$$DA = 145426 \left[1 - \left(\frac{P_0/P_{SL}}{T/T_{SL}} \right)^b \right]$$

Where:

DA = density altitude in feet
P_0 = atmospheric (static) pressure
P_{SL} = standard sea level atmospheric pressure (101.325 kPa)
T = true (static) air temperature in <u>Kelvin</u> (K) [add 273.15 to the <u>Celsius</u> (C)] figure
T_{SL} = standard sea level air temperature (288.15 K)
b = 0.235

Great! Science is wonderful, and I'm glad there's a Northwest Airlines aeronautical engineer at Pittsburg airport with his calculator. Unfortunately, he just learned that his wife is leaving him for her supervisor at the real estate agency, and his car was just towed away because he forgot to put five quarters in the meter. His weight calculations were made ten minutes after his wife gave him the bad news. Just to be spiteful, she also threw out his baseball cards that he had lovingly collected since he was nine years old. She obviously hated him and had some serious issues.

We're all interdependent. We count on the guy running perpendicular to us to stop at his red light before we go on our green light. We can wait to make sure he stops. If he shoots the red light, we can scream at him, give him the finger, blow our horn, and then continue through the intersection.

What do we do if that Northwest Airlines employee hits the wrong button on his calculator trying to figure out how much weight our plane can carry? Tough shit, it's death by milkshakes and potato chips for us. I'd rather walk across America than ride in a jet plane. It's unnatural, and it's burning up all the oxygen in our upper atmosphere.

I have a theory. As you know, I'm a runner and am well proportioned for my height. It's easy for me to have contempt for those who are overweight such as the wide-body comment I made earlier. This is unkind, and I do apologize to all those who the government has classified as overweight or obese. It's not your fault. You are simply reacting to the stresses of the modern world. You eat too much because it dulls your mind. The blood rushes to your stomach and leaves your brain in the background.

All the environmental destruction, lack of universal healthcare, wars in the Middle East, the financial meltdown and the economy going into the toilet, sexual and marital issues, children falling victims to a vicious media or to drugs, hopelessness for your future, and for the future of mankind: Shit, who can blame you for having an extra Dunkin' Donut covered with jelly, stuffed with custard filling, and sprinkled with white confectioners sugar? I eat them all the time. Good thing I'm walking across the country. If I weren't I'd probably weight 546 lbs. You've heard the expression, Try to walk in the other guy's shoes. It's easy for me to be critical because walking is melting whatever excess I had. If I were walking in your shoes, I wouldn't be walking at all. I would be sitting on my butt watching *American Idol* while I scarfed down chocolate-crème-coated animals, vegetables, and minerals. I think I sympathize.

The Dobbs' home was just as inviting as the living room at their inn. They both knew that I couldn't linger and had to be on my way. Mr. Dobbs handed me a new map, and Adele said I wouldn't be needing MapQuest or GPS because I will get a new map at each of my stops. Wow, my father did a lot of planning for this journey. What if I had said no? Would he have picked one of my brothers or sisters? None of them would have done this in a thousand years. I guess I answered my own question.

The new route was between Old Forge, New York and Euclid, Ohio. The Dobbs offered to take me back to town to resume my journey, but I felt like walking along the lakes. The countryside is beautiful, and the sun was shining although it was still quite cool. They were both standing on their front porch and we waved to each other as I walked away into the morning mist. They couldn't see that I was crying. I couldn't tell if they were. If this trip ended tomorrow, it would have been worth it just to meet Adele and Thomas Dobbs.

I'm in good shape. All my clothes are freshly laundered; I can smell the fabric softener that Adele used. I have two extra meals in my backpack because there is a long stretch of road without restaurants. I may need new shoes soon; the snow and salt have weakened the fabric. They will probably last another couple of hundred miles, though. Some people I talked to before my trip suggested that I wear waterproof boots, but they are too big and heavy. Adele suggested that I buy polypropylene liners and wear them under my socks. She said that moisture, either in the form of sweat or rain, can cause blisters. The poly wicks away moisture into the next layer. They didn't have any in Old Forge, but I'll try to find them along the way. They did have a bicycle shop, and I bought a small rearview mirror that cyclists mount on their helmets. It's only one inch in diameter and has a wide field. I jury-rigged it with wire to my straw hat, and as soon as it gets warm enough to wear the hat, it will show me how closely cars are approaching from behind.

The last eighty miles have been relatively easy walking. I almost got hit by a motorcycle, of all things. I don't think even that little mirror would have helped me. The guy was going so fast he had to round the corner close to the shoulder as the road turned to the right. His right knee barely scraped my left leg as he roared by at over seventy miles an hour. I don't think he ever saw me, because he was sitting low for the least wind resistance, and wore one of those full-face helmets with a dark plastic shield. I didn't have time to react; he went by too fast. I don't like the numerical odds. X number of miles = one incident of a near accident. With XX miles to go, there would then be a possible total of 18 near accidents. Let's hope not. One of those near accidents could turn into an actual accident. I guess this is another one of those moments where I'm seriously thinking of bagging this goose chase. I'm not young and stupid enough to think I'm immortal. I tell myself the universe is looking out for me and nothing bad will happen. I guess that was really a prayer. *PLEASE* don't let me get squashed like a squirrel, very bad Juju.

Guess what I just did? I crossed the state line into Pennsylvania. I'm only a couple of miles from Lake Erie, so I'm going to visit it just to say that I saw it. This is my second state, and I'm very happy. The weather has changed dramatically. It's now close to May, and the daytime temperature goes into the seventies since I left the mountains. I've gotten rid of my heavy coat and gloves. I gave them to a pilgrim who was going west to east and was headed for the Adirondacks. Those mountains are just plain cold. Thomas Dobbs told me that on more than one occasion they had a frost in every month of the year. Just thinking about a July frost made me keep my wool cap, and besides, I've grown attached to it. I might need it on some cold morning.

I've got only about twenty miles to walk through Pennsylvania before crossing into Ohio. My next stop, Euclid, is only a day's walk after I cross the border. That's where my father met my mother. There is no doubt that there will be some kind of connection, although the name of

56

the people I'm going to meet is not the same as my mother's family. Her maiden name was Orwell, and the people I'm to see in Euclid are named Jefferson. Interestingly enough, Orwell and Jefferson are both towns in Ohio that are near Euclid.

I crossed into Ohio yesterday and was walking along Highway 6. I was in the Smugsburg city limits and I noticed a sign, "Visit Corporate Cavern in Smugsburg, and see the primitive cave painting." It was only two miles out of my way, and I was curious. I paid five dollars by dropping the bills into a large locked metal tube with a slit in the top. The tube seemed to lead to an underground storage vault. I think it's impressive that admission is on the honor system, because there was no way of telling how much money I really put in there. I was standing in a small cave about fifteen feet long, six feet wide, and ten feet high. The outside of the cave was painted red and there was a spotlight shining on the far wall.

This is the primitive cave painting I found.

I walked farther into the cave and noticed the following names on the near wall, which was painted red, and also illuminated by a spotlight:

THANK YOU FOR CONTRIBUTING

George Bush
Dick Cheney
Condoleezza Rice
Donald Rumsfeld
Alberto Gonzales
Karl Rove
Rupert Murdock
Sarah Palin
Newt Gingrich
Rush Limbaugh
Ann Coulter
Glenn Beck

A metal door slammed shut just as I was about to walk outside, and the lights went out. After an hour of darkness, which seemed like eight years, another light came on and shone on a blue wall with 12 more signatures.

THANK YOU FOR CONTRIBUTING

Nancy Pelosi
Ben Bernanke
Chris Dodd
Ben Nelson
Joe Lieberman

Bill Clinton
Charlie Rangel
Rod Blagojevich
Elliot Spitzer
John Edwards
Blanche Lincoln

Then a cylinder appeared down a chute, like those we use at a bank's drive-up window. The instructions were clear: Pay ten dollars or no exit. The lights went out again and it felt like another eight years of darkness. Finally, I deposited two five-dollar bills in the chute, it disappeared into the wall, and the door opened. Looks like they got me coming and going.

At first the sunlight hurt my eyes, but it didn't take me long to readjust. There are many such red and blue caves in America, all controlled by the corporations. It's actually quite a franchise. The same twenty-four signatures are on all the walls. You can't go anywhere without paying this tribute money.

I'm ten miles from Euclid. Although I'm out in farm country, I smell a lot of car fumes and now I see why. There's a large field, I guess it's about one hundred acres, and there are several thousand cars parked there. More are arriving as I approach the site. There's a stage set up with a desk and two podiums. Perhaps a play is going to be performed. There are thousands of lawn chairs in neat rows and WHAT? All the people are completely naked. Whoa! This is Ohio, not the French Rivera. Now I see a lot of network sound and camera trucks, and two large helicopters are parked on the field. I've got to know what's going on here.

"Excuse me, ma'am, why is everyone naked and what's going to be performed here?"

"Welcome to the Pleasant Valley Nudist Society. I'm sorry, sir, but if you want to sit down, you will have to take your clothes off."

"Oh no, not me, ma'am, I'll just watch from across the road. What's going on here?"

"There's going to be an au naturel debate between Sarah Palin and Hillary Clinton."

Everyone is naked here, even the camera crews. There are a few hundred people standing where I am, about 400 feet in front of the podiums. Like me, they have all their clothes on. Most of them have binoculars, and some have brought their own lawn chairs while others sit on top of their SUVs. There are a few recreational vehicles with direct TV antennas. I heard one of the people say that the debate is being broadcast on channel 558, the Nudity Channel. They have many events now scheduled to be shot. Last month they had a nude exhibitionist game between the New York Mets and the New York Yankees. There were some problems with inside pitches and head-first slides into second base, but other than that the game went smoothly.

Both of the podiums are made of clear Plexiglas. They are not completely see-through, however, because there are ripples in the glass, where private parts would otherwise be displayed. I feel this is not in the spirit of the Pleasant Valley Nudist Society, and I'm glad I didn't pay the fifty-dollar fee. This is one time when total clarity would have been appreciated.

The moderator, a short, round man with glasses, read from his notes. He was standing between the podiums and held a microphone in his left hand. Obviously shy, he held his notes over his private parts. Again, this disturbed me as not being in the spirit of Pleasant Valley.

He was about to speak.

"Ladies and gentlemen, in the spirit of full disclosure and transparency in government, the Pleasant Valley Nudist Society is proud to welcome two of America's most ample personalities. Please welcome Sarah Palin and Hillary Clinton."

The crowd clapped wildly.

"The subject of this afternoon's debate will be who speaks more for the common man, Democrats, Republicans, men, or women. We have also asked the speakers to be specific about what they like best about America, and what needs to be improved or changed. Our goal is to arrive at the naked truth." (This got a few chuckles and moans from the audience.) "Each speaker is limited to three minutes with a two minute rebuttal from her opponent on the same topic."

They drew for high card from Mrs. Palin's poker deck to see who went first. Mrs. Palin drew an ace, and Mrs. Clinton drew the four of clubs, but demanded a recount. On the second draw, this time using Mrs. Clinton's poker deck, Mrs. Palin drew the nine of diamonds, and Mrs. Clinton drew an ace. However, this was the same ace of spades that Mrs. Palin had drawn; it had markings from her deck. Mrs. Clinton was then accused of palming, and the moderator awarded the first question to Mrs. Palin.

"We're proud to present our moderator for this afternoon's debate. Please welcome Britney Spears."

When Britney Spears was introduced, everyone booed because she was fully clothed. I don't get it. She teases the American people by flashing glimpses of her anatomy here and there, getting in and out of cars. But when she has a chance for full disclosure, she keeps her clothes on. Britney sat in front of the two speakers with her back to the audience. TV cameras photographed her from the front, however and the view was placed on huge monitors fifteen feet off the ground on either side. She had a fat notebook with photos of little doggies on the covers. She asked her first question:

"Mrs. Palin, can you really see Russia from your house?"

"You betcha. Not only can I see Russia, but I can see the Western tip of China. This is a small world, and I thank God every day that America is in the center of this beautiful earth. There is so much suffering in the world. Not everyone has a Ford Explorer, you know. I was surprised when I found out that most people didn't drive one. Yes siree, we sure are lucky."

"Mrs. Clinton, your comments?"

"China? She says she can see the Western tip of China? That's the coffee cup you broke yesterday, lying on your kitchen floor, you stupid twat."

"Mrs. Clinton, please refrain from calling Mrs. Palin names. She gets enough of that from intelligent people all across America.

"The next question is for you, Mrs. Clinton. Do you believe that Congress deserves lifetime pensions and paid healthcare for their entire families for the rest of their lives?"

"Democratic Senators and Representatives do. The Republicans don't really care because they own the insurance and health industries that provide the shitty service to the rest of us. Not one Republican voted for President Obama's heathcare package, not one! They are not warm and fuzzy."

"Mrs. Palin?"

"Yes, well naturally I disagree with ol' Hill here. Aw shucks, girl, I'm a Republican, and I'm warm and fuzzy. I love baby seals clubbed only once, and cute fuzzy little wolves shot only twice, and those big white polar bears, well I guess you have to shoot them three or four times. That's the kind of can-do attitude I will bring to America when I run for President. I believe in universal healthcare for every American who can afford it."

"The next question is for Mrs. Palin. Do you favor drilling for more oil off our unspoiled coasts, or do favor some other form of energy?"

"Dad gum, I wasn't expecting that one. Let me see, hold on a second, I have some notes here somewhere. Oh, I favor quotas on the number of Hispanic people who can enter....whoops, I'm sorry, wrong notes. Well, let me see, I've got something written on my tummy. Would someone get me a mirror? For those of you who think I'm stupid, I had a member of my staff write these notes backwards on my tummy so I could read them with this mirror. Yes, here's my position on energy. When I'm President we will have enough oil to power America. Oil worked for us in the past, and for pity's sake, there's more in the ground, we just gotta go find it! So, a little oil leaked in the Gulf. What are we going to do with all those gas stations and Ford Explorers, just throw them away?"

"Time's up, Mrs. Palin. Mrs. Clinton, your comments, please."

"If I am elected President, America won't have to worry about its energy future. I will put a bag over Sarah Palin's head and collect enough BIOGAS to power the world."

The debate ended an hour later. I had as much fun watching the people in the audience as I did listening to the speakers. I also learned a lot about sex from this experience:

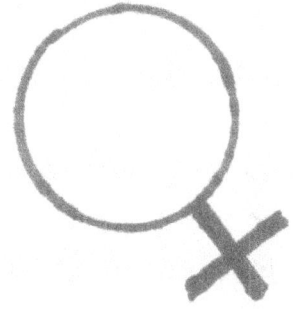

All I Know About Sex

Boys have Penises
    and girls have Venuses.

Women have Vaginas
    and men have Viagras.

Eventually I'll tell you why Joan and I split up, but I don't know you well enough yet. You really don't know much about my personal life, especially my past. You don't know my dreams or my fears. So far we've traveled together as new friends, people who have just met. As I mentioned in the Prologue, there is no omniscient narrator in this book, so he can't describe how I look, my facial expression, the tone of my voice, or my body language to give you a glimpse of my character. I will have to tell you what I am doing, and what I am thinking, and you will have to decide whether I'm worthwhile knowing or not.

I promise to be honest, or at least as honest as I can be if I'm not fooling myself. I'll tell you one thing, since I'm in a telling mood: I've made some mistakes in my life. Actually, I could go easier on myself and say that if mistakes are part of the play, then my mistakes are certainly going to be part of this memoir. There is a danger in walking alone on all these forgotten byways. A person could easily turn inward and become totally self-absorbed, *my* journey, *my* feet, *my* aches and pains, *my* thoughts, desires, and actions.

This is usually the way most American adolescents begin their lives, and I was no exception. It's taken me ten years to realize that there is a world full of *other* people. I know it sounds so basic, but I still don't quite have my life in balance. I don't know who said it, but the self is a dead end. In the last few years, I have been happiest when I've helped someone who has had a need. I used to have a fiery temper and absolutely no patience. I still revert to my old negative ways given the right stimulus. For months on end I can become surly, selfish, and bitter.

In two days I will visit the Jefferson family in Euclid. Tonight I'm sleeping in the Kirtland's Rest Motor Hotel. This is a perfectly typical motel except for the unusual decorations. The carpet on the floor continues up the wall and stops about five feet off the floor on two sides of the room. There's a molding on the wall hiding the edge of the carpet. Screwed into the carpet that is climbing up the walls are various decorations. There are four drawers, as in a chest of drawers, that are neatly stacked and screwed into the carpet. They don't open; they can't open because they are stuck into the carpet, and the carpet is stuck into the wall.

On the other carpeted wall, there are five mounted and framed photographs of 1950s pickup trucks also stuck into the carpet. There is a plastic globe light over a half-round table that has a telephone, and that also serves as a desk. This globe light is three feet in diameter and has every color of plastic known to man stuck to it in little squares. There is only a sixty-watt bulb in the lamp so when you turn it on, it gives no light. It only makes the lamp glow.

There is a vibrator in the bed with a coin slot. I put in fifty cents and the damned thing shook so violently my socks came off. It lasted exactly two minutes and then it abruptly stopped. I don't even want to think about what has gone on in this bed. In the night table is a pristine, practically unread Gideon Bible, and next to the Bible is a well-worn copy of *Valley of the Dolls*.

God bless America.

CHAPTER FOUR
Euclid, Ohio to Nappanee, Indiana

I don't have much to download into my computer this evening, but I do have an idea. I'm in another motel, called the Days and Nights Lodge, seven miles from Euclid. Have you ever heard of WBDY in Chicago? They have the strongest station in the Midwest. At night I used to listen to their jazz show in Vermont. During the day it still puts out a signal hundreds of miles. It's nine p.m. here on the outskirts of my second destination and time for the Shorty Jones show. I listen to him every night, and Thursday night he has the Doctor Prozak hour.

I have a short wire with a male connector at either end. It goes from the line-out on my SONY radio to the line-in on my computer. Since I don't have much to report, I decided to record the Shorty Jones show and make it a part of today's diary. The show is just starting. Shorty Jones always gives an introduction for Doctor Prozak.

"Okay, Middle America, I'm Shorty Jones, and you got me on your radio and I got you as a listener. Pleased to meet you on this fine Thursday evening. Tonight the Doctor is in. After I tell you about him I'll take my first caller.

"Dr. Connor Prozak studied at the University of Talledega and received a fellowship from the Sam Houston Institute of Technology (S.H.I.T.) in Texas. Dr. Prozak was nominated for the Nobel Prize in Medicine three times by his mother and has a controlling interest in Prozak Pharmaceuticals. He is a frequent speaker on the Republican Geriatric Circuit, and his name is often mentioned as a possible Vice-Presidential candidate or as the party's choice for Surgeon General.

"Dr. Prozak writes a column in the *Midwest Journal of Medicine*, which is now part of the Prozak Publishing and Cable-Entertainment Group. WBDY in Chicago is proud to have him answering those difficult day-to-day questions from our listening audience. Dr. Prozak has a wonderful collection of quotes from the world's greatest minds. He quotes from them before he gives *his* answers. It's amazing how fast he can find just the right passage. Finally, at the end, he will give you a 'Germ of the Day' to live by. The Shorty Jones Show welcomes Dr. Prozak. Oh, and please remember folks, don't give him your real names. Make up a name, such as Stumped in Smugsburg. This is very important for insurance purposes. Are you ready for the first caller, Doctor?"

"Oh yeah, bring 'em on."

"Go ahead, this is Shorty Jones, you're on the air."

"Hello, Dr. Prozak. I earned a masters degree in business administration from Cleveland State, worked hard to get my CPA and just passed the test, but there's a problem. I no longer like accounting, and I believe I dislike business altogether, but I don't know what else I can do. Call me Confused in Smugsburg."

Of all the damnable waste of human life that ever was invented, clerking is the very worst.

George Bernard Shaw

"Wow, you really are Confused. I realized that I hated business when I had my first part-time job in high school. I'm not surprised that you've studied for seven years before you realized that it's not for you; pampered people with thick glasses are slower on the uptake than we creative types. Actually, the way you vacillate makes you well suited to business management, so think twice before abandoning CPA plans. The world needs people who can press calculator buttons all day and have the skills to improve the bottom line. Payables and receivables are as important to people like you as love and honor are to people like me. You can sit on your ass all day, you never have to work outside in that miserable crisp autumn air, and you can buy enough insurance to protect your future median family there in Smugsburg."

Your Germ of the Day:
I must accept my fate. Corporate America needs me. I may not be lively at cocktail parties, but it's a sacrifice I must make. To audit, to calculate, to reconcile; that is the thing.

"Hello, this is Shorty Jones, what is your question for the Doctor?"

"Doctor Prozak?"

"Yes, go ahead, you're speaking to Connor Prozak."

"Doctor Prozak, please settle an argument between me and my mother-in-law. I say the toilet paper goes with the loose end hanging down at the back. She says the loose end goes over the top. Which one of us is correct? I guess I'm Fastidious in Fernwood."

Advertising is the rattling of a stick inside a swill bucket.
George Orwell

"Pleased to meet you, Fastidious. I'm so glad you took the time to call me about this issue. Its importance is underappreciated. Americans should be concerned with issues the rest of the world finds trivial; it adds to our international appeal. We don't have to worry about having enough food and water like the rest of mankind, so we should concern ourselves with better and more meaningful problems.

"Before I answer, I'd also like to mention that I wish the media would devote more time to advertising pet deodorants and disposable hair curlers. Which brand of chocolate caramel-covered cocoa puffs is best for my Pekingese? Is there a toilet seat polish that will really shine sitting after sitting? Do they make a kitchen remote for my toaster and can opener? I'm tired of getting up and down.

"Back to the toilet paper. It should be pulled apart at each perforation and stacked neatly to the left of the bowl, fourteen inches off the floor, right next to a current issue of either *House Beautiful* or *TV Guide*."

"Shorty Jones Show, go ahead, you're on the air."

"Doctor Prozak, I'm worried. My daughter is a senior in high school this year, and she brought home four new friends for me to meet. The girls have shaved heads with weird tattoos on their scalps, and the boys have earrings in their noses and wear leather chokers. They don't speak English and have lots of small plastic bags filled with white powder. If I tell my daughter not to see them, she'll do just the opposite. What can I do? I'm Freaked in Philly."

Somewhere on this globe, every ten seconds, there is a woman giving birth to a child. She must be found and stopped.
Sam Levenson

"Don't despair, Freaked. I get many questions like yours. Raising kids in the twenty-first century is tough, but you hold the key to solving your problem and don't realize it. Since your daughter will do the opposite of what you say, I suggest the following: Shave your head and get a full scalp tattoo in five different colors. Wear tight leather pants and a chain vest. When your daughter comes home with her friends, have loud, violent, heavy-metal music playing and

74

give them all a big hug. Within two weeks your daughter will probably become a nun. Be careful, though, that her friends don't get too attached to you."

Your Germ of the Day:
I will give my children reverse guidelines. If I want them to stay in, I'll tell them to go out. I'll tell them college is for nerds, and only dweebs take piano lessons. I'll sit back and watch them "rebel" against me.

"This next call is unusual, Doctor. I've got a phone line with three extensions. Shorty Jones Show, go ahead all."

"Doctor? Is it wrong to sit with my hair in curlers in front of the TV, and watch more than four soap operas a day while I eat potato chips? My husband says I should get him a beer. I'm usually Supine in Sarasota."

"Doctor Prozak, that's easy for her to say, but does my wife have the right to complain if I sit with a six-pack of beer, and watch more than four football games on Sunday? I'm Unhappy in Sarasota."

"Doc, my parents always give me a hard time. Is it harmful to watch four straight hours of MTV instead of doing my homework? I plug in headphones so I don't bother them, and although I bring in plenty of munchies and soda, my room is mostly clean, except for the rug and the bed. I'm Unloved in Sarasota."

Energy experts have announced the development of a new fuel made from human brain tissue. It's called Assohol.
George Carlin

"People, people, I don't believe you've been introduced to each other. Although you all have the same address, you obviously each live in your own room. Keep up the good work. You make a wonderful, modern, American family."

Model Family Germ of the Day:
Don't let anyone steal your remote.

The show went on for another half hour. I learn something every night from Shorty Jones. As I walk through the Midwest, I'll be recording snippets of the most interesting items.

I've arrived in Euclid. My destination is a tidy three-story house on 222nd Street near Lakeshore Boulevard. I met the Jeffersons. Dr. William Jefferson was raised by my mother's parents. He is black, and his wife Jennifer is white. My mother and he never got along, and I don't remember her ever mentioning him. They have three grown children. Wow, did I get an earful about my father's visit in 1974.

It seems that at first the Orwell family hated my father. When he came back from Aberdeen for my mother, he had to sneak her out in the middle of the night. Two years after they were married, they visited Euclid. Mr. and Mrs. Orwell still hadn't forgiven Papa Jack for stealing their daughter and Mr. Orwell started a fight. Dr. Jefferson said that my father refused to fight back because he would never forgive himself for punching his wife's father. He got a split lip and a black eye, but although he didn't know it at the time, he also won the respect of his in-laws. I never met my maternal grandparents; they were both dead by the time I was born.

Dr. Jefferson told me that Papa Jack paid all the hospital bills in the old folks' final days. William Jefferson's father ran off when he was seven, and his mother died when he was nine. The Orwell family took him in when they were in their fifties. My mother, an only child, had long ago left with my father, and the Orwells didn't think twice about giving him a home. I'm puzzled because I didn't see any mixed-race connection in my mother's past. Dr. Jefferson and family are from a different generation.

My father paid for Dr. Jefferson's education. He's a vet with a practice not far from here. His home reminds me of the set of *All Creatures Great and Small* that used to run on PBS television. He has a cute little white dog with only three legs. You should see him move; he's faster than I am. There are two other dogs, including a huge black Newfoundland, and five cats. One of the cats is missing a tail. There are photos and paintings of animals everywhere. His son, William Jr., is about to get his doctorate and enter the practice, and Rhonda, his daughter, is also studying to be a vet. This will be a wonderful family practice. I wish that our family was as close, but there's too much money. Money is a wedge that knifes between family members. All my siblings have been trying to outmaneuver each other to get in my parents' good graces. They each hate it when the other gains favor. When Jonathan was accepted into medical school, my sister said "Quack, quack" at the dinner table. And so it goes.

On Saturday morning a package arrived from Old Forge, New York. Adele Dobbs had found two pairs of poly sock liners and sent them to the Jeffersons' home. I love the Dobbs. At lunchtime the Jeffersons took me to the Albert W. Henn Mansion in Sims Park. This is a brick English Tudor Revival home on thirty acres with a bird sanctuary on the shores of Lake Erie. We took a picnic lunch. I thought New England and New York had all the pretty scenery, but this place is beautiful. In so many ways Ohio, Indiana, Nebraska, and Iowa are the true weathervanes of America. In the middle of the country there aren't any extreme political or social movements like the ones that start in New York or California. There isn't the glitz of Las Vegas, or Miami to the south, or the opulence of Aspen, or Stowe to the north. When a Democratic presidential candidate carries one of these states, he has to earn it. They won't vote for a phony. Republicans usually rule, whether or not they are phonies. I wish I could change that, but we have a long way to go.

William asked me if I had had any trouble with the police. He seemed surprised when I said no. He gave me my next map. I'm to walk from Euclid to Nappanee, Indiana. The person I'm to see next is Caroline McGregor.

Walking conditions are absolutely perfect. As I record this message, the temperature is sixty-two degrees with low humidity. And Highway 24 is flat with no hills. I felt energetic, hopeful, and positive after meeting the Jeffersons, but now I feel down. There's nothing like walking to free my thoughts. They sneak out when I least expect it.

Here's another family that talks about my father as if he were a saint. Dr. Jekyll and Mr. Hyde. If I ever needed a reason to continue on this journey, this contradiction has provided it. By the time I reach Aberdeen, I hope to know exactly why he was so kind to all these people and so surly to his own family. But it's early days yet, and as I walk through the West, I may learn that he was an impossible bastard.

The last two days have been wet, and I needed my rain slicker. I crossed into Indiana and am right outside the town of Waterloo. Today I'm going for a record walk. There are footraces across America. Appropriately enough they are called Trans-America footraces. The runners average 46 miles per day for 64 days. I like to run, but 64 straight days is more than a bit much for me. I wonder what I can do in one day. I've really picked up the pace. My goal is 35 miles today.

You would not believe what just happened. As I was walking along Route 24 at 11:30 a.m. a very bright light stopped me in my tracks. There, in the middle of the road, descending through the rainy mist was a huge figure bathed in yellow sunlight. He had a long beard and was at least twenty feet tall. He had such a loud voice that my ears rang for hours afterwards. He told me his name was Moses and he had returned to Earth to present mankind with a new set of Commandments. Naturally I asked him, "Why me?" and he answered: "David, because you're the first schlep who wandered down the road. Besides, I've decided that Americans are most in need. Most of you pay no attention to the first Ten Commandments, but you had better follow these ten, or else." Then he disappeared straight up through the clouds, and the road was once again dark and rainy. All I could feel were my knees shaking.

In my hands were two tablets made of some kind of stone. They didn't look like real stone, but some sort of composite. I didn't understand the writing. It wasn't Aramaic or Hebrew, but some form of English. When I turned one of the tablets over it said *Made in China*. Then it dawned on me that they were written in Pig Latin. This is a unique gift from the heavens that we have been given. I translated them, and I freely share these commandments with you.

I – Thou shalt not have sex with a Republican in or out of wedlock. No begetting or begatting is to commence. The race must not propagate.

II – Thou shalt not have impure thoughts about Hillary Clinton.

III – Youse guys must tithe to the Temple of Bernanke. However, you keep the 10% and give Uncle Ben the 90%.

IV – Thou shalt not study Palintology. It is the forbidden science of lower life forms. It is a study that condemns all practitioners to the rotten, nasty fires of fucking hell.

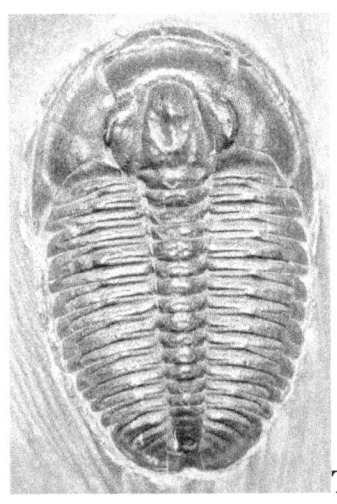TRILOBITE

Paleontology is the study of fossils

Palintology is the study of assholes

V – Thou shalt always obey, trust, listen to, follow the instructions of, sacrifice for, believe in, and welcome no member of Congress. A special place has been reserved for them in the afterlife and we strongly suggest you plan on arriving at a different final destination.

VI – Thou shalt not watch television.

VII – Thou shalt not have impure thoughts about Nancy Pelosi.

VIII – Thou shalt not covet thy neighbor's Lexus.

IX – Thou shalt not drink tea.

X – Thou shalt not worship graven images. This would exclude the IRS, CIA, FAA, SEC, FCC, FBI, FSA, who need your prayers and all your money.

As I write this in my computer, I'm staying at a Howard Johnson in the town of NoName, Indiana, two miles from where I started this morning. Let me tell you what happened. I was walking along Highway 24 when the county sheriff stopped his patrol car in front of me. He got out, and as I approached he asked me to stop. He asked where I was from and where I was going. I told him that it was every American's right to be afforded free movement without explanation, when that citizen is law-abiding. Identifications are unnecessary as long as no charges have been filed.

That was not what he wanted to hear. He told me to remove my backpack and pushed me against the side of his cruiser. He slapped handcuffs on me and stuffed me in the back of the car. I hit the side of my head and it still smarts. He then got on his radio and asked for backup. Another sheriff's car arrived with two more deputies, and one of them got in the back seat and asked me some more questions, but he was much nastier.

"Who the hell are you, boy, and what are you doing walking on Highway 24? What's in this backpack? Where are you from, Iraq? Do you have any chemicals that could poison our water supply? Are you carrying anything that could harm the people of Indiana?"

I admit right now that I could have put an end to this outrage by producing my photo ID driver's license or my passport. I could have told them what I was doing and provided the address of Caroline McGregor in Nappanee, but I didn't do it because I was furious.

They took me to a jail cell in their wonderful town of NoName, and put on latex gloves before they patted me down. They confiscated my backpack and sniffed inside my canteen. They emptied my backpack onto the large wooden table where we were sitting and went through every pocket. They ruined the food I was carrying by chopping it up with a hunting knife, and the questions kept on coming. They were desperately trying to find something to book me for.

"What's on this computer?" They made me turn it on. The dumb fool didn't know how to do it. His partner then scrolled through the list of books I had stored. I was in the middle of reading the poetry and drawings of Edward Randall and one of them came up on the screen.

WEST TERRE HAUTE, THE WAY GOD WANTS IT

Of all the drawings that could have been on my computer! Unfortunately, West Terre Haute is in Indiana, and the sheriffs, who were white, were deeply offended. They didn't say anything to my face, and I suppose that's progress. If this were the 1950s, I probably would have been beaten with a rubber hose. If we were in the 1930s and a little further South, they may have been looking for a tree and a rope. I did hear the fat guy tell his partner in the other room, "First time I've seen a mongrel with blue eyes." The other deputy said, "Yeah, but this mongrel has a valid passport. We have to let him go."

They did a complete background check. I don't even have a speeding ticket. They made me take a breathalyzer test. They said it showed a trace of alcohol. I told them I never drank alcohol, so it was impossible to have a trace in my blood because alcohol doesn't occur naturally in the body. I said there was something wrong with his tester. This only made the deputy angry. They were very disappointed. They read all my notes and saw who I would be visiting, but they made no comment. They told me I had five minutes to pack my things and hit the road.

Before I left, I told them I was a reporter. I called up my old webpage from *The Burlington Free Press* on my computer so they could see me at work. As soon as they knew I was a newspaperman, they got very nervous. The fat deputy leaned on the edge of the desk and said, "Boy, if I were you I'd hitch a ride. These roads can get very unfriendly, if you follow my drift." If you wrote this in a movie script, it would be laughable. The sheriff with the big gut is too much of a stereotype, totally not believable.

I still can't believe it. I was out of there in two minutes. I never once cursed, raised my voice, or gave them any reason to hold me. I wanted them to know that I hated them as much as they hated me, but I didn't want to spend time in their lockup. This memoir is my response. I'm protecting the town by calling it NoName; I have faith that most of the people who live there would be upset if they could have seen the way I was treated. I'm not mentioning the officers' names; I hope they can see themselves and change the way they treat ordinary citizens whose skin is a slightly darker shade than their own.

I know I tend to simplify complex issues. I'm not a political sophisticate, but we're in for a lot of trouble in this country if dark-skinned people, including Mexicans, Puerto Ricans, East Indians, Middle-Easterners, Africans, and West Indian Americans can't walk the streets and highways without fear. If the terrorists succeed in getting us to turn on ourselves, it will be far more deadly than an armed attack. They will have destroyed our country's soul.

I did 35 miles in one day. I'm tired but happy. Another police officer stopped me. Actually it was an Indiana state trooper who pulled alongside me as I was walking. I was ready for a fight. Quite frankly, I'd had enough of tin authority figures. He asked if he could give me a ride or if I needed anything. I was so shocked I started stuttering. I told him I was walking across the country to write a book, and he actually pulled the car over and asked me what was the most interesting thing I'd see so far, and what did I think of Indiana. I told him about the incident at the Sheriff's Department, and he asked if I wanted to file a complaint. I told him no, but he should be aware of their misconduct. I took his photo, we shook hands, and he went on his way. Same state, same road, different outcome. This peace officer was a gentleman and a humanitarian.

I've learned an important lesson on this trip, now that I'm almost 840 miles from Burlington. I've learned not to pre-judge people. I don't automatically assume that a person is going to do me good or ill. I have to be ready for anything. I guess I can describe my stance as neutral: not guarded, but neutral. I will respond to kindness with kindness, and nastiness with either nastiness or kindness, depending on how big the nasty person is.

Before I arrive at my next destination, I usually Google the place to learn all about it. I check the history, scenic attractions, look at the photographs and anything else of interest. I deliberately refrained from checking the Internet for Nappanee, Indiana. I wanted to be surprised at what I found when I arrived.

I was surprised. About two miles out of town I was passed by two black horse-and-buggy rigs. I recognized the people immediately as Amish. I flagged down a Nappanee police officer and asked her if this was Amish country, and she was glad to give me some additional information. She was as friendly as the Indiana state trooper. I'm beginning to like this state after all.

Do you know what I learned? Nappanee is the center of one of the largest Amish settlements in the United States, with over 2,500 of them. The police officer, Nancy Timmons, spoke warmly of their presence in the community. She said that they connect with one another heart-to-heart in a way that is often foreign to modern communications.

Whoa! This is a cop talking, the fuzz, a Dickless Tracy who I would have expected to be a Femi-Nazi. She continued.

"Here you'll find that a handshake is all that is necessary to do business with your neighbor. *Time* magazine voted Nappanee one of the top ten small towns in America that has re-invented itself to face the challenges of tomorrow. David, before you leave you should sit down to a traditional Amish haystack supper. You can take home some bologna and cheese that will be better than anything you ever had. That is, if you have room in your backpack. You take care, I got a call."

As quickly as she entered my life, Officer Nancy Timmons was gone. I shouted, "Be safe!" as she roared away. She left about ten feet of rubber; must have been an important call. It was probably a cat caught up a tree, or a housewife locked out of her car. Nothing bad could ever possibly happen here. Yeah, I know, the bad guys are everywhere, but this town seems so idyllic. Now there's an amazing woman. Police officer? She should be mayor.

Caroline McGregor lives on North Main Street in a large, rambling house that used to be an inn. She has two women living with her. They are technically housemates, not roommates. The three of them share expenses. The house is so big they each have complete privacy. Caroline is twenty-five years old and is absolutely gorgeous. Whoa! When I met her I just stood there staring. She has the reddest hair I've ever seen, is five foot seven, curvaceous in all the important places, has green eyes, an engaging smile, a beautiful voice, and I've known her all of three minutes. She is wearing a green cotton dress that matches her eyes.

CHAPTER FIVE
Nappanee, Indiana to Nappanee, Indiana

Caroline said that my timing was perfect for dinner. Her housemates had their own kitchen, and she had already prepared a meal in hers. A little girl walked into the room and threw her arms around Caroline.

"Sara Ann, say hello to David."

"Hello, David."

"Sara Ann is my daughter."

"Oh," was all I could think of to say, but then I recovered, smiled, and made a big fuss over the beautiful child. She had the same color hair as her mother.

"I've been a single mom for about two years, and Sara Ann is three."

"Oh," I said again, but how different the same word can sound.

The three of us sat down to dinner, and I know I was being very rude. I could not take my eyes off Caroline. I asked her how she knew my father, and she told me she didn't, but her parents did. I asked her what their relationship was with Papa Jack, and she couldn't tell me because her parents were no longer alive.

"I was hoping *you* could tell *me*. Our family attorney called and said you would be visiting. I went to see him, and he gave me a map for you. I appreciate your calling me yesterday. You must have this walking thing down to a science; you were within a half hour of when you said you would arrive."

"Sorry I was late," I quipped. "If I'd known how pretty you and Sara Ann are, I would have been a week early." I can't believe I said that. I was blushing as much as she was. All she did was smile. She put down the ladle she was using to scoop out a delicious beef stew, walked over to my chair, and kissed me on top of my head.

"Would you care for some wine or a beer?"

"No thank you, I don't drink alcohol. I'm a real square. I don't believe in using any mind-altering substances. You go right ahead. Any kind of fruit drink or water will be fine for me." I was puzzled because when I opened the refrigerator to help take out some orange juice, there was no beer or wine. Sara Ann really took to me and was sitting on my lap, playing with my food. Caroline made a move to take her away, but I held up my hand and asked her not to. "Please don't think me rude, but were you ever married?"

"You're not being rude at all. I like you and already know that we can be friends. Yes, I was married but my husband and I divorced. He is currently in jail on a drug distribution charge. He became a heavy user of both drugs and alcohol, became abusive and ruined our lives. At first, I didn't have a clue that he was using drugs. He concealed it from me for a year. The alcohol abuse came later. I was stupid, naïve, and am still bitter, but I have a daughter to raise. When you told me you didn't even drink alcohol, I almost lost it right here in this kitchen. It's been very hard."

"So, when you offered me beer or wine, you were hoping I would say no? A lot of people drink a glass or two of wine, and it doesn't mean they are addicts. What if I had said yes?"

"I'm sorry to have misled you. I would have excused myself for not having any. I'm really sorry, David, but I have an extreme fear and sensitivity about exposing my daughter to any more unhappiness."

While I was talking to Caroline, and staring into those green eyes, Sara Ann, who was now sitting in her own chair, accidentally knocked her steaming-hot bowl of stew into my lap. I jumped up quickly, just as Caroline was bending down to help clean it up. We both laughed. I said "Ow!" and we just stood there, our faces one foot apart. Neither of us could pull away from looking deep into each other's eyes.

I'm writing this at 1:00 a.m. from my room. We talked for seven hours. All I can say is that I don't believe this is happening to me. How could I have fallen in love so quickly and so totally? I actually wondered if I had been hit by a car and landed in Heaven. I know it's corny, but when you truly give thanks and are grateful, it has to be simple, pure and simple. Unfortunately many people only pray or meditate when they are in trouble or need something.

I guess by now you know that I'm a Buddhist. Actually, Caroline and I were both born Methodists. My mother was half Catholic, half Methodist, and my father didn't belong to any church, but I know he meditated and prayed. His parents were Presbyterian and Catholic, and his grandmother was Jewish. His great-grandmother was Islamic. My religious background is as varied as my ethnicity. I have been drawn to Buddhism, and have been reading a lot about it. It's a gentle, peaceful religion and a great antidote to the fundamentalist madness. Those sheriffs in NoName could never have treated me the way they did if they meditated to the Tara, or Kwan Yin. It seems strange to think of that fat deputy sitting on a meditation bench chanting Om Mani Padme Hum over and over again. I'll bet they all go to church on Sunday and think they're pure.

I went to Methodist Sunday school but really don't believe any of it. Yeah, I know the arguments, there has to be a Prime Mover, something can't come from nothing, everything must have a beginning. This is Thomas Aquinas stuff. It's just as likely that the universe has always existed.

I know, you're jumping up and down screaming, "It can't have always existed because everything that exists must have had a beginning!" You and I are in a doo loop. That is precisely my point, we don't understand it.

It's interesting to study the scientific explanations. In the last century, astronomers decided that the formation of the universe started when two suns collided. Absolutely, they were sure of it, but whoops, the theory changed. The current cause, and I'm sure it's proclaimed with equal certainty, says that all matter started with something the size of a pea, an exploding pea. They base this theory on the fact that the universe seems to be expanding. How everything got into this pea, and how the pea came about, are different subjects. What if there is a cosmic can of peas, and there are several thousand parallel universes full of exploding peas? That's a whole bunch of aliens with strange belief systems.

I love all the different religions humans have created to explain who they are, where they came from, and hopefully where they are going. There are many Gods: Jehovah, Jesus Christ, The Holy Ghost, Allah, The Great Spirit, Yahweh, and a host of other deities who are vying for our tithes.

Here are some of the sects:

Pressedbyterians

Starchedbyterians

Ironedbyterians

The more liberal Tumbledrybyterians

And the avant-garde Blowdriedbyterians

Baptists, with their female auxiliary, the Paptests

RhythmMethodists, very preoccupied with procreation

Catholics (who are taking quite a licking at the moment)

Islam (If they don't stop strapping bombs to their underwear, there will be none of them left.)

The Church of Christ of Latter Day Saints, also known as Mormons (They are latter day because they want to convince you they're holy every time they wake you up at 7:00 a.m. on a Saturday morning. Some of them are also called Muns. A Mun is a male nun. They're breaking new ground here.)

Unitarians and their offshoot, the Parliamentarians, basically a philosophical social club awash in constant rhetoric.

Jehovah's Witnesses who, like the Muns, will visit you at 7:00 a. m. on a Saturday morning. They hand you "The Watchtower" and other pamphlets. Whatever you do, don't accept one because you are guaranteed a visit the next Saturday morning at 7:00 a.m. This sect is especially tough because they are such sweet people, so it's very hard to shout "get lost!"

Scientologists, who are anything but sweet.

Episcopalians, who are really Catholics in alien form.

Jews, who can be cool when they're not kvetching.

Buddhism, an earth-based religion with a sense of the preciousness of all beings. These are the teachings I really like. I'm convinced that my primitive attempts at meditation, unenlightened as they may be, are responsible for controlling the rage that seems to live inside me. We are all connected. I went to a Buddhist lecture in Burlington and the teacher screamed at the top of her lungs, "Wake up!" This warning has been reverberating inside me ever since.

Back to the here and now. I think I know what's on your mind. I've known this woman less than twenty-four hours; how could I possibly believe that I've found such happiness? How could I possibly be in love? She asked me if I could stay for a few more days and I said yes. To be truthful, I wish I could stay here for the rest of my life.

Let me tell you how this happened. Someone once asked Carl Sandburg, at least I think it was Carl Sandburg, how long it took him to write a poem. The poem in question was a short one of less than thirty lines. He replied that it took about twenty years. He had to experience the subject of that poem for twenty years before it was ready to leap from his mind onto the page. The act of writing it was probably as long as it took me to realize that Caroline was the person I wanted to be with. I was ready. I told her about Joan, and why we broke up, and everything else I could think of. We have each been preparing to meet the other for many years. When it happened, all the work had already been done.

Caroline is very sensitive to the fact that she could not just admit a new boyfriend into the house without an explanation to Sara Ann. She told the child that I was a good and kind man, and I would be staying for a while. Sara Ann said, in a very loud voice, "Good, I need a new daddy." I can tell that Caroline wants to move slowly. She sure as hell isn't going to jump into bed with me until she knows me better, damn it!

Caroline's housemate, Nancy, is looking after Sara Ann, and Caroline and I are going to see a series of four one-act plays at the Tyler Theater in Elkhart. Her other housemate, Sydney Boylan, is starring in two of the plays. She plays Mary Louver in "Split Screen." This is a unique production that has one actor offstage saying what the onstage actor is really thinking. Since this is an amateur production, they allowed me to record it. Actor's Equity has strict rules against recorders or photographs unless you are the press, which I also am, or at least was. I still have my press card.

I'll read the intro from the old-fashioned description in the program:

Split Screen

A one-act play,
Wherein we get a chance to observe the actions of
Salespeople at a dinner meeting,
While we simultaneously hear their thoughts.
(Their thoughts are written in italics.)

Cast of characters:

Molly Idunno - Sales Secretary
Simon Fuehrer- Director of Sales
Nathan Folger - East Coast Sales Manager
Mary Louver - Salesperson
Ralph Terra - Veteran Salesperson
Turk Bulk – Salesperson

(These notes on the play are mine.)

The curtain opens and we see the six characters sitting at a corner booth in a fine French restaurant. It is the kind of place with thirty-seven different appetizers on the menu and a wine list that goes back to 1914. There are four servers catering to their every whim and fancy. Simon Fuehrer asks Molly for a stack of handouts, which he distributes to all present.

ONSTAGE ACTION (DIALOGUE)	OFFSTAGE VOICES (THOUGHTS)

Simon

I'm glad we all have a chance to be here tonight. I'm looking forward to working out a strategy for the next quarter. Please feel free to order anything on the menu.

Shit, the Knicks are playing the Bulls, hope I can end this in time to watch the game.

Nathan

We need to redefine our territories. Our East Coast sales are down nine percent from this time last year. We have to raise everyone's quotas and go get the business.

Simon, you couldn't work out a strategy to get from your seat to the bathroom, you asshole. You shouldn't be the director of sales, I should be the director.

Simon

That's a good point, Nathan, we must aggressively pursue new business or our market share will continue to drop.

Take a tranquilizer, you dickbrain. You'll burn out long before you come near taking my job. I'll decide what's on the agenda.

Molly

Mr. Folger, should I take minutes of this meeting or can I eat dinner also?

Shit, I forgot my tape recorder.

Simon

We need to have a record of what we are discussing, so yes, you need to take notes. When you get back to the office tomorrow, please transcribe them and send them to everybody present.

The stupid bimbo forgot her tape recorder again. I'll be lucky if understands every third word. Oh what a rack, I love it when she reaches for a glass of water.

Turk

Nathan, I don't know why we don't got parts available for the Fulcrumb line.

(nothing)

Turk

What's the point of making the sale if
nobody gonna ship the parts? The order
ain't complete and I get no commission.

(nothing)

Nathan

I know it's a pain but you absolutely have
to stay on top of parts and service. Keep
after them to send the orders. It's just as
important to service an account after the
sale. The customer must have confidence
that we can deliver.

*Turk, you are a joke. The boss's
son-in-law. Where did she find
you, on Muscle Beach? Don't got,
don't got, learn how to speak
English, try oiling your brain
instead of your biceps.*

Mary

I'm the new person here, and since I just
started working for Fulcrumb & Minsk,
I'd like to know if there is any support in
terms of product seminars or other events.
Is there up-to-date product literature?

*Uh oh, I think I made the wrong
decision. Fulcrumb & Minsk is
on the way down. I'll pretend to
be interested and hang on long
enough until I get some
experience and then go to the
competition.*

Ralph

I guess I have been with Fulcrumb the
longest. Relax, folks, I've seen dozens of
ups and downs in this business. You have
to learn to enjoy the good times and suck
it up when the going gets nasty. We all
must work as a team.

*Another college kid who thinks
she knows everything. Product
seminar, bullshit. This product
line will be dead in less than a
year. I wonder if the Bulls are
beating the Knicks.*

Simon

Nathan, I want you to work with Mary
and see that she understands the product
line and introduce her to the key accounts
in her territory. That used to be your old
stomping grounds and she can benefit
from your expertise and contacts.

*I didn't like the way Molly
smiled at you. If you make a
move on my property, you are
history. You'll like Mary. Skinny
little college girl who hates your
guts. I can already feel the vibes.
This should keep you on the road
awhile, numbnuts. Stay cozy.*

The servers bring an ample supply of French Chardonnay, Cabernet Sauvignon, and two magnums of Gewurztraminer. There are no objectors or abstainers. The appetizers are followed by quail, duck, scallops, and Rock Cornish game hens with truffles.

Nathan

I've asked Ralph to show Mary the ropes. He has the most experience, and we are going to redefine the territories. She will have some of his accounts while he travels to new places. I've asked Molly to prepare the schedules.

Nice try, you old sack of shit. Stick me out on the road for two months, no way. I hate to tell you, Simon old boy, but Ralph and the Service Manager have been doing Molly for over a year. I don't want your secretary but I will have your job.

Simon

I have already made arrangements for the three of you to travel out tomorrow night. It is extremely important that she have the proper guidance, and between you and Ralph, she'll be a pro in no time. I have also asked the Service Manager to visit some key accounts. This will demonstrate

You don't know it yet, Ralphie ol' buddy, but your and the Service Manager's new territory is Northern Canada. I'm moving Nathan's office from Boston to Fargo. That will leave just Molly and me in the sales office.

Turk

How come nobody showed me the ropes? I wish I had somebody to introduce me to new accounts. It's hard just walking in without knowing nobody. When am I gonna get a company car? I need a cool car. Got to look important to sell good.

(nothing)

Simon

Your own car is fine for now. We do pay generous mileage. Nobody sees your car after you leave it in the parking lot. You don't need to have a new one to sell Fulcrumb and Minsk products.

This is turning into a good meeting after all. I missed the basketball game but I slam-dunked Nathan, Ralph, and now Turk.

Mary

I notice that our commission schedule is patterned after high volume companies. We don't have nearly as many sales, so shouldn't the base salary be higher, or do the percentages go up as sales increase?

These people are horrid. I don't care if I upset the whole bunch. I'm going to talk about money, benefits, and women's rights. I want to see Simon and Nathan squirm.

Simon

The commission is based on incentive clauses which are designed to stimulate the most sales while giving the sales-person a good territorial base for future gains. Our bonus system usually fills whatever voids occur.

You are going to make the same money no matter what you do. If you sell many accounts we'll bog you down with late deliveries and poor customer service. Don't try to pin me down any further or you'll end up a shipping clerk in the mail room.

Mary

That's a non-response and a cheap one. You and Nathan have expense accounts for restaurants like this one. Ours doesn't include enough money to take a client to lunch at McDonalds. I must have better support to commit myself to arduous travel, cold calls, and dealing with hostile purchasing agents.

The gloves are off, you two-bit pimp. The whole sales manage-ment staff, including the vacant blond, should be going door-to-door selling vacuum cleaners. You're not going to exploit me with promises of bonuses. The only bonus you should get is when Molly sits on your lap.

Nathan

Simon, Mary has some genuine concerns here. I've drafted, with Molly's help, a new commission schedule that rewards

This ought to make both of them steam. Simon will go off the deep end because I mentioned Molly,

extra effort. It gives every salesperson the potential of six-figure incomes. We will put that in place before she officially starts in the field on Monday.

and Mary will fume because she knows it's all corporate double-talk. She'll take out her rage on Simon and he will look out of control. Everyone will see his incompetence.

The waitstaff brings more wine in ice buckets and removes the corks. Empty glasses are quickly refilled.

Six-figure income, my skinny ass. Sure, including the cents columns. I am not going to break my skinny ass and then hold my hat in my teeth waiting for the all-benevolent management to shake their fat asses and put a measly tip inside. I want some guarantees now or I don't go outside and break my skinny ass, got it boys?

Let's put it all on the table, shall we? Let's see how good you all are at fighting. I've got nothing to lose so I'm willing to go all the way here. The worst thing you could say is "you're fired," and I don't give a shit. It's your move Honey buns.

The waitstaff removes the dinner dishes and bring their guests the dessert menu. They also bring a pastry cart the size of a small barge. It is filled with Austrian and French delights, mostly chocolate, custard, whipped cream in exotic combinations. Turk orders the largest mousse with custard and whipped cream. He also orders seven-nut ice cream from the dessert menu. They remove the six empty wine bottles and bring after-dinner liqueurs on a rolling server made of walnut. The glasses are turned upside down on a lace-patterned cloth. Simon pours his glass full of Drambuie and looks at Mary.

In the next sequence, both the off-stage voices of the actors' minds and the actors on stage are saying the same thing at the same time.

Simon

Mary, if you can sell as good as you can curse you'll be a millionaire in six months. There are no guarantees here, sweetie pie. It's called working for a living. You get your ass out there and sell. We pay you money to live. If you don't want the job, I can find twenty people who would love to take your place, so shut the hell up.

Turk

My mother-in-law, Mrs. Fulcrumb, told me that I would someday be her right hand man. I tink you people better had try to do better. Someday I'm going to be the boss, and I don't like what I'm hearing. **(no offstage voice)**

Nathan

Turk, you're a jerk. Christ, are you still eating? What a slob. If you'd stop stuffing your face long enough to let a thought out, you might try to understand our difficulties. Don't threaten me! The day you become the boss is the day I go to the competition.

Ralph

Turk, old boy, old buddy, would you pash me the Bailey's Irish Cream? Thank you, thank you. It is imposhible for people for people for people to agree on everything. Imposhible. We should work as a team.

Simon

Here's another wasted night. I could have been home watching the fucking basketball game, but no, I have to sit here and listen to a bunch of whiners, a greedy feminist, and back-stabbing morons. Listen, you overrated bunch of third-rate dweebs, I'm in charge. What I say goes. You either do it or I will find someone else who will. If you don't like it, get the hell out of here.

Nathan

Listen to Mr. Big. Listen to Mr. Independent. Listen to the man in charge. Sure you don't need us. You can do everything yourself. You and Molly, of course.

Har, har, har hardy har har. Without me, you would be dead last in the entire U.S. I'm sick and tired of you doing nothing while you make 275 thousand a year. You have the leadership skills of a lemming and the energy of a slug.

Mr. Folger, could I stop taking notes now? You are all talking so fast my hand is beginning to hurt and I've got nothing to drink.

The waitstaff clears the table and stands impatiently near the group. The restaurant is officially closed and the clean-up crew wants to go home. Turk orders one last chocolate mousse and Ralph has another cordial. Simon picks up his Chardonnay and flings it at Nathan, hitting him square in the chest. Nathan drops his pastry and the goo slides down his tie and onto his lap. Turk flings his mousse at Simon but hits Mary instead. Molly screams. All six then fling everything they can get their hands on at each other while the waitstaff is pleading in French, "Madames! Messieurs! Madames! Messieurs!" The curtain falls.

Sydney did a great job as Mary Louver. She was the only character I liked in that play.

We called Nancy and asked her to put Sara Ann to bed. The two of us parked by a beautiful stream and rolled down the car windows. The sound of the water and the crickets was soothing. We sat in the car with our arms around each other. I think she feels the same way about me as I do about her. I'm afraid to go any further because I might scare her off. She has been badly damaged by her ex-husband, and I want her to feel safe with me. Caroline and I are both in a state of blissful shock. I called my brother in Burlington, and the first thing he said was, "But you've only known her a few days!"

I called Adele Dobbs in Old Forge and told her that I met Caroline and that I was abandoning the trip. She was upset and made a suggestion. She said that although she didn't know all the details, it was vitally important for me to walk to Aberdeen, Washington. She advised me to take Caroline and Sara Ann with me. Adele is a very sweet woman, but I told her that Caroline has her own life in Nappanee, and it was much too dangerous for her and her daughter to travel with me. Adele said Caroline could be my sag wagon, and we could still spend every night together. A sag wagon is a van that bicycle clubs use during century rides of one hundred miles or more, in case they have mechanical or other trouble. I told Adele that neither of us are independently wealthy, and Caroline needs to work at her job to support herself and Sara Ann. She's a licensed speech therapist who specializes in autistic children. I thanked Adele for her suggestions, but she really got insistent that I continue on my journey. I didn't tell Adele that we are not sleeping together.

I'm writing this journal entry seven days after I spoke with Adele. I've been living in the house with Caroline and Sara Ann for one week. This was the best week I've ever spent in my life. Yesterday evening, the two of us spent the night together. I'm not going to tell you the details; we both deserve privacy. I feel like I've been dormant through a long winter and have just now emerged. It reminds me of a poem by Edward Randall.

SPRING RUN

Do I have your permission
to tap the maple trees?

My 82-year-old neighbor places
old-style buckets around the sentinels
that stand in our front yard.

He will again visit the entire street.

In the late afternoon sunlight I can see
their life's blood dripping down,
a very good run today.

For me, March sugaring time is the
beginning of all things wondrous.
Everything has been so still
beneath the deep snow.

Soon the crocus will peek out as
once again the earth cheats death.

Maple yawns, stretches her branches and
thanks the sun for longer, brighter,
warmer Sunday afternoons.

After so many frozen nights
even the buzzing of a black fly
will sound like music.

Why not move to Florida or to
coastal Carolina?
Why not be green forever,
never dormant?

Smooth would not be smooth without rough.
Light would not be light without darkness.
Warmth would not be warmth without cold.

A joyous spring would be less a joyous spring
without the severe Vermont winter.

The longer the dormancy,
the brighter the crocus.

We got a letter in the mail today. I say *we* because it was addressed to Caroline McGregor & David Hall at this address. It was from Adele and Thomas Dobbs. Along with the letter was a check for fifteen thousand dollars. The letter gave us additional suggestions of how and why we should make the journey. She said the money should take care of the entire rest of our trip, and if we needed more to ask.

Caroline needs three weeks to reach a stopping point in her practice. She cannot abandon two children she has been working with. The timing is as good as it gets, because autism is a new specialty for her and she hasn't yet made long-term commitments. Once you start working with a child, she said, you can't just disappear. That would do more harm than good. This woman has a golden core. I told my brother to sell my three-year-old Honda and get the best price he could for it, because Caroline has a car, and I could use the money. I also sent a photograph of Caroline and Sara Ann to my family. Jonathan and I talked for an hour two nights ago. He's never shy with his opinion. He told me that if I didn't marry Caroline, I would be irredeemable.

Adele called again with another idea. Caroline has a sturdy car, but it's a small Toyota Yaris. Adele suggested we put on a trailer hitch and buy a pop-up camper to tow with us. We can then use campgrounds instead of motels and hotels. My brother's letter arrived today with a check for ten thousand dollars. He said I still have my car and it was not a loan. Jonathan has no strings. It was a generous brotherly act.

The very act of accepting money from Adele says that we will make the trip. If I'm staying in Nappanee, I've got to return the fifteen thousand immediately. I want to return it and Caroline does not. We've already had our first disagreement.

CHAPTER SIX
Nappanee, Indiana to Dyersville, Iowa

As I write this, Caroline, Sara Ann, and I are in the Powahassett Camping Area, ten miles from Valparaiso, Indiana and about twenty miles from the Illinois state line. The first night we spent in a motel because there were no camping areas along Highway 30. Camping is something that neither of us is good at. Right now it's absolutely pouring, there's a thunderstorm raging, and the hail is pounding the car and camper. We are very uneasy; the wind is shaking everything to pieces. I say *we* are uneasy, but I do not include Sara Ann, who is having an absolute ball. Every time she sees lightning, and then hears the thunder, she laughs.

I didn't admit this in the first paragraph of this chapter, but obviously Caroline got her way. I kept telling her that making this trip together was a bad idea, too much hardship, too many unknowns, and not good for Sara Ann. I'm completely overmatched. We are going to have a very interesting relationship because I can't say no. If she can't win on logic, she will pout. If that doesn't work, she will sniffle. She already knows that I will do anything she wants to keep her from crying. This is extortion. This is blackmail. This is grand manipulation. This is the way I want to live the rest of my life, with an extortionistic, blackmailing manipulator. Caroline loves me, and I love her and Sara Ann, end of argument. Everything else is negotiable. Do you know how blessed I feel that she cares enough to want to travel with me?

There are lots of logistical considerations when traveling with a three-year-old. Sara Ann is as smart as I was at fourteen, and she doesn't miss anything. She even taunted Caroline and me by saying that she wanted a beer. She remembered our conversation in the kitchen on the day we met. So because of Sherlock Sara, our amorous displays have been severely curtailed, and I'm a wreck. After doing without for so long, you think I would be happy with an occasional quiet roll when Sara Ann is asleep, but not so. I wish we had a camper with two rooms and a live-in nanny. I keep joking with Caroline that I'm going to lock Sara in the car. The truth is that it's bad for a child to see her mother making love. It appears like violence and is disturbing. We constructed a curtain, and make quiet love only when we know she's asleep.

The pop-up camper has a current converter that runs off the car battery. I can recharge all my electronic goodies, and it hardly draws any current. We have an LED lantern that shines for 200 hours on four D batteries. It throws light 360 degrees and is very bright. Because we now have a camper, I've taken my mountain tent and sleeping bag out of my backpack and saved six pounds.

Do you know what is absolutely amazing? We say goodbye in the morning as if I'm going off to work. We plan our route, and Caroline and Sara are waiting for me when I arrive at my destination. If there are no motels nearby, Caroline has the camper set up and a hot meal waiting. She is always near the side of the road, and when I see the car and camper ahead of me, even though it's at the end of my walk, I always run the last hundred yards to meet them. During the day Caroline takes Sara to various places of interest and tells me about them while we eat. This routine has been wonderful for the last ten days. We are almost completely through Illinois, and are stopped in Morrison about twelve miles from Clinton, Iowa. You don't know how tempted I am to drive to the next destination. I still don't like leaving Caroline and Sara alone all day.

Clinton is right on the Mississippi River. The river forms the boundary between Illinois and Iowa. The person we met this afternoon is Roger McIntire. Mr. McIntire is almost ninety years old and is very hard of hearing. Even with his hearing aid turned on, we had to talk loudly to be heard. Sometimes the exchange was rather comic. He also realized it, and we had a good laugh. He asked the three of us if we wanted crackers and cheese, and Caroline said she would love some cheese. So Mr. McIntire said, you don't have to say please, you can have anything you want. I said thank you for your hospitality, and he said it's two miles south, is everything all right? Good doctors there, though.

He showed us a photograph. I have the same one in my collection, and it shows three people sitting on a split log fence. One of them is my great-grandfather, and the other two are a young boy and a woman. Turns out that it's Mr. McIntire and his mother. He told us that they had walked with my great-grandfather because they were homeless and traveling to stay with her brother in Sioux City Iowa, 400 miles away. The bank foreclosed on the family farm, Mr. McIntire's father had died the year before, and all their possessions were sold with the farm. They each carried a suitcase, but they were too heavy for a woman and a young boy. My great-grandfather ended up carrying both suitcases, while Roger carried his knapsack. The year was 1933. Here's yet another example of one of my ancestors helping someone along his journey.

Mr. McIntire is now living with his son and his family. His mind is sharp, and his son John told us that he remembers and knows everything, even the smallest details of conversations held decades ago. Halfway through the evening we got an example of what John was talking about. Mr. McIntire told us all about Clinton's history. He spoke of log rafts being floated down the Mississippi. He said that by 1892, production of lumber had risen to more than 195 million board feet. He told us about the lumber barons who built the mansions on 5th, 6th, and 7th Avenues. He said Clinton lost 403 people in the last census, and the population was now 27,039 people. He said there are 56 churches. Then he said something I didn't quite understand. He said before my journey was ended, I would walk in my ancestor's shoes, first my great-grandfather's, then my grandfather's, and finally my father's. Those were his exact words.

After meeting Adele and Thomas Dobbs, and now Roger McIntire, I'm convinced that old age doesn't have to mean decrepitude. I've had some wrong-headed notions. Being old is a state of mind. I know some people in their twenties and thirties who are very old.

The most interesting stories of all are the ones he told of the Great Depression. I can't imagine what it was like to live through that. He said I should learn more about it since my own great-grandfather traveled across the country during this terrible time. In many ways, Sam Hall had the toughest journey. Mr. McIntire came back to Clinton after World War II. He served with the Marines in the Pacific and won a slew of medals. He is still as tall and gangly as he was in the photo of him in his Master Sergeant's uniform, about my height. When my grandfather and father made their trips in 1955 and 1974, they stayed with Mr. McIntire in his old house a half-mile from the river. He handed us our next map. The route is between Clinton, Iowa and Dixon, South Dakota, a distance of 596 miles. He said this would be the longest leg of our journey. When we arrive, we are to see Mapeahwechastah, also known as Jake. He said his name translated from the Sioux means the "Man in the Cloud."

We spent one night at John McIntire's house, and as is now our custom, we planned our next meeting place. I'm writing this the following evening after a scary, worry-filled, harrowing day. I arrived at our destination along Highway 20, in the town of Galena. I walked through the town and saw nobody. On June 5th it gets dark about 8:30 p.m., and I waited for them to appear from 5:00 onward. Finally at 7:45 an Iowa State Trooper stopped and asked me if I was David Hall. I said yes, and was begging God for Caroline and Sara Ann to be safe.

She ran over some tractor parts that had fallen off a flat-bed truck, and both the rear tire of the Yaris and a camper tire got cut and went flat. It took forever for a repair person to find a replacement for the camper. The trooper said to stay put, she would be along in about an hour. I nearly kissed him, I was so relieved. She showed up at 9:15.

Tomorrow we are buying Caroline a cellphone. I don't know why we didn't think of it earlier. I have a computer, shortwave radio, digital recorder, digital camera, a Blackberry, backup disks and adapters of all varieties, so why doesn't Caroline have a cellphone? We can be in constant communication all day. I must admit, I have always had some reservations about them, especially when I learned that they may be killing off the honeybees. I hate it when some inconsiderate person is yelling into his or her phone as if there weren't another person within fifty feet. Unfortunately, they are usually on line in front of you at the supermarket checkout or the bank, or even right behind you in a movie theater. Even so, we will buy her one. Sara Ann will cry and want one also.

I also purchased a wireless modem for my computer so I can access the Internet from our camper, without using any motel phone connections. Now I really am an electronic pilgrim. I can use my Blackberry or my computer.

Tomorrow we will meet in Dyersville. That's where they filmed the movie *Field of Dreams* with Kevin Costner and Amy Madigan. Caroline will go ahead to Waterloo, pick up the phone, get supplies and clothes for Sara Ann, and come back to Dyersville. I should arrive between 5:30 and 6:00.

I already mentioned that my great-grandfather's name was Sam Hall, and that there is a folk song with the same name. In 1701 a chimney sweep named Sam Hall was hanged for burglary. The original lyrics were written by an English comic minstrel named C.W. Ross, in the 1850s. This version is kind of a hybrid of four or five that have been sung on both sides of the Atlantic, by people like Johnny Cash and

114

The Dubliners.   Even the great poet Carl Sandburg had his version.

Oh my name it is Sam Hall, it is Sam Hall.
Yes my name it is Sam Hall, it is Sam Hall.
My name it is Sam Hall, and I hate you one and all.
Damn your eyes.

I killed a man they say, so they say.
I killed a man they say, so they say.
I smashed his rotten head, and I left him there for dead.
Damn his eyes.

So it's up the rope I go, up I go.
Yes it's up the rope I go, up I go.
A swingin I must go, o'er you bastards down below.
Damn your eyes.

Now the preacher he did come, he did come.
Yes the preacher he did come, he did come.
And he looked so Goddamn glum, as he talked of kingdom come.
Damn his eyes.

I saw Molly in the crowd, in the crowd.
Yes I saw Molly in the crowd, in the crowd.
And I hollered right out loud, hey Molly ain't you proud?
Damn your eyes.

Oh my name it is Sam Hall, it is Sam Hall.

115

Yes my name it is Sam Hall, it is Sam Hall.
I'll see you all in hell, yes I'll see you all in hell.
Damn your eyes.

Well, they didn't sing this song on *Sesame Street*, but I just wanted to share the lyrics.

It's warm today, high temperature will probably be in the low eighties. Time to buy some shorts. I am traveling lighter now, with no jacket and only one long-sleeved white cotton shirt. I listen to the weather forecast in the morning, and if there is no rain, I also leave my rain slicker behind. Having Caroline with me has made this trip so much easier. I feel like a pampered executive out for his daily constitutional.

I've been reading about the Great Depression, especially about how it affected Iowa, since this is the state I'm walking through. I'll paraphrase George Santayana, the philosopher, who said that those who don't remember history are condemned to repeat it. Did you know that the Iowa farmers were already in a depression since the 1920s? In the rest of the United States, people were buying automobiles and appliances, and it looked like the economy was robust. But there was a cancer in the land. Although businesses showed substantial increases in profits due to increased production, workers got a very small share of the wealth. At the same time, huge tax cuts for the wealthy were given to the top five percent. The end result was that in 1929, the top 0.1 percent of rich Americans had income equal to the bottom 42 percent.

Does this sound familiar?

Due to overproduction after World War I, improper farming techniques, and no crop rotation, the topsoil was depleted. In 1930, a severe drought hit the Plains states. This area, including Iowa, came to be known as the Dust Bowl. Thousands of small farmers lost everything, as Roger McIntire's family had done. Many migrated to California. In 1933, the year of Sam Hall's trip, the worst dust storm of all time hit the Plains. First the dust clouds blew into Chicago, and the dust fell like snow. It dumped four pounds of debris for every person in the city. A few days later the same storm reached the East, and red snow fell on New England.

By 1932, unemployment was 25 percent. Homeless people built shacks out of old crates and formed shantytowns, which were called "Hoovervilles" out of bitterness toward Republican President Herbert Hoover. He refused to provide relief and instead proposed to cut government spending. He insisted that the economy was sound and that prosperity would soon return.

Does this sound familiar?

In 1932, Franklin D. Roosevelt defeated Herbert Hoover and instituted his New Deal. Joy at Roosevelt's victory soon gave way to another fear. The Supreme Court of Butler, McReynolds, Sutherland, and Van Devanter voted to invalidate almost all the New Deal provisions. In 1935, a fifth Justice, Owen Roberts, who was appointed by Hoover, voted with those four to form a conservative majority. In a six-to-three ruling, they defeated Roosevelt's farm program.

Does this sound familiar?

On the side of the road in Ames, Iowa, they burned life-sized effigies of the judges, calling them the Horsemen of the

Apocalypse. I wonder if there will be Bushvilles in tomorrow's America? I've seen thousands of abandoned houses and homeless people in every state. President Obama has inherited the Republican and Wall Street mess, and quite frankly, I don't think he has the power to make any changes. The corporate culture is just too strong. I think of the military/industrial/government complex as a symphony orchestra. Obama is the conductor, but he is not facing the musicians. He is facing us, the audience, and is waving his baton wildly while he tries to dazzle us with his rhetoric to assure us he's in control. The orchestra is playing whatever it wants to without his direction. Unfortunately, it may be a death march for the American Republic.

I'm walking along Highway 20 and passed a sign that says, "Welcome to East Dubuque, 1933."

Whoa! A Ford Focus just passed the sign and then disappeared. On the other side, out of nowhere comes a Model A Ford. What the hell is going on! When I look behind me, everything is as it should be, but ahead of me things are very different. Two more cars have gone by, along with a truck with a stake body. They are all from the 1930s, and their engines sound like four chipmunks spitting. I walked back across to the other side of the sign and everything is normal, in my time. I crossed over again and the same time-warp thing happened. What the fuck!

I'm getting some very weird looks from the drivers and from the people in houses alongside the road. There is a broken down old car, it's also a Ford, but it looks older. I believe this one is a model T. There is a large family gathered around it. All their worldly possessions are inside, and they have a little girl who is sick. A handsome woman is taking a photograph of the family, and the mother of the sick child has just said, "We don't want to go where we'll be a nuisance to anybody." My God, the picture-taker looks like Dorothea Lange, the great Depression-era photographer. I've studied her in my photography class at UVM.

I remember what Roger McIntire said: Before my journey was ended, I would walk in my ancestor's shoes. First my great-grandfather's, then my grandfather's, and finally my father's. I'm really frightened. I'm stopping behind this large tree to gather myself. I'll turn on my radio and see if the programming is modern. Perhaps I can hear WBDY in Chicago.

I can hear it all right. They played "Stormy Weather," sung by Ethel Waters. The next song was "Shadow Waltz," sung by Bing Crosby. Now they are playing "Love is the Sweetest Thing," sung by Ray Noble. Holy shit, this is not the twenty-first century. I wonder if I'm dead. This can't be a dream because I've never heard this song before, and I never heard of Ray Noble. I've got to keep going. How else can I meet Caroline? Perhaps on the other side of town I'll get back to my own time.

"Hey boy, where you from? Them's funny-lookin' shoes."

I thought quickly. "I'm from Chicago, bought them up there."

"If I were you, I'd go back to Chicago. There ain't nuthin' here no more."

I stepped off the road and poured water from my canteen and mixed it with dirt. I spread mud all over my white-mesh walking shoes to hide them. Damn, it's a brand new pair.

There's a farmhouse up ahead and a hundred people are gathered around. There's an auctioneer with a bullhorn. This is a farm foreclosure. Half the men wear fedoras and half wear caps. Many wear shabby clothes.

"Hey boy, you're not from around here, you a Republican?"

"No sir, I hate Herbert Hoover, he's ruining the country. Iowa would have been better off without him." It occurred to me that modern day Iowa would have been much better off without Congress.

I'm hungry, and there's a small eatery up ahead but I dare not stop. My money is different. My quarters are just silver-coated copper, and the dates are all post-2000. In 1933, they were pure silver. My paper money also has today's dates on them. At least I think they do, let me check. Yup, all of me is the future. If anybody here searches me, I'll be sent to a lunatic asylum, or they'll say they found an alien time traveler, and turn me over to the U.S. Army.

"Hey mister, that's a funny watch you got. How come there are only two numbers?"

"It's a new-fangled watch I bought in Chicago. It also tells the temperature, 82 degrees." The teenaged girl and her younger sister studied my atomic clock watch intently. As soon as they were out of sight I took it off and stuffed it in my pocket.

These farmer's faces are so different from those I've seen on my travels so far. In spite of the hard times, the people don't have a mean look. They aren't predatory, and they help each other. If we went to twenty-five percent unemployment today, and there wasn't enough food to eat... I can't envision what would happen. I don't want to envision it.

You have no idea how many antiques I've seen alongside the road. I guess these weren't antiques in 1933, just trash. I wonder how much a Ford Focus will be worth in 2074? How about my disposable felt-tipped pen?

This Alligator wrench and the inkwell are great finds, and I'm stuffing them in my pocket. On the handle it says "Alligator wrench, Pat. Feb. 8. 1898." There's no rust on it, so someone must have lost it recently. There's a lot of traffic and broken down vehicles. I've been passed by two more families who are leaving town. In 1939 John Steinbeck wrote *The Grapes of Wrath*. The Joad family was just like the people I've met in East Dubuque. There were hundreds of thousands of people headed West desperately looking for something to do. They had hungry kids, no place to live, and they would do anything to earn a dollar. A dollar, hell, twenty-five cents would have fed the family.

I think I see the East Dubuque welcome sign on the far edge of town. There's a ramshackle house fairly close to the road just before it. There's wash hanging on a clothesline. There are sheets with holes in them and blue sewn-on patches. A woman is using a washtub, and her baby is crying at her feet while her daughter helps her with the wash. I heard her husband when he came outside to yell at the little girl.

"Nellie, you left the Goddamned cover off the tin and the flour is full of bugs. How many times do I have to tell you to put the damn cover on the flour?"

A 1930s car is approaching me and as it gets closer, I can read that it's a Buick. There is a well-dressed couple inside. We are both even with the East Dubuque sign, and as it drives past the sign, it disappears. On the other side of the sign it morphs into a big Blue Lexus SUV and passes by me. I look back over my shoulder and the town is still the way it was in 1933, but ahead of me is my world. The Alligator

122

wrench and the inkwell have disappeared from my pocket, but my photos remain in the camera. I have to stop. My knees are shaking and I'm hyperventilating. How will I explain this to Caroline?

CHAPTER SEVEN
Dyersville, Iowa to Dixon, South Dakota

Caroline and Sara were quite upbeat until they saw me. I was as pale as an Englishman. The first thing I did after explaining East Dubuque 1933 was show them the photographs I took. Caroline is a very religious woman, and she had no trouble believing that this happened. I insisted that it had to be some sort of mirage, hypnosis, or delusion. Perhaps Mr. McIntire caused it when he insisted that I would walk in my great-grandfather's shoes. Caroline insisted that it was God talking to me.

I gave her lessons on how to operate the cellphone she had bought and made a call to John McIntire's house. John was in tears and told me that his father, Roger McIntire, had died two days after we left. The funeral was today. He insisted that we not return to Clinton, but continue on our journey. Caroline said that the real prophets and saints are probably farmers from Iowa. How can you argue with that? It seems so totally illogical and ridiculous, but it's probably as true as believing in the Holy Ghost. As Kevin Costner said in his film, *Field of Dreams*, "This isn't heaven, this is Iowa."

I have reached another one of those times when I seriously want to bag this trip and return to my happy little apartment on South Union Street in Burlington, or back to Caroline's house in Nappanee. I don't need and positively can't handle any more other-worldly experiences.

We were about to make love last night when Caroline said, "What's this, what's going on?" As she spoke, Sara Ann, who we thought was fast asleep, giggled. Caroline screamed as she encountered a good-sized green snake that the holy terror had placed in our camper bed. This is not good. They are totally harmless, but Sara doesn't know the difference between a green garden snake, a coral snake, copperhead snake, rattlesnake, or whatever else kind of snake they have in this part of the country. She cried when I put it outside because she wanted to keep it as a pet. Not a chance. For obvious reasons, Caroline was no longer interested in sex. Sara Ann is adorable but devilish. She's much too bright.

I'm now 1,118 miles from Burlington, Vermont, finished with about one third of my trip, which has now become *our* trip. Iowa is huge. It goes on forever and I feel walked out. My health is good, but the routine is getting to me. I fondly remember being in the Adirondack Mountains of New York State, walking through the snow. I say fondly because the temperature today is abnormally high. It's 1:30 p.m. and 94 degrees, 109 in the sun. There are annoying biting flies that always seem to find the spot where I didn't rub insect repellent. They have mosquitoes so mean in Iowa that they bite me right through my cotton shirt. To add insult to injury, I just heard on the radio that the temperature in Houston is only 88. I've been wearing my straw hat but need additional protection for my neck. I'm now carrying two canteens, and refill them often. I'm also carrying salt pills. So far, I've never been refused when I've asked for water. No matter whether it's at a gas station, restaurant, or from a garden hose at a private home, water is freely given. If I asked for the family car, or a couple of hundred dollars, the answer would probably be no. So how do we measure generosity? Do we give only if it doesn't hurt, or do we give if it hurts a little? The most generous people of all are those who give when they themselves could use what they are giving away, like those people did in 1933 East Dubuque. It's not true generosity if we give away something we don't need or want. It's like courage. If we do a deed that other people think is brave, but we aren't afraid, it's not real courage. Courage is action in the face of fear. We're afraid, but we act in spite of the fear. Thanks for the water anyway; I am grateful.

I've gotten into some good conversations when I ask for water. The lines I hear the most are, where are you from, and where are you going. When I tell them what I'm doing, that's when the responses vary. I've gotten everything from golly gee, watcha doing that for, to Aunt Martha and Uncle George rode across Iowa by bicycle, to it's too hot, or it's too windy, bet your feet are sore, and the most common response if I take a person's photograph is, are you going to put me in your book? Some people tell me to watch out for trucks.

The trucks are a problem. Actually, I'm the problem. I'm walking alongside roads, and roads were made for trucks and not for me. Trucks are wide. On a two-lane road, when two trucks pass in opposite directions, they take up the entire road and sometimes part of the shoulder. That's where I'm walking, on the shoulder. The little rearview mirror on my straw hat has helped, and trucks are generally loud, so I can hear them approaching. Some sections of all these highways have very busy truck traffic. I've had to step off the shoulder into a drainage ditch on many occasions. On these busy roads, I walk as far to the right as possible, and sometimes I don't see what's in the grass. It's great when mowers cut everything ten feet from the edge of the road, but this has not always been the case. Yesterday I stepped in broken glass and cut the bottom of my shoe, but thankfully not my foot. I also saw a rattlesnake, at least I think it was a rattlesnake, but it was on grass that had just been cut. If the grass had been tall, I would not have seen it and I could have been bitten. Yesterday evening I bought and added a snake-bite kit to my backpack.

We've had three days over 90 degrees and I'm drained. It's Saturday, June 21st, and we are in Lawton, Iowa, about eight miles from Sioux City. Sioux City is where Nebraska, Iowa, and South Dakota meet. Tomorrow's goal is Elk Point. I really feel like celebrating when we cross the South Dakota line. We talked about my taking a day off and playing along the Missouri River. Perhaps we can take a boat ride. Unfortunately, Dakota is over 450 miles long. I don't have the right attitude any more. Caroline and Sara Ann have changed my perspective on life. Instead of wanting to meet everyone along the way, I have a greater need to be with them. I don't understand how they can handle the boredom. Much of this country is so much like itself. That probably needs more explanation. Every town we pass through has a Main Street. I wonder how many Main Streets there are in the United States? There's a good assignment for people who have too much time on their hands. Great research project for a Republican-controlled Congress.

If you were traveling in Italy, would every town and city have a street named Strada Principale? I don't think so. Or perhaps in every town in Germany there's a street named

Hauptstraße, or in France, Rue Principale, or in Portugal, Rua Principal, or in Norwegian, Hovedgate. I'm finished showing off my language skills. That's something I haven't mentioned yet. I speak Italian, German, French, Portuguese, and Spanish. I don't speak Norwegian but was able to construct Main Street from stuff I've read. To me language is music. I hear rhythms in many places. There's a great old movie called *Eddie and the Cruisers: Eddie lives*. Eddie is forming a band in Montreal and he lectures to everyone while they are practicing. The band was missing notes and he was trying to get them together. He says, "I was in the desert once, but it ain't quiet. I heard things I never heard before. If you know what to listen for, it ain't quiet out there. That's the sound I want us to capture." Well, the logic may need a little bending and stretching, but he made an interesting point. I hear rhythms in the passing of several cars over a rough spot in the pavement. The wind makes music in the telephone wires. The crickets, car tires, and moaning wires together, create a symphony. I downloaded a CD from my computer into my digital recorder, and I'm learning Russian as I walk. By the time I get to Washington, I'll know how to say главная улица.

Back to boredom and sameness. Before television, mega-corporations and franchises, each Main Street was different. Now we all use the same products, watch the same shows on the tube, and have the same conversations at work about what we saw on the tube the night before. Just think about it, it's positively frightening. We can all look at photographs of weapons of mass destruction, as held up by a well-respected and trusted American general. We can all go to war in Iraq based on what we've seen and heard. We can all watch a Presidential news conference and hear him say, "Read my lips, no new taxes," or "I did not have sex with that woman," or "Yes, the economy is robust, and America is safer now." We can all watch as a cheap entertainer exposes herself during a football game. We can all watch as some foul-mouthed comic on any night show makes a half-dozen crude, lewd, downright disgusting jokes about bodily parts or his husband or wife.

There are Bible stories about falling towers, people turning to salt, and God smiting a satiated bunch of sodomizing, selfish, pleasure-seeking, greedy slobs who were probably driving metallic-blue Lexus SUVs.

I hate statistics. The easiest way to lie is by quoting the great God Mathematica, but here's something to ruin your evening. In 2006, the total U.S. combat deaths in Iraq totaled 822. In New York City and Philadelphia, only two of our cities, the total deaths from homicides in 2006 were 982. The population of Iraq, in predominantly hostile territory was 27,500,000 people. The population of New York and Philadelphia combined was 9,700,000. I'm not going to tell you how many homicides were committed in the United States in 2007, or 2008, or '09, because each year will be different. I'll bet that the total is greater than the population of the city you're living in. As Walt Kelly said through his genius comic strip hero, Pogo, "We have met the enemy and he is us."

This is your brain after you snort
whatever it is you are snorting.

This is your brain after you have
consumed two sixpacks.

This is your brain after
eight hours on the job.

This is your brain after you watch
five hours of American Idol.

This is your brain after you slam
Your head into concrete fifty times.

This is your brain after you listen
to the President of the United States.

We are taking the day off. Actually we are taking two days off. We're in camping spot number 11, in the Scenic Area campground on the Missouri River, in Sioux City. It's almost time for the Shorty Jones show, and I'm just lying here in a camp hammock that Caroline bought me. It's stretched between two trees so that I'm facing the river while I swing back and forth. Sara Ann is lying next to me and Caroline is rocking us. As she pulls the hammock to her she kisses each one of us alternately. Naturally Sara Ann is laughing. We had a prayer service for Roger McIntire and spoke again with his son. I also talked to Jonathan, who insisted that I call my mother. My tactful mom wanted to talk to Caroline and asked her if she was serious, or are we just friends. Caroline was patient and politely told her that we are a couple. I was somewhat less cordial because without actually hearing the questions, I could imagine what she was asking. Why are families such a pain in the ass? I didn't hear, "How's your trip going, tell me more about Caroline, that photo of her is great, she sure is pretty, do you need anything?" Nothing. I'm glad I no longer look for approval from any of my siblings or my mother. At least Jonathan has been great.

I'm going to put my headphones on because the Shorty Jones show can be somewhat indelicate. It's funny, but the language I hear on his show is the same as that used by the dirty comics, only for a higher purpose. Sort of like when Allen Ginsberg wrote, "America, go fuck yourself with your atom bomb." Perhaps it's a rationalization. I only like noise when I'm making it. Yesterday was improv night on the show, and tonight they have another of Shorty's skits. He writes his own material and he, his wife Karen, and the other actors do a great job. I love radio drama. You can use your own imagination and are not glued in one spot, staring into the blue void. The music has started and it's time for the show. It's an organ playing "Love is a Many Splendored Thing."

Harold and Lydia

Welcome, welcome, welcome.
Hello Judy, hello Steven, so glad you could come to our party. And here's Jenny and Charles, good deal, everyone arrived at the same time. Jenny, you never met my wife.

Lydia! Lydia! they're here. Lydia, I want you to meet Jenny. Jenny, Lydia and I have been married for two years, and she's the best little hostess in Smugsburg. Lydia, you already know Charles from the company banquet.
Oh yes, hello, and there's Judy and Steven, so glad you could come.

Chorus: All the actors are repeating each of these words at the same time.

Hug, hug, hug, hug, hug
Kiss, kiss, kiss, kiss, kiss
Hug, hug, hug, hug, hug

What is that fabulous aroma, Lydia?
Oh, Lydia made the best veal a-la-marsala you are ever going to taste, let me take your coats and pour you a libation.

Name your poison, Steve, and how about you and you and you?

Pour, pour, pour, pour, pour
Drink, drink, drink, drink, drink
Talk, talk, talk, talk, talk

Harold made me this fabulous butcher-block table, took him over three months to do it. Isn't it sturdy? I'm so proud of his fine work.

And Lydia made me this cooking apron, whatdaya think, guys, do I look like I belong in the kitchen or what?

Laugh, laugh, laugh, laugh, laugh
Drink, drink, drink, drink, drink
Eat, eat, eat, eat, eat

That was delicious, would anyone care for some espresso or some Earl Gray tea? Oh Lydia, I'm so glad to finally meet you. You are sooo lucky, Charles tells me that all Harold does is talk about the two of you and about how much he adores you, makes me sooo jealous, but old Charles isn't half-bad, now is he?

Compare, compare, compare, compare, compare
Outdo, outdo, outdo, outdo, outdo
One up, one up, one up, one up, one up

Lydia has the dessert tray. We made hot Bavarian fudge twirls. Put a dab of whipped cream on these dark beauties

133

and you are in for a treat. Lydia, you didn't take them out of the oven yet?

I thought you were going to do that, Harold, while I made the coffee.

Confusion, confusion, confusion, confusion, confusion
Burned, burned, burned, burned, burned
Disappointment, disappointment, disappointment,
disappointment, disappointment

We're sorry about the dessert, let me give each of you a scoop of butter pecan ice cream instead. Harold, I worked for two hours making those fudge twirls and you go and leave them in the oven.

You told me you were going to get them, Lydia.

Silence, silence, silence, silence, silence
Nervous guests, nervous guests, nervous guests, nervous
guests, nervous guests
Whispering, whispering, whispering, whispering,
whispering

Harold, you miserable idiot, you had only two jobs to do. I asked you to pour the drinks and get the damned dessert. I've spent all day making the rest of the meal, you rot-brain.

Listen twaddle-bottom, you said you would get the dessert. You've had so much wine that you can't remember your own low-life family name.

Indigestion, indigestion, indigestion, indigestion,
indigestion
Embarrassment, embarrassment, embarrassment,
embarrassment, embarrassment
Early exit, early exit, early exit, early exit, early exit

Now look what you've done, everybody went home. You can stick what's left of this meal in your ear, you useless, stupid whore.

And you can cram all your dimwitted co-workers in your ear, you pompous fool. Everybody in your whole division makes more money than you do because you are no stinking good at your job, you are a simpleton who will stay a jerk-clerk for the rest of his mediocre life.

It doesn't seem to stop you from buying every dumb-assed useless trinket you can find, now does it bitch-face?

Thrown dishes, thrown dishes, thrown dishes, thrown
dishes, thrown dishes
Damage, damage, damage, damage, damage
Crying, crying, crying, crying, crying

I saw the way you looked at Charlie, you stupid slut, what were you doing playing footsie under the table or maybe a little crotch grab?

At least he has one, you eunuch, vomit on your mother's grave for raising such a moron like you.

You say that again about my mother, scunge-bucket, and I'll rearrange your face.

Go ahead and try it, eunuch.

Clenched fists, clenched fists, clenched fists, clenched fists,
clenched fists
Rage, rage, rage, rage, rage
Scream, scream, scream, scream, scream

Oh boo hoo, Harold, we're having our first fight.

Golly, I guess you're right, Lydia.

Oh, what are your friends going to think of us now?

Oh, they know we love each other, Snuggle-bunny, not to worry.

Can we invite them over again for Thanksgiving, Pumpkin? Oh boo hoo, I'm sorry,

Oh boo hoo, me too.

Boo hoo, boo hoo, boo hoo, boo hoo, boo hoo
Hug, hug, hug, hug, hug
Kiss, kiss, kiss, kiss, kiss

The organ again plays "Love is a Many Splendored Thing." That was vintage Shorty Jones. I was laughing so hard that I woke up Sara Ann. She scampered over to the bed and kept trying to take the headphone jack out of the radio because she wanted to hear it. She now knows there is something on the radio that she is not permitted to listen to. I'll give her two days before she stays up past her bedtime and tries to turn the radio on. She's even memorized where it is on the dial. She's also strong for a little girl. We were playing catch and she threw the ball over the camper into the lake. One of the other camper's dogs got the ball and brought it back to her. It was a beautiful yellow Labrador retriever. Yes, she now wants a yellow Labrador retriever. She's perfected her mother's pout and hurt expression if she doesn't get what she wants. Thankfully Caroline agreed with me that there wouldn't be enough space in the car for such a big dog. Sara Ann, not to be outdone, reminded us that we could get a puppy and it wouldn't be big until the trip was over. She is going to be four years old in two months, and she can match wits with us. What's she going to be like at thirteen?

Caroline and I share a love of books. Even when Sara Ann was one year old, Caroline read to her. I'm convinced that's why she's so smart. In addition to the books on my computer, there's another dozen scattered throughout the car and camper. There is a great poem by Edward Randall that he wrote when he was looking at his bookcase.

WINDCHIMES

ting with voices of shell and glass.

Mumble clunks of bamboo reeds
hung above the window
sound click clacks of talk.

We stare at the bookcase and

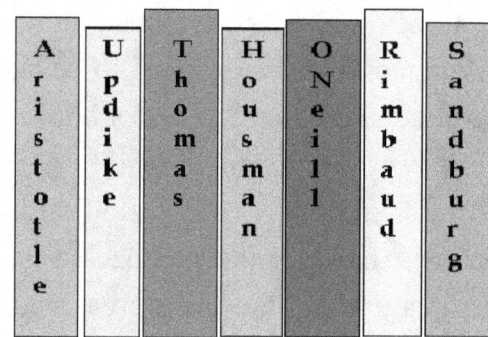

Stare back at us.

They wonder if, as we sing
we remember aged choruses
of vintage words that have been
written for us.

They see the darkened silhouettes of lost cities.

They know the sound of sand
and the color of music.

We string new beads of glass and bamboo.

An ancient spirit enters our song
while our windchimes
chant homage in awe.

I get a restful, peaceful feeling when I think of my home library. I have two floor-to-ceiling bookcases, one on either side of my desk, which is right by a picture window that looks out onto Lake Champlain. There are wind chimes overhead, a Green Tara statue on the right, and two Foo Dogs on the left side. Between them are all the reference books I use, Strunk and White, Thesaurus, Webster's Dictionary, etc. I remember Papa Jack's office. He had a huge walnut-veneered desk that was very old, but the rest of the room was austere. He didn't surround himself with things he liked, except for a photo of my mother. He had two large side tables that were covered with work items. He had his computer on one of them. On the other were all kinds of electronic parts, semi-conductor wafers, and test equipment, but no knickknacks.

I'm back on the road, and I crossed into South Dakota three days ago. I felt refreshed after two days off in the campground, but it continues to be very hot. Rain is forecast for tomorrow, and I'm going to walk. I prefer cloudy days to break the heat. Caroline suggested that I should walk for four days and then rest for two. I'm averaging twenty-five miles per day, so that would be over one hundred miles a week. By the time I reach western Washington, I should be on schedule. I don't think November will be a problem. Perhaps there's bad weather in the East, but it's looking good here. I've been taking advantage of the increased daylight by starting out at five a.m. I walk for six straight hours and stop for lunch between eleven and twelve. I then walk until three or four, depending on where Caroline is set up. Every three days we check in to a motel, and I resume my walk from the exact spot where I stopped, even if we have to backtrack for a couple of miles. Caroline says I'm obsessive about this, but once I bend the rules, I know what will happen.   More riding, less walking.   I called Mapeahwechastah yesterday and told him to expect us tomorrow. Dixon is within our sights. He sounds interesting and told us where to cross Lake Francis Case. He wants us to call him Jake, like all his friends do. He absolutely insisted we spend an extra day on the lake. I know nothing about it, but am going to research it this evening.

Wow, this is a huge lake. It's 107 miles long and there are 540 miles of shoreline.   Guess what we saw?   We saw burning bluffs. What are burning bluffs? There's oil-bearing shale along the lakeshore.   Lightning strikes or chemical reactions ignite the shale, which may then smoke for years. Lewis and Clark observed the phenomenon on their expedition in 1804.   I'm starting to get into the higher elevations. By the time we get to Dixon we will be at 1,800 feet.

Caroline and Sara Ann were waiting for me at Jake's house. I'll tell you right now that there aren't any Saks stores, French restaurants, or shops selling Gucci handbags in Dixon. It's the smallest of any of the towns our contacts live in. The total population is 119. It's about 60 percent German and 18 percent Native American. Half the Native American population is Sioux, as is Jake and his family. It's a poor community dollar-wise. The per capita income is only $14, 219. Jake's father met my grandfather Bill Hall on his trek in 1955. Jake's dad was named Brave Eagle, but his friends also called him Jake.   It was such a simple and beautiful friendship. Bill Hall needed a place to sleep and Brave Eagle provided it.   Brave Eagle's Harley Davidson motorcycle was broken and my grandfather fixed it. Jake, Jr.

still has the bike. It's a white and red 1936 Knucklehead with one of those suicide shifter knobs on the tank. You have to take your left hand off the handlebars to change gears. Jake takes it to the huge Sturgis, South Dakota motorcycle rally every year. Jake built his own house; he's an excellent carpenter. He proudly showed us the wooden floor he put in the living room, and the sewing cabinet he built for his wife. Jake taught me how to drive the Harley. Sara Ann was totally ripped that I didn't give her a ride, but I wasn't confident enough to carry her. Jake sat her in the seat in front of him and took her for a short ride around the neighborhood. She was yelling "Whee!" from the time she sat down to the time she got off the bike. You guessed it. Mommy, can I have a Harley?

I don't know how much education Jake has, but his wisdom is far greater than mine. Before we left, he spoke of my grandfather's visit.

"David, your grandfather made a choice when he helped my father fix his Harley. He could have just left after spending the night, but he chose to repay my father's kindness to him.

"I learned this parable from an old Cherokee squaw named Dancing Bear in Oklahoma. Her people tell that, one evening at the campfire, a Cherokee chief instructed his grandson about a battle that goes on inside all people, every day.

"He said, *My son, the battle is between two wolves inside us all.*

One wolf is Evil - It is anger, envy, jealousy, sorrow, regret, greed, arrogance, self-pity, guilt, resentment,

141

inferiority, lies, false pride, superiority, fear, rigidity, pessimism and ego.

The other is Good - It is joy, peace, love, hope, serenity, humility, kindness, benevolence, empathy, generosity, truth, compassion, patience, service, gratitude, laughter, resonance, optimism, and faith.

The grandson thought about it for a minute and then asked his grandfather, Which wolf wins?

The old chief replied simply, The one you feed."

It was amazing the way Jake rattled off those choices. It reminded me of a poem by Edward Randall.

Choose, choose, choose, choose, choose, choose, choose, choose, CHOOSE!

I am the captain of my ship,	or	I am the third mate of my fate,
I am the master of my soul.		I am a soul out of control.
I am whole and entire,	or	I pray to anyone with power,
The universe is within me.		Forgive me, forgive me, forgive me.
I never hate or fear the unknown,	or	I like X-rated comedy and
I love to read a good book.		I love everyone who is just like me.
I praise the dawn,	or	Leave me alone,
And thank God for another day.		I've got taxes to do.
To be is to do and I scream I am,	or	I do what I have to do,
I jump straight up a grab a star.		And I am what I do.

Smooth	or	Rough
Hot	or	Cold
Fast	or	Slow
Love	or	Hate
Ecstasy	or	Misery
A Prius	or	A Humvee

Luciano Pavarotti	or	Snoop Doggy Dogg
Albert Schweitzer	or	George W. Bush
Manicotti	or	McDonalds
Lauren Bacall	or	Britney Spears

Choose, choose, choose, choose, choose, choose, choose, choose, CHOOSE!

Jake doesn't have a computer, and my father sent everything to him via U.S. mail. Our next map takes us from Dixon, South Dakota to Miles City, Montana. We are traveling northwest and will cut through the extreme northeastern corner of Wyoming for a few miles before entering Montana. The person we are to see in Miles City is a rancher named Colin Cleary.

CHAPTER EIGHT
Dixon, South Dakota to Miles City, Montana

Montana is big, 640 miles long as you plot out the roads I'm going to walk. It's all mountains, and if flattened out, would be twice the size of Texas. I'll probably cover twelve hundred miles, most of it straight up and down. Good grief, why didn't my ancestors go farther south? I'm tempted to buy roller blades and tie them to my pack. When I reach the crest of a hill, I could put them on and coast down the other side. Caroline said it would be too dangerous, and she's probably right. I've always loved the *idea* of Montana. I've never been here before. It's the place where I always dreamed of living. Do you remember the movie *Hunt for Red October*? Sam Neill played the executive officer on the Russian submarine, talking to the skipper played by Sean Connery. They were planning on defecting to the United States. Neill said, "I think I will live in Montana, and I will drive a pickup truck, or maybe even a recreational vehicle. Will they let me do that, no papers?"

I don't know what it is about Montana. Perhaps it's the name. *Montana* is so strong-sounding. If you say it in a low voice, the ground shakes beneath you. Of course, in Spanish it means "mountain." The only other state in the union that I can think of that is named for its geography is my home state of Vermont, which means "green mountain." I tell myself that there are no wimps in these hills. I'm probably just kidding myself; there are plenty of wimps in Vermont.

I had an insight that may help unravel the Papa Jack mystery, specifically why he was so hard on me. Colin Cleary is the man we are going to meet in Miles City. A Tom Cleary is currently the president of my father's company, Hall Digital Networks. When I phoned Colin, I asked if he was related to Tom, and he told me Tom's his son. I didn't ask how Tom had found his way to Vermont. There's plenty of time for that discussion when we arrive.

Here's the insight: I met Tom Cleary on at least four occasions. The last time was when he was a production manager, about to be named vice-president in charge of manufacturing. My father always spoke highly of him at home. "He's a natural leader. You can't teach a man what he should know instinctively, and Tom already knows," and other comments like that.

Here's the interesting part. On the two occasions when I saw Papa Jack and Tom Cleary together, Jack was always rude and surly to him. I remember a company picnic held at Red Rocks Park in South Burlington. I was working part-time in the testing lab while attending UVM, so I was there at the picnic. Tom made a comment about work, and Papa Jack rudely dismissed his rather good observation. I felt sorry for Tom and wanted to apologize for my father's behavior, but I said nothing. Now the guy runs the place.

At the time of my father's death, Papa Jack was Chairman of the Board. He sold his interest in Hall Digital Networks to the employees. It is known, on the basis of how much the stock was worth, that his share totaled about forty million dollars. He also had other investments. No one knows what the hell he did with most of it, except for what I've told you about. Perhaps he gave it to some old whore he met in Aberdeen. My mother is set for life. With the trust funds and the value of the homes, she's worth over twenty million.

I remember Christmas time when the family would exchange presents. Papa Jack was so uncomfortable sitting in the living room that he always sat as far away from the tree as he could. He hated to be thanked. My sisters would make a big fuss over their expensive presents, which of course were all bought by my mother. They would run over and give him a hug. He never said "You're welcome," and he never said thank you for any of the gifts we gave him. He sat there with a forced smile and grunted. That still doesn't explain why all my brothers and sisters got two million dollars each while I got nada. Caroline says that perhaps Papa Jack treated me the way he treated Tom Cleary for a reason, a reason that will only become clear when we reach Aberdeen.

My merry band is camped along Highway 323, just before it joins Highway 12, approximately 10 miles from our destination. Montana gets the all-American state award for the most rifle-racks in rear windows of pickup trucks, the most *full* rifle-racks in rear windows of pickup trucks. All throughout my walk, I've heard gunfire. I've seen several groups of cowboys target shooting or perhaps hunting prairie dogs, secular humanists, or whatever else is in season around here. I've also not seen any African-Americans. I hope I'm just paranoid. Tomorrow we meet Colin Cleary in Miles City. Caroline will get there ahead of me.

Do you know what is absolutely magnificent in Montana? At night the stars are incredible. The state slogan is "Big Sky

Country," and I see what they mean. There's very little humidity and no ambient light from large cities. We have a horizon-to-horizon planetarium right outside our camper. We can see constellations with the naked eye. We bought a small telescope, and I'm now contemplating the origin of the universe while I eat ravioli and meat sauce. We have a great propane stove with two burners and a little refrigerator. Caroline bought some decent cheese ravioli and a jar of sauce. We also have green beans with almonds, and chocolate fudge pudding with oatmeal cookies and whipped cream for desert. Now this is camping. We heard wolves last night, or coyotes, or some kind of wild-dog creature. I don't know the difference, but this critter was howling. He or she was joined by his buddies, and for a while three of them were harmonizing. Whoa! I hope they don't come too close.

The Shorty Jones show comes on in a half hour. Monday night is Shorty-Circuit night. Shorty saves the nutso stuff for this show, and it's impossible to predict what he will have on. Last Monday it was an interview with Mickey Smarmy, the right-wing talk show host. Ten minutes into the show they were shouting at each other, and at the twenty-minute mark Smarmy walked out. Shorty got him so tied in knots, Smarmy said right on the air that all the faggots in America should get AIDS and die. Shorty also got him to admit that it isn't wrong to kill for oil. The quote everyone is talking about is "Towel-heads aren't going to hold this country hostage. If they aren't going to give us crude at a reasonable price, we're just going to have to go over there and get it ourselves."

Tonight's show is about to start. The music is playing "God Save the Queen," but I have no idea why.

Hunter Safety Course

Reginald?

Yes, Percival?

I do love these hunting trips to Montana, don't you?

Oh yes, yes, and how about Brewster and Winston, this is your first time here with us. Hope you are ready for some action.

Can't wait, we're delighted you asked us to accompany you. The Cambridge Society and the men's club can get a bit tedious about now, don't you think?

Haw har haw har haw haw haw har har

While the girls are back home playing bridge, it's the four of us flying from London into Great Falls, and then driving on Highway 89 in Percy's rented Mark XI, to the great Montana wilderness. Oh look, Cuddles packed us a kit of biscuits.

Five months ago Brewster and I decided to grow beards for the hunt, we hear that is THE traditional thing to do up here. Look, you can already see some fuzz on my lip and chin, smashing isn't it? Vivian has been looking at me funny lately, says my face always seems dirty.

Haw har haw har haw haw haw har har

Where exactly is your hunting lodge, Reggie? I hear it's near Black Eagle, and is it large enough for the four of us to have a first class trip?

My hunting lodge *is* Black Eagle, I bought the whole town.

Haw har haw har haw haw haw har har

We'll be staying at the Cedars. It's a great old bungalow with a wrap-around porch, and listen boys, I've converted the maid's quarters to a billiard room with complete bar. The maids will have to sleep with us.

OOOOOOOOOOH

There's over nine thousand acres, and sometimes the elk come right up next to the lodge and you have a real good view from the bay window over the bar.

Last year I got so excited when I saw one through the window I shot right through the glass.

Did you get him?

Her, it was a cow and no, I got the window frame instead, and ruined half a case of Macallan Single Malt.

I thought we couldn't shoot cows, milk and that sort of thing?

You took eleven shots, Reggie.

Well, if I were using my shotgun like I wanted to instead of that stupid 9mm you bought me, I would have hit something.

Oh most definitely, you would have also hit the porch swing and ruined a case of Chivas Regal along with the Macallan.

Haw har haw har haw haw haw har har

Brewster and Winston, what kind of rifles did you bring?

We each bought 458 magnum drillings with 44 magnum revolvers and mace as backups. We hear that elk can be fierce if you just wound them, so we thought we should be safe.

Absolutely, I concur. Percy splashed some cow scent on his coat last year and this huge eight point bull elk snuck up on him while he was hiding behind a big boulder, and haw haw, and haw, you should have seen, haw har haw, you should have seen him scamper up that rock with his pants half off. Percy bought us all blaze orange designer hunting outfits with matching skinning bags. He had them custom made at Abercrombie and Fitch.

OOOOOOOOOOH

Before we get there, we thought that we would give you two new fellas a crash hunter-safety-course, just to be prudent.

Percy, do we have to do that even if we own the land and the town?

Absolutely, we must never use our privileged positions to take advantage of existing laws and people in a foreign place.

Okay, Reggie, hold up the first photograph. Brewster, what is this?

It's a black and white spotted animal with a bell around its neck.

Right, good show Brewster. It has a built in target. Hold up the second photograph, now Winston, what is this? Whoops, sorry, wrong photograph. How, haw haw, how, har, did Cuddles get in there, and where did she get those leopard knickers? That sneaky little slyboots is always trying to get me in trouble, haw. Forget that one. Okay now, Winston, what is this?

It's a sheepfawn with a very wooly coat.

Right again, and it's over the legal limit, very tasty. And what are these, Brewster?

Those are deer with small horns, no, those are male goatfawns.

No, Brewster, you need a bit more work, those are miniature cow moose.

No, that isn't so Percival, those are male moose calves. You can tell because they have no udders.

Male cow moose don't need udders, but I'm not sure about male sheepfawns.

No, wait Reggie, its a herd of male and doe mice, both kinds are there.

Oh what the hell, we'll blast them and check the field guides later,

Haw har haw har haw haw haw har har

"God Save the Queen" is again being played and the show is over. Well, what a coincidence, a British hunting party in Montana. We had some great sound effects during the show because we again heard gunfire. I have no idea what or why they are shooting at night.

Miles City is not like any city in New England. It's probably not like any city in America, except possibly for another part of Montana. I'm only a few miles from where I'm supposed to be, but I don't see any sign of Caroline. I got an information packet about the city from the post office on my way through town. Listen to this; I'm quoting from the brochure:

"Miles City was, and sometimes still is - the real Frontier. August 1876 marks the end of thousands of years of wilderness history and the beginning of Wild West history. Miles City was at the epicenter of this history and has been immortalized by authors and historic characters alike.

"Originally established as a military reservation by Colonel (soon to be General) Nelson A. Miles, Miles Town followed soon to meet the needs of the soldiers. Some rumor that Miles Town was established simply around drinking, gambling, dancing and prostitution. But the real truth of the matter is that it WAS! Nelson Miles was a temperance man and booted the saloon owners out of the fort property. The original Miles Town located 2.5 miles down river was literally built from driftwood around a barrel of booze. The soldiers knew where to find entertainment and soon followed.

"The Frontier was changing rapidly as US forces drove the Indians into reservation lifestyle. Trapping, Lush Grasslands and Reliable River Transportation made Miles Town more valuable than just booze and entertainment. So called 'Reputable' businesses followed and on February 22, 1877 *Miles Town site Co.* was officially formed."

Whoa! I couldn't find the Miles City Opera Company, or the Haiku Club. I did find out that there's a Bucking Horse Sale every year. People come from all over the country to pick horses for their rodeos. There's a parade, a three-day Cowboy Mardi Gras, gun and coin shows, barbecues, and a quick-draw contest. I wonder if they use live bullets.

There's a Cowtown Beef Breeders show every February when Main Street displays some of the best young bulls in the region. The show allows people to meet one-on-one, with leisurely conversation about breeding programs. On my way out of town I passed Spotted Eagle Park in Miles City. Here's what was written on the plaque at the entrance.

"This scenic park plays host to many different outdoor activities. With a non-motorized boating area, fishing and swimming, you can enjoy most of your favorite water sports. There is also a shooting gallery with private skeet shooting and an archery range. Sand beaches make a perfect spot for picnics and volleyball. A dirt biking area, plenty of room for nature walks, hiking, mountain biking and camping make Spotted Eagle an outdoor sporting paradise."

Thank God there's a shooting gallery, with private skeet shooting and an archery range. The people should never be too far away from their Winchesters, even when picnicking with the family.

I've been walking along a fence that has gone on for miles. I see a gate up ahead and there's Caroline and Sara Ann in the Toyota. There are two pickup trucks stopped alongside her. There's a big gate with a wooden arch above it. In the middle of the arch is kind of a western logo that looks like this.

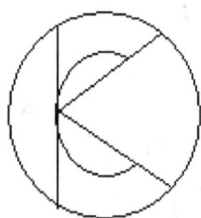

Under the logo are the words "Circle CK Ranch." I guess this is the same logo they use to brand their cattle. I wonder if they still do that. How would you like to have a red-hot iron burn Circle CK onto your ass?

A couple of cowboys are talking to her, and I can feel them drooling from a quarter of a mile away. Caroline and I hugged each other, and she told me she had to meet me at the gate because the house is two miles from the road. The two cowboys just stared at me. They were not happy or welcoming looks. She told me the men worked for Colin Cleary and were just being friendly. We are on his land, and I have been walking alongside it for over five miles.

Do you remember the old TV western, *Bonanza?* The Cartwright family had a Ponderosa. That place was a flea-trap compared to this home. This house is as big as Fort Apache. Half the wood in the Rocky Mountains was used to construct it. There are not one but three American flags, one at either end, and one in the middle. It is about seventy feet high and is large enough to be seen from New York City. Is Mr. Cleary afraid of being mistaken for a damn foreigner? Caroline said he is a very nice person, but then she says that everyone is a very nice person.

Colin Cleary and I shook hands. He tried to squeeze my hand as hard as he could. I saw it coming, I have an instinct for this sort of thing, and I squeezed back with all my might. I didn't hear anything crack, but I didn't feel any pain either. The handshake contest was a draw. The old buzzard was about seventy, and his face looked like the back of a sea turtle. He appeared stitched together in segments as if he was beaten by sun, wind, and rain and then air-dried until he was well-cracked. He should have worn a cowboy hat, but he likes to show off his full jet-black head of probably-dyed hair. He had a grin like Jack Palance just before he was about to cut your throat with a skinning knife.

The first thing we saw when we entered the living room were stuffed animals mounted all over the woodwork: bison, elk, mule deer, black bear, grizzly bear, big-horn sheep, mountain lion, coyotes, and a couple of wolves. A wolverine-looking animal with snarling fangs was mounted, standing on a half-sawn log, in the middle of the huge dining room table. I hope we eat somewhere else. Cleary's place reminded me of Teddy Roosevelt's home in Oyster Bay on Long Island. He had all the animals he'd shot in Africa mounted throughout. He had ashtrays made of elephants' feet, and many other objects made with the creative use of animal parts. By the way, Teddy Roosevelt was one of the visitors to the Miles City Club.

I knew it. "To Colin Cleary, with admiration and affection," was written on an 11 x 14 mounted photograph of Ronald Reagan. We were shown to our room by one of his staff. I saw nine cars in the parking lot. He has a very large staff. The room is thirty by fifty feet. Listen to what is in this room. There's no way you could guess, so don't even try. There are the journals of Henry David Thoreau on a beautiful roll-top desk. On the wall is a portrait of a mother and child by Mary Cassatt. Whoa! An original portrait. There is an entire shelf of poetry books above the desk, and a sound system with four speakers. The CDs are a collection of jazz, world music, and folk music. A violin and bow sit on an eight-sided table along with a Scrabble game and a deck of cards. A Martin D18 guitar is sitting on a stand next to our bed.

There's an unlocked gun case with half a dozen rifles, the kind with a lever underneath. The octagonal barrels have an aged brown patina and one says 38.55. On the desk there is a gorgeous statue of Kwan Yin riding a Foo Dog. Next to her is a meditation singing cup, and next to that is an engraved purple-bronze temple bell. There are prairie wildflowers in a vase next to the bed and a box of imported semisweet chocolate candies. Framed above the table on yellowed paper in very old script is the following quote:

A person will worship something, have no doubt
about that.

We may think that our tribute is paid in secret
in the dark recesses of our hearts, but it will out.

That which dominates our imaginations and our thoughts,
will determine our lives and character.

Therefore, it behooves us to be careful what we worship, for what we are worshipping, we are becoming."

Ralph Waldo Emerson.

Okay, so much for my pre-conceived notions. There's more to this guy than I thought. There's another portrait on the wall of a younger Colin Cleary, an attractive woman who is or was his wife, and a youngster who is definitely Tom Cleary.

"I'm glad you like the room. Is Sara Ann happy?" Colin asked.

"How could she not be, your hospitality is so gracious," Caroline said.

Sara Ann has her own adjoining room next to ours with a little rocking-horse, a toy chest, and a tank full of the most beautiful angel fish I've ever seen.

"This was my wife's favorite room, and most of her things are still in it. Can't bear to part with them, although it's been five years since she died. I ought to get my Winchesters out of there, they don't quite fit with her Buddhist statues. Tom takes after his mother, another Democrat. Are you a damned Democrat just like your father?"

Aha, I thought, that explains it, his wife's things. I said, "No sir, I'm not a damned Democrat, even worse than that, I'm a damned Independent, just like Bernie Sanders." I thought he would he would split in two, he was laughing so hard.

"You know, David, I'd keep Caroline close to you. There are about 350 cowboys in this county alone who have never seen a woman with hair as red as hers."

I explained to him that closeness is based on mutual love and trust, and I didn't need to keep her alongside me all the time. I was waiting for Caroline to say something, but all she did was smile and look coy.

"He was just trying to be friendly and pay me a compliment, that's what cowboys do," she said after dinner when we were alone in our room.

A woman always knows when the timing is perfect, at least a woman like Caroline. She could tell that I was more than a bit jealous of all the attention she was getting. We haven't mentioned the "M" word, I guess because each one of us is afraid of scaring the other off.

"David, they wouldn't bother me as much if I had a wedding ring on my finger."

Whoa! Now what do I do? My whole past life up till now, my present life in this room on Cleary's ranch, and my whole future life flashed in a tri-panel right out front in my consciousness. Past, present, and future, right there, no time to duck, impossible to change the subject.

"I was hoping you would let me mention it first, and I'm sorry I didn't. If you want to get married on a mountain top in Nepal, and then have a honeymoon in Antarctica in our camper, I would consider myself the luckiest man in Montana."

"Why just Montana?" she asked, as she turned out the light.

I laughed, and she knew she'd been set up.

We both slept until seven-thirty, which is very late for us. We probably would have slept until nine if Sara Ann hadn't climbed on the bed. She couldn't find any snakes or toads to put under the covers, so she did the next best thing. She used the mattress between us as a trampoline. I got dressed and grabbed the Martin D18 off the stand. I always carry picks, and I played and sang a James Taylor song, "The secret of life is enjoying the passing of time." I'm always singing around our camp, but this is the first time they have heard me play. Sara Ann would not let me stop, and my stock rose considerably with Caroline.

Do you know what they call guitar players who don't have girlfriends? Hopeless. When we came down for breakfast, only Colin was there at the table. His associates, other house guests, and staff were nowhere to be seen. He complimented me on my playing, said he heard it faintly but I sounded good. The guitar belonged to his wife, Kristin.

"I'm surprised you didn't ask me all about my relationship with your father, and how Tom got to Vermont and became president of Jack's company. I'm also surprised that you didn't ask for your next map and who you are to see. I am so very sorry you lost Papa Jack. It was much too early, much too soon."

I thanked him for his sympathy, and I told him that I figured he would tell me when he was ready. He said that I really wasn't an Independent, because I was a person of few words, who showed tact and restraint. All liberal Democrats, and Independents, and Unitarians talk too damned much. He got me laughing with that one. He knows that I like Thoreau's journals and that Thoreau was a Unitarian.

The Circle CK ranch was bought by Colin and Kristin in 1965, and they added to it over the years. At one time he had several thousand head of beef cattle, but now he's sold off most of the herd. When he was young he went on several cattle drives. They slept on the ground and did all the things you see in the old movies, except kill Indians. The family made a fortune in the stock market, of all things. His father bought IBM when it was only one dollar a share. He bought fifty thousand shares. I can just imagine what the return was on that investment.

Papa Jack stayed with Colin and Kristin Cleary for three days. My father was bitten by a rattlesnake. Luckily for him the snake had just killed something and the reptile's poison sacs were nearly empty. Colin saw my father on the side of the road cutting his own leg with a pocket knife. Colin didn't have a snakebite kit, so he sucked and spit out the poison. Papa Jack pulled the 38 from his pocket and at a distance of twenty-five feet shot the snake between the eyes. Colin and Papa Jack were best friends from that moment on. They took Papa Jack to the hospital and he was fine. He told Colin that he would always be in his debt.

It seems that some of the business trips Tom and my father made were actually back to Miles City to visit the Cleary family. Why didn't he mention it to us? Why didn't Tom Cleary mention it to us at my father's funeral? This is a tight-lipped bunch of macho cowboys. Perhaps there's a secret society. You aren't permitted to express any emotions or show caring towards your own family, only outsiders. Colin told Papa Jack that his son was graduating from Boston University and wanted to stay in New England. My father insisted that he come to work for Hall Digital Networks. Not only did I learn that my father was a standup guy, but was literally a straight-shooter.

We stayed for three days, just like my father had done, and didn't want to leave. For the first time on our journey we have two contacts in the same state. Missoula, Montana is our next destination, and we are to see Mrs. Olive Beatrice Sheridan.

I can no longer claim that I've never met a Republican I liked, but I do have one complaint. When we said goodbye my guard was down, and after we hugged each other, Colin shook my hand. It still hurts.

CHAPTER NINE
Miles City, Montana to Miles City, Montana

I'm glad I slept last night in the pop-up camper with my baby instead of on the ground in my mountain tent. In this part of the country there isn't a Howard Johnson's every thirty miles. We're on Route 59, headed toward Highway 200. Lewistown is still almost two hundred miles away. When we get there we're going to ride the Charlie Russell Chew Choo that Colin told us about. It's a dinner-train trip that goes through a half-mile-long tunnel. They cross three historic trestles, and the fare includes a full course prime rib dinner and dessert. Colin said that when you least expect it, masked bandits try to rob the train. I'm glad they will stage a holdup because I'm beginning to miss the sound of gunfire. We haven't heard any for the last twelve hours. We bought Sara Ann a little cowgirl hat with a rose embroidered on the front. There are wild roses everywhere, and as I write this we're in Rosebud County. I like it when counties are named for flowers or have otherwise picturesque names. There are a lot of them in Montana: Prairie, Powder River, Big Horn, Yellowstone, Beaverhead, Sweet Grass, Mussel Shell. Vermont county names are boring by comparison: Washington, Franklin, Windsor, Bennington, Windham, Addison, ho-hum.

There are areas here where our cellphones don't work very well. It's good to know that the entire earth isn't yet covered with relay towers. I tried to call Caroline. She could hear me but she was breaking up, and I only got every third word until she completely faded out. The words I did hear were *surprise, new Smokey Joe grill, shish kabob,* and *silk nightgown.* If that's not enough to keep a man walking, he would have to be very, very old, or dead.

We got permission to camp on a ranch between Rock Springs and Cohagen. I should say that Caroline got permission. All she has to do is drive anywhere with the Indiana plates on her car, and with the way she looks, she could probably get any rancher in the state to give her half of what he owns.

You are not going to believe what I just got. That sneaky Colin gave Caroline the Martin D18 Guitar, and she hid it in the camper. I just called to thank him but he's in Billings until tomorrow. All I have to do is buy a new set of strings, and it will sound fabulous. There's a like-new, plush-lined case with it. Kristen Cleary had the instrument for many decades, and it's mellowed out. There's no way a new instrument can sound as good. Playing a guitar makes the top vibrate and this ages and conditions the wood. I took my flat and finger picks and placed them in the case. The new Smokey Joe grill is a beauty and is the perfect size for the three of us. There's a tag on it that says "Made in the USA." Martin guitars are still made in Pennsylvania. Everything else, including the former Vice President's eyeglasses, and hairpiece, is made in China.

It's Shorty Circuit night and it's time for the show. I'm just going to lie here and listen while I watch Caroline comb her hair as she reads a one-month-old copy of *The New Yorker.*

The music is playing, "Love is a Many Splendored Thing."

163

"Good evening, America. I'm confused. I thought I knew the score, or at least my gender. As you know, Shorty Jones has a Personals website. I'm proud to say that so far, 743 people have found each other through my online dating service. As we stated, all ads are welcome except obscene or lewd entries, but I should also have banned ambiguity. Let me read a few to you so you can hear what I'm talking about. I'm convinced, after looking at this week's personals, that there are really six or more sexes."

1- He
2- She
3- She He
4- He She
5- He She He
6- She He She

"I always read these because I never know when I'm going to find a ripe tomato. Who says I can't respond to an ad on my own website?"

He, 29, loves sports, movies, and taking that special someone to a candlelit dinner. I'm six foot two, have dark hair, and love kids and animals. Looking for a special non-smoking She for friendship and ...who knows?   Box 3493

He, 44, loves classical music, reading, and baking bread. I love to collect old motorcycles and I love to travel. Looking for She 25-45 with same interests.   Box 7114

She He, 41, loves to go to the big city and dance in exciting night clubs. I also love to shop, and do needlepoint. Searching for another She He who believes in magic and who wants to share my wonderful life.   Box 8484

"All of this seems simple enough. The first two ads are guys looking for women, and the third is a gay guy looking for another gay guy. Fine, no problem, but I kept reading."

She, 34, petite, blond hair and blue eyes, looking for a best friend and ???. I love Siamese cats, water skiing, and am tired of working as a secretary. Looking for a romantic He, 55-65, who knows how to treat a She.   Box 1652

She, 51, full figured, with dynamite moves is looking for a rare someone who's He enough to keep up with me. No crybabies or wormboys.   Box 9937

He She, 26, sick of stereotypes and dishonest people who just want to take you for a ride, seeking a straight-shooting He She, looks unimportant. Must be non-smoker and enjoy living in the country.   Box 5547

"So far, so good. The first two are women who are looking for men. The first guy should be rich, and the second guy had better be tough. The third ad is for a gay country woman wanting to share her place with another gay woman. I should have stopped reading here, but I continued."

He, 47, wants to share large lakeside condo with She He and He She. Must be willing to contribute to the mortgage payments. Own room and private parking guaranteed. If you are responsible and want to share this picturesque location, write. Box 1371

"Now the sorting becomes difficult. I think I know what this person wants. He is a hetero male who wants a gay male and gay female to share his home. He chose this system because he doesn't want sexual entanglements to complicate the living arrangements. He probably paid too much for his lakeside condo and needs to be bailed out."

He She He, 35, award-winning painter and sculptor, wishes to share 4,000 square foot home with another He She He, She He She, She He or He She. I want to build a loving community where everything is shared. He's or She's should please not write. Box 6767

"I need a sex therapist to translate this one. I think Box 6767 is a bisexual male who wants to share his home with either a bisexual male, bisexual female, a gay male, or a gay female. No heteros need apply."

He She, 42, and She He, 44, wish to find traveling partners for a trip to California in our motor home. If you are an attractive She He She or He She He, He or She who has a spirit of adventure, and are a good driver, please send photo to... Box 4545

"Box 4545 are a gay couple of opposite sexes who are traveling together and want either bisexual or heterosexual companionship, or both. There's more."

He and He She He, both 29, and She, 25, wish to meet two He's and a She in order to explore life's mysteries. We have a lakeside condo and share a wall with Box 9937. The adjoining bedrooms in each condo have a connecting door and there is one king-size bed in each room. There are two jet ski boats for everyone's use. Send photo and signed statement of medical history to... Box 3366

She He She, 31, with houseboat on Lake Michigan, wishes to meet He She He's and He's on the Illinois shore, and bring them on Monday, Wednesday, and Friday to join She He's and She's on the Indiana shore. On Tuesday, Thursday, Saturday, and Sunday, She He She, 31, wishes to meet She He She's and She's on the Indiana shore and bring them to join He She's and He's on the Michigan shore. Please send photo and food preferences. For the sake of simplicity, my goal is to find people who all like the same kind of food.
    Box 9182

Former She, now a He, 52, wishes to find an It It. Must be abstract, cubical, and enjoy anagrams. If you are a legitimate It It and enjoy the poetry of Ezra Pound, the wisdom of Dick Cheney, and like listening to dada data discs, I want to be your partner. Please send a copy of your birth certificate and tell me how many times you changed your sex before becoming an It It. Box 1911

The music is playing, "Love is a Many Splendored Thing." It fades into the weather report. I know some It Its, gender neutral people. They make great nannies and can sing very high notes.

Holy spumoni! Caroline just put on the most beautiful, slinky, dark-green satin nightgown I've ever seen. Gotta go.

I'm up early this morning. Caroline and Sara Ann are still sleeping. The early light has begun to show, but the sun has not yet appeared on the horizon. There is a gentle breeze blowing and the prairie grass is swaying with each air current. It's so quiet that I can hear the rustling. I found a jewel-like piece of rose quartz, very clear with a deep rose coloring, and I have an idea. I took another rock and chipped several pieces off the rose quartz. I took the best one and made an engagement ring out of grass and the quartz cabochon. I wrapped the grass around the stone so it shows through. I'm going to give it to Caroline at breakfast.

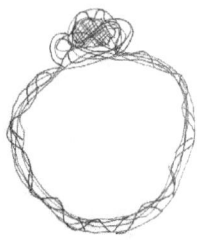

It's getting harder and harder to leave them behind each morning. My mileage has increased. I'm capable of doing thirty-five miles per day, and now I'm taking only one day off instead of three. My new goal is two hundred miles per week. I know the journey is important, but we have a sign on the back of the camper, "Aberdeen or Bust." I just want to get there quickly before I bust.

Everything tastes better when you are camping. Three biscuits, red-currant jelly, and a cup of coffee is a banquet. I need a lot of food because my metabolism is racing. Since Caroline mentioned the "M" word, I have been the one to beg and plead. I want to get married as soon as we can, in the next town where there's a Methodist preacher, since that seems to be what we are. Caroline is so coy, she doesn't say yes or no, she just smiles. What is that supposed to mean? I want to buy her a diamond ring, and a gold wedding band for each of us. I don't have much money, but I can afford it. I wish she would respond, give me a sign, a nod, something. It's gotten so bad that now I insist that we stop at the very next jewelry store we see. This woman is driving me crazy.

I'm slow. You, the reader, probably got what was happening long before I was aware. This is exactly what she wants me to do, sweat. It such a classic male-female communication. She broached the marriage subject at Cleary's ranch and hasn't mentioned it since. She flutters away when I bring it up. This is the old playing-hard-to-get routine. Since there is doubt, I must try harder, I must up the ante. What will she want next? I can just imagine the conversation.

"David, I always wanted to live on the ocean; do you want to live in California?"

"Anyplace is fine."

"David, I like a front porch with a swing like my house in Nappanee."

"A porch swing is fine."

"David, can we buy Sara Ann a rocking horse and a Labrador retriever?"

A rocking horse and a Labrador retriever are fine.

A house made of rubies and emeralds is fine.

A horse stable in the living room is fine.

A walk-in closet seventy-feet-long is fine.

Yes, your friends and gerbil collection can live with us.

Yes, you can listen to all your Swiss yodeling records all day.

"You can have anything you want, and I will do anything you want." I took the rose quartz ring out of my shirt pocket and finally blurted it out. "Damn it, are you or aren't you going to marry me?" Sara Ann giggled, sat between us and looked at Caroline and me, over and over again like she was at a tennis match. She then turned to Caroline and said, "You better say yes because I need a new daddy."

Caroline said she wants to wait until we have time to ourselves when the trip is over, but she did put on the ring. She wants us to get off the road, and I don't suppose I blame her. All of a sudden she started crying, changed her mind and said, "I will marry you anytime because I don't want you to think that I'm waiting to see if you get a lot of money."

The thought never occurred to me. I insisted that we wait so we can do it right, have our families and friends there, sleep in our own bed without my having to walk away the next morning.

Relationships are weird. Now our positions have completely reversed themselves. I, knowing that she wanted to get married after the trip, insisted that we wait. Caroline, knowing that I wanted to get married right away, insisted we do it as soon as possible. There are so many things that we agree on. Getting married is one of them. The details need a little work, but the joy is shared. Indifference to money and everything associated with money is something else we have in common. This reminds me of a poem by Edward Randall,

Ten Million Dollars

If I had ten million dollars
I would buy new strings for my guitar.

I would find you the most beautiful
antique vase and fill it with a bouquet
of wildflowers and green ferns gathered from
the entire Champlain valley.

I would go to the animal shelter
and find us a new kitten.

If I had ten million dollars
I would buy you another book of poetry
and each of us a new paddle
for our white canoe.

I would open the curtains wider
to let in more sunlight.

If I had ten million dollars
I would play boccie in the backyard
with all the neighborhood children.

I would try to grow
Italian curly-leaf basil and oregano
in clay pots hung along our back porch.

I just had my afternoon meal, a turkey and cheese sandwich that Caroline stuffed in my backpack, and I refilled my canteens at a gas station. I got a call on my Blackberry, and as has happened several times before, I can only hear bits of the conversation before losing the contact completely. This time I heard Caroline crying, and the words "Holy Rosary." She had planned to ride up ahead to scout our next stopping point on Route 200. I'm talking into this damned tape recorder, and I don't know what's going on. My cellphone is ineffective so I'm going to flag down the first motorist I see coming toward me.

Thanks for nothing, asshole. The first two people drove right by my waving arms and didn't stop. My phone is ringing again.

"Hello, David Hall, this is Victor Tyrone. I met you at Mr. Cleary's ranch. Where are you now?"

"I'm about ten miles from Route 200."

"Start walking back toward Miles City. I should be there in an hour."

"What happened, where's Caroline?"

"There's been an accident. Caroline and Sara Ann were taken to the Holy Rosary Healthcare Center on Wilson Street in Miles City. By the time I reach you, we should know the extent of their injuries. The state police told me the car and camper were totaled. I'm very sorry."

Victor Tyrone was one of the cowboys who was ogling Caroline when I met her at the gate to Cleary's ranch. He showed up when he said and I got in his pickup truck. I thanked him for going to so much trouble, and he told me that the car and camper were put on a flatbed truck and taken back to Colin Cleary's place. We passed the spot where it happened, and I saw broken glass, and Sara Ann's cowgirl hat was in a ditch alongside the road. I grabbed it and got back in the truck. We tried to use the cellphone but it still faded in and out. That's when Mr. Tyrone got on my nerves.

"You shouldn't let a lady like that and her baby wander out by themselves in this country. It's too dangerous. I don't want any thanks from you, boy, I'm doing this for the lady."

"Are you a cowboy?" I asked him. "Because if you are, that makes you a boy also. You don't call me boy unless you want to fight. Do I make myself clear? After this is over, you and me will go round and round. Leave your damned guns at home and just bring your fists, cowboy. You don't scare me. I don't give a shit what you think of our arrangements. I appreciate your coming out to get me, but I'm sure Colin asked you to do that. If you have anything else to say, wait until this is over. You'll get your chance."

Tyrone glared at me as he dropped me off in front of the healthcare center, and said he would see me back at the ranch. I ran to the receptionist, who led me to Caroline. I threw my arms around her and was crying like a baby. She told me that she was fine, but Sara Ann has a broken leg. Colin was sitting with her and said we could stay in the same room back at his house until Sara Ann felt well enough to travel. The doctor said it was a simple fracture, and they put on a plaster cast. Colin said we were lucky it wasn't worse. A driver approaching Caroline went way over the centerline of the road onto her side. She didn't have time to react, and he hit the left rear of the Toyota. Luckily the child seat was on the right side of the car. The camper took the brunt of the impact and was totally destroyed. The driver of the vehicle was cited by the Montana State Police because he was under the influence. He is also at the medical center with a concussion, and he needed his head stitched up. I don't care if his head falls off and rolls down the hall.

Sara Ann was in good spirits. She cried at first, but we told her she would be fine after her leg healed. We promised to get her a rocking horse and a Labrador retriever like the one that brought back her ball at the state park. We also had to promise her that we would get married, and yes, her puppy could sleep in the bed with her. What is it about the McGregor girls? I am so overmatched.

It was many hours before we returned to the Circle CK ranch. Victor Tyrone was the first person to meet us and took me aside. He said from one boy to another he did apologize. He said that Caroline was in good hands, and he would help us if he could. We shook on it, and it was over.

I inspected the car and when I saw it, and I got weak-kneed. It was a miracle that either of them survived. Nearly everything in the camper was destroyed, including that wonderful Martin guitar. The computer was in the back seat of the Toyota. The outside of the screen was cracked but it still worked. I was able to salvage some clothes and most of the books. Neither of those vehicles will ever be used again. Colin said that he would arrange for the insurance agent to make his inspection.

The three of us were finally alone in the bed. I looked at the empty guitar stand and thought how would I have felt if there was an empty space where Caroline or Sara Ann were lying. I told Caroline, I absolutely insisted, that we go back to Nappanee immediately, and end the trip. There is no way that we can travel with Sara Ann, her car has been destroyed, and there was no way on God's earth I would leave them alone to wander about the countryside. This was my objection in the very beginning, but I let Caroline talk me out of it. Not this time. The trip is over.

I called Jonathan and told him what happened. He gave us medical advice, and then he said something I didn't expect. I told him that we were going back to Nappanee, and he agreed that I should accompany Caroline and Sara Ann back home. Then he said that I must continue on my journey from where I left off in Miles City. I went absolutely ballistic and was shouting on the phone. I told him he couldn't give me any reason why I would want to abandon

Caroline and return to the road for that idiotic quest. He said he couldn't tell me all the details, but I simply had to go through with it. He asked to speak with Caroline, and they talked for fifteen minutes. He talked, she listened and said no or yes a few times. When they were through I took the phone and thanked Jonathan for his concern. I demanded he tell me about these mysterious "details," but he said he couldn't. I controlled my anger and again said that the trip was over. I hung up.

I asked Caroline what Jonathan told her, and she said that it wasn't money at the end of my journey. People needed help and we were the only ones who could provide it. He said the quest was a chain and each person I see is a link that's necessary to complete the circle. He said I was the key. I asked her if he said anything else, and she said he asked her if she would permit me to finish the trip while she waited in Nappanee. She refused to agree and would only stay in Indiana long enough for Sara Ann to heal. She then wanted to fly to the nearest city on my journey, rent a camper, and continue right along with me like we did before.

I positively refused to allow it and am writing this from the porch of her house. Sara Ann has a new puppy. She's the cutest little yellow Labrador retriever you ever saw. The cast comes off Sara's leg in a week or so, and the three of us are very happy. Caroline just called me inside. Adele McIntire is on the phone.

CHAPTER TEN
Miles City, Montana to Missoula, Montana

I don't want to talk about it. I know you paid good money for this book and I owe you an explanation, but I refuse to discuss it. The title of this chapter is misleading because I am not going to give up the hundred miles I trekked away from Miles City. I'm resuming the trip alone from the town of Jordan, on Route 200. Lewistown means nothing to me now. There will be no dinner excursion. There is only

walking, walking,

walking, walking,

walking, walking,

walking, walking,

walking, walking,

walking, walking,

walking, walking,

walking, walking,

walking, walking,

walking, walking,

and walking.

I've got about forty pounds on my back and plan on camping often, since there's nothing but cow shit as far as the eye can see. I have my cellphone and whenever civilization shows its head around here, every seven hundred miles or so, I may be able to make a phone call or possibly even find a toilet. I promised Caroline I would call every day, but told her not to worry if she didn't hear from me due to transmitting conditions. It's the same with the wireless modem on my computer. If the cellphone doesn't work, the modem doesn't either.

It's now August eleven, and I'm ten miles from Great Falls, Montana. The city is good-sized, about 60,000 people, and I plan on recharging myself and my electronic equipment at the first decent motel I can find. I still look forward to my shower. Right now it's a cold shower. Both my body and my mind need a cold shower. Fuck, it's hot, and I'm miserably unhappy. There is only one fact that makes me feel better. The distance from Burlington, Vermont to Great Falls, Montana is 2,290 miles. The distance from Great Falls, Montana, to Aberdeen, Washington is 735 miles. This is according to the computer mapping system. I've actually traveled a much longer distance but the ratio should be the same. I have less than a third of my trip to go, and have been averaging thirty-five miles per day. If I have to travel another 850 miles, divided by 35, that equals 24 days. Add a couple extra for meeting people along the way and I should be in Aberdeen ahead of schedule. Fuck, I'm miserable.

I'm staying at the La Quinta Inn on 5th Street in Great Falls. It was right near Highway 89 where I've been walking. I'll say one thing for not having Caroline meet me at the end of each day. Stopping has become an adventure. I'm meeting more people because I have to ask permission to camp. Two nights ago, I got invited to sleep in a tractor shed. This may not seem like much, but it was pouring rain and the sound of the water on the metal roof was music. I had it too easy spending every night in that camper, next to the red-haired woman with the dark-green satin nightgown. Fuck, I'm miserable.

The high point of my day is talking to Caroline. As you know, the Blackberries have miniature built-in cameras. So far I've used it three times and can't keep from feeling devastated that we aren't in the same room. Rather than comforting me to see her face, it's making me even more miserable. I can tell that it's doing the opposite for her and Sara Ann. I had to walk around the room and show them the view out the window. When I see an interesting sight along the road, and I'm in transmitting range, I am going to call Caroline and show her what I've found. I guess this is a remarkable technology. Back in Lewis and Clark's day it was, Goodbye Dear, see you in a few years. Keep the bed warm.

You might find this fact interesting. Of all the motels, hotels, inns, and private homes I've stayed at on my journey, I have never turned on the television set if there was one in the room, and there usually is. I'm a radio man. It's almost time for Shorty Jones. Tonight is Thursday and he will have Doctor Prozak on. I feel like calling in; perhaps I can break through. I should probably place my call about five minutes before the show starts. They must get thousands of callers.

The show is about to begin, and I placed my call. I'm on hold, no telling if I can get through.

"Hello America, Happy Thursday to ya'll, or should I say to all you well-adjusted normal people. Just in case some of you aren't normal, or are even weird, we have Dr. Prozak with us tonight to help.

"Are you ready for the first caller, Doctor?"

"I most certainly am."

"Go ahead, this is Shorty Jones, you're on the air."

"Hello, Dr. Prozak. I have an office job and I like to eat. I hate exercising but my doctor says I have to. What type of exercises do you suggest? I'm Mellow in Marshland."

Health nuts are going to feel stupid someday, lying in hospitals dying of nothing.
Redd Foxx

"Poor Mellow. The best exercise you can get is to go pound your doctor. You already said that you hate working out, so what is your doctor trying to do? If you listen to him you'll be a physically-fit mental case. I find that people who force themselves to be fit doing something they hate develop a very mean look. Anyone who gets up at 4:30 a.m., eats mega-bars, and drinks tonic that tastes like sweat isn't going to be all cuddly after dinner. Avoid them."

Your Germ of the Day:
Today I will eat and drink what I want to and have a second helping of everything. I will hire a maid and someone to do all my yard work. I will buy spandex clothes

and laugh at everyone who wiggles their funny aerobic butts to rap music in some stupid YMCA.

"You're on the Shorty Jones show, go ahead."

"Good evening, Dr. Prozak. My ex-wife of 20 years is making trouble. As a new divorcee, I pay child support but now she wants more money, and part of our house. That's not fair! What can I do? Call me Dr. Valium from Smugsburg."

I am a marvelous housekeeper. Every time I leave a man I keep his house.
Zsa Zsa Gabor

"Good evening, Dr. Valium. I can tell that you are a psychiatrist. This is outrageous! All your wife did for 20 years is cook, clean house, and raise two children. She makes $7.50 an hour, which is enough to get by. It took years for you to build up your medical practice; it's not your fault that your income has increased to $437,000 in the last year. Your ex doesn't have to be a maid. Her mother can take care of the children while she goes back to college. Just because she put you through medical school, hey, that was a long time ago and now you have a new family, three time-share condos, and a two-masted schooner to worry about. She should get off your back."

Your Germ of the Day:

Today I will be firm. My psychiatric training has prepared me well to deal with the unpleasant, trying, unfinished business of my first marriage. Isn't everyone entitled to a starter marriage?

"We're talking with Dr. Connor Prozak. Actually, you are talking with him and I'm just sitting here listening. I'm Shorty Jones, and it's time for my next caller."

"Dr. Prozak, I'm really discouraged. I write true-romance short stories but nobody wants to publish any. So far this year I've received 76 rejection slips. All my stories involve Ralph and Blanche and take place in the law firm of Stoke, Guano and Sift. Should I change my characters or my setting? I'm Rejected in Riverville."

Dear Contributor: Thank you for not sending us anything lately. It suits our present needs.
                    Charles Schulz

"Hello, Rejected. Don't give up on Ralph and Blanche just yet. Many writers got hundreds of rejection slips before their first story was published. I wouldn't change characters or settings, but I might suggest some additions. You need titillating sex, preferably coupled with violence that degrades the human spirit. You also need to add every foul-mouthed, rotten curse you can dream up. Your characters need to spit and throw up a lot and commit crude acts with brooms, chairs, and their pets. If you make these editorial changes, you will also be successful on cable TV."

Your Germ of the Day:
I will not be discouraged. Tonight I will re-write my story.
I'll make it filthy and horrible and make sure there are at
least sixteen pauses in the action for commercial time. I will
also plan six sequels.

"Shorty Jones, go ahead."

"Hello, Doctor. My roommate (I'll call her Sophie) has developed some bizarre behavior. At 3 a.m. I hear a strange scratching and growling coming from her room. I notice a green mist rolling out from under her door. I smell garlic and then hear a flapping sound and a dog howl. During the day she seems normal. Is Sophie all right, or should I try to find out what's going on with her? Call me Uneasy in Utah."

Something wicked this way comes.
William Shakespeare

"I can see why you are uneasy. I'm glad you are concerned about 'Sophie'. Only a good friend would show such compassion; she's very lucky. Her symptoms are becoming more common, and I've run into hundreds of people with a similar problem. She must have been listening to Rush Limbaugh, Ann Coulter, or Bill O'Reilly earlier in the evening, and she's having an allergic reaction. Tomorrow make sure she listens to Yanni and don't give her access to a radio or TV. The symptoms should disappear in a few days."

Your Germ of the Day:
If any of my friends should listen to right-wing talk shows.,
I'll be ready to help them with understanding and plenty of
laxatives. I will keep something soothing at the ready to
counter any squalking, strident pedantry they may
encounter. I will tie a string of garlic cloves and wear it
around my neck just in case....

"Last caller for the Doctor, go ahead."

"Dr. Prozak, I'm walking across the country. Why don't Americans behave like Americans? I'm the Walking Man."

In the United States there is more space where nobody is
than where anybody is. That is what makes America what
it is.

Gertrude Stein

"Hello, Walking Man. Are you a Communist? How should Americans behave? They have no manners, too much money, drink too much, and burn too much gas. Do you expect to find culture and refinement in Dry Gulch? You are completely misguided. Americans always behave exactly like Americans."

Your American Germ of the Day:
As I walk through this great country, I will not speak
English. I will wear strange linen pants with loose tops and
a funny foreign cloth headdress. I will stop at every gas
station I see and ask them if I can use their restroom to cook

up a batch of goat meat and couscous. I will marvel at how well I have been treated.

I made it on the show as the last caller. Shorty Jones is quite a genius, and I'm still laughing as I write this. He does both voices, himself and Dr. Prozak. I'll bet he has books of quotes opened and arranged by subject, and he probably has hundreds memorized. He fires them out so quickly.

After breakfast in La Quinta's restaurant, I went back to my room. Caroline called me and Sara Ann was sitting next to her as usual. She said she had something to show me and panned the camera-phone to a guitar stand. On the stand was a brand new Martin D18 with a red bow tied around the neck. She said that I have to mellow it out, and it will probably take forty years. I wonder if God will give us that long. Sara Ann wants me to play rock music. She thinks that rock and roll was invented for her rocking horse. All she likes is music to rock by. The cast on her leg is covered with signatures. It's supposed to come off tomorrow, and she doesn't want it removed.

As I left the hotel I was listening to the radio with a single earbud. I do this so I can hear both the music and the traffic. I sat on a bench and adjusted my backpack when the news came on:

Eleven U. S. airmen, the crew of a B-29 shot down over Korea, have been released after two years imprisonment in Red China. After crossing the bridge onto the free soil of Hong Kong, they all headed for baths, hot running water, and American soda, a taste of home after their grim ordeal.

A bus boycott has begun in Montgomery, Alabama. A colored woman by the name of Rosa Parks refused to give up her seat to a white person.

And in sports, Sterling Moss has claimed the checkered flag to earn his first Grand Prix victory.

Now back to our hit parade.

The station played three songs: "The Ballad of Davy Crockett" by Bill Hayes, "Angels in the Sky," by The Crew Cuts, and "Birth of the Boogy" by Bill Haley and His Comets.

I turned around to look behind me and the hotel was gone. There was a movie theater in its place. Parked in the street in front of me, with the showroom invoice still stuck to the rear window, was a brand new blue and white 1955 Chevy Bel Air.

I sat down again on the bench and tried to gather myself. Okay, this has happened before and I got through it. I did an inventory check and everything was functioning. My wallet contents were unchanged. I quickly grabbed my cellphone, but it was non-functional and completely dead except for static. The computer was working, but of course there was no Internet connection. I'm not attracting as much attention as I did in 1933 East Dubuque, but I'm still dreadfully out of place. I'm going to find out all I can about this time and take hundreds of photographs. I'm glad I recharged the camera's batteries and downloaded all the photos into the computer.

My grandfather took photos of Great Falls in 1955. I have them on my computer, and I'm going to access them right now. On second thought, I will walk away from here to a less conspicuous place. A color computer screen is bound to draw a dozen onlookers. I remember a Ray Bradbury story about a time-traveling agency. They took people on excursions back into the past. They warned all time-travelers not to wander off the path because if they so much as stepped on a blade of grass, they might alter history. That's exactly what happened. Someone strayed off the trail, and when they got back to their own time, there were changes. The language was slightly different, letters of the alphabet were different, even the color of the grass was weird. I wonder if I would have the same effect if I showed people a glimpse into the future, or told them who was going to win the World Series for the next ten years. What would happen if I saved someone's life who would have otherwise have died? There could be major consequences. It's an interesting notion, but I have absolutely no intention of testing my theory.

I have the same food problem I had before because my money's no good. I had a big breakfast and stuffed some English muffins, cheese, and several apples into my food bag, but after that, it's a home-cooked meal or nothing. I wonder if I'll get back to the twenty-first century when I reach the other side of Great Falls. This time, I'm in no hurry. You should see the cars, they are really cool. There's a big dark-green car that looks like a sow bug. It's a DeSoto. Here's another, a Kaiser, model Henry J. God, these things were death-traps. The dashboards were made of steel and actually came to a point. There were no seatbelts, head restraints, or airbags. Shit, I just picked up a discarded newspaper and listen to these prices:

New Ford is $1,606

Gas is 23 cents a gallon

Bread is 18 cents a loaf

Eggs are 61 cents a dozen

Ten-pound bag of potatoes is 53 cents

I see houses for sale for under twenty thousand dollars. There are several listed for less money than Caroline paid for her car. Speaking of cars, there are a lot of squealing tires. It seems that the locals like to drag-race from stoplights. I also notice quite a few cars with blue smoke coming from their tailpipes, and there's a smell of burning oil. I guess the people of 1955 thought the supply was endless. The fashions are interesting, but everyone looks the same. The only variation I see is a slight one between people of color and white people. There's much more diversity and self-expression in dress in our time. Ah, yes, the Age of Conformity. GI's returned home from the war, and the perfect Leave It To Beaver families were created all over America. I see a few beatnik-types here and there, but I suspect they are affecting the dress and have none of the sensibilities. After all, this is Montana, not Greenwich Village.

I've just looked through my grandfather's photos, and there's an inn where he stayed that's right on Route 200. I'm going to stop in and chat with the owner and see if I can learn anything about him. I don't know if I am arriving before or after Bill made his trip. I don't know when his photos were taken.

I'm approaching the Pinehurst Inn, and there's a delightful front porch with rocking chairs set up. It's in the shade about seventy-five feet from the road. A rawboned woman, maybe the owner, walks up to me.

"Sorry mister, we're full up, and we aren't serving dinner for five hours."

I could see this wasn't the case. As a matter of fact, the parking lot was nearly empty.

"No problem, ma'am, I was just wondering if you remember this man." I made the bold move of opening my computer and displaying a photograph of my grandfather sitting in the green wicker rocking chair. She quickly called her husband, and they both just stared at the screen.

"How did you ever get those pretty colors on that screen? Is that a television set? Look Dustin, there's our place, right there, how did you do that?"

"I'm from Chicago, and this is my grandf....er, my second cousin, Bill. This screen is my invention. I have a company that makes these."

"Your cousin? Bill Hall is your cousin? I never would have known. You're so dark, I mean..."

"Must be the Italian part of my family."

"Land sakes alive, why didn't you say so? Please come on in. We have plenty of rooms available. Can I fix you something to eat?"

My stomach hurt, I was sick inside, but I kept at it. We sat in the guests' living room, which had a pool table, a library with Reader's Digest condensed books, and a Dumont television set in the corner. Three guests were camped in front of the screen watching the "George Gobel Show." The next two shows were "Dragnet" and "I Love Lucy," and they kept everyone entertained. The entire inn smelled of tobacco. Everyone was smoking, and a thin layer of nicotine covered everything. When no one was looking, I grabbed a few paper towels and cleaned the TV screen. One of the guests said, "Did ya get a new TV?" Mr. Grebbs, oh did I tell you, the owners are Mr. and Mrs. Grebbs, had a ashtray next to his pack of Camels. I studied the pack and noticed that the animal had one hump, so I said to him that it isn't a camel. So he said, "It isn't a Chesterfield," whatever that is. So I says to him, I says, "It only has one hump so it's a dromedary." So he says to me, he says, "I don't care if they call it a rhinoceros, it will still taste the same."

Mrs. Grebbs said, "Bill Hall stayed here for three days last month. He was traveling across the country on foot, can you imagine that. He is an extremely cultured man, and knows a lot about art and music. He was tired from his journey, and the first night he must have slept for twelve hours. When he woke up he was like an uncaged tornado. We had some roof tiles and rain gutters that had come loose after a storm. We were going to hire a contractor to fix them, but Bill climbed up on the roof and took care of everything."

"Did my cousin ever talk about his family or his home?"

"You know, David, it's odd, but he did talk about his father. It seems that his dad also walked across the country. His father's name was..."

"Sam Hall."

"That's it, Sam Hall. Sam was very hard on Bill. He threw him out of the house and said that he would never give him anything unless he walked across the country. Isn't that odd?"

Mrs. Grebbs took a Swanson TV Brand Frozen Dinner out of the oven and handed it to me. I insisted that I should do something to earn my meal like my "cousin" had done, but I was given every accommodation, since I had blue eyes and was obviously Italian.

Mr. Grebbs talked about the Godless Russians and said that they wanted to conquer the world. He promised they would never set foot in Montana. He had an M1 Garand, like the one he used in the Second War. He also had three hundred rounds of surplus 30-06 full metal jacket ammo. He coughed and said, "Those Russians had better not come anywhere near the Pinehurst Inn." Then the subject changed to UFOs. The newspapers were full of accounts of alien sightings. There were strange glowing discs sighted all over Great Falls.

So this is 1955 Montana. "I Love Lucy," UFOs, TV dinners, the "Ballad of Davy Crockett," Chevy V8s, Gillette blue blades, condensed books, and Godless Russians. I spent a half-hour lying to them about the screen they saw. I told them it was like a television screen that held photographs. They wanted to buy one, but I said it was still in the research and development stage. They asked me how much it would cost, and I said thirty-nine dollars. Mr. Grebbs said that was way too expensive for a novelty item, and it would never sell. He said people are just going to use their regular old albums because with my screen, you can see only one photo at a time and you have to open it up. I should have told him he could get a job as a notebook product development consultant at

192

Hewlett Packard, but he wouldn't have known what I was talking about. I feel a little bit like God, knowing what will happen to them all, not as individuals, but to their world.

I wonder if I was ever visited by someone going back in time to my era. Perhaps if I was sitting at home this traveler would tell me, you know, the Washington Nationals are going to win the World Series next year, and in 2016, Paris Hilton will become President of the United States. He could tell me how I ended up. If Caroline and I had any kids, if I ever got my books published, if global warming wrecked the planet. I don't want to know, and I want to get out of 1955. I'm leaving before dawn, when everyone's asleep. I'll leave a note thanking the Grebbs for their hospitality. I feel like leaving another message: an African-American person slept here.

What do these names have in common? *Hudson, DeSoto, Packard, Kaiser, Nash Rambler, Studebaker, Frasier.* They are all names of cars alive in 1955 that are extinct today. I can think of a few more political names that I wish were extinct, but I'll let you fill in your own blanks.

I'm almost out of the Great Falls city limits. Look what I found alongside the road.

There's an Anvil Brand Work Clothes pocket knife, a fishing lure, a hair curler, two Buffalo nickels, a Bugs Bunny Pez dispenser, and I have no idea what that round thing is with the wooden handles. I put the knife and the nickels in my pocket.

Thankfully, on the other side of the Great Falls city limits sign, I walked back into now. Once again the objects disappeared from my pocket. I just noticed something: all the cars were loaded with chrome. In today's cars, I don't see any chrome and I miss it. Those huge bumpers were all shiny and reflected the sunlight. So this is what my grandfather saw. And guess what else he did? He smoked. The Grebbs took some photos of him I never saw before, and he was sitting in the same wicker rocker. Between his fingers was a cigarette. Mrs. Grebbs said he had his own pack, so this was not an occasional event. How the hell could he smoke and still walk across the country? As soon as I was away from the city, I phoned Caroline and told her what happened. She said she was constantly praying for me. I told her not to stop.

The distance between Great Falls and Missoula is 165 miles, and I did it in seven days. I didn't make it all the way to Mrs. Olive Beatrice Sheridan's house, but I should be there by ten tomorrow morning. I called her and expected to hear an older woman's voice, but she sounds like a young person. I just realized how dumb that statement is. How the hell can I tell if someone is 35 or 75 by the sound of their voice? Adele Dobbs sounds no different than Caroline on the telephone.

I arrived in Missoula, and met Olive Sheridan. She's a high school physical education teacher, and her husband is a math teacher in the same school. They have two children aged ten and seven. I'll tell you all about their home and who her mother was.

In chapter two I mentioned my older brother Seth and the gross-out contests, and I also mentioned my older sister, who can be somewhat cranky at times, the one who threw up on the rug, but I didn't tell you that her name is Jennifer. Seth and Jennifer were there to greet me at the Sheridan house. This is getting interesting.

CHAPTER ELEVEN
Missoula, Montana to Coeur d'Alene, Idaho

Olive Sheridan's mother was a nurse during the Vietnam War. She came home after her service and went to work in the hospital. She met my father under unusual circumstances. It seems he took a dump in a remote camping area and got poison oak all over his bottom and private parts, and he was exhausted and dehydrated. Mrs. Sheridan treated the poor man, and then let him stay at her mother's house until he was fit to travel. My father never forgot the kindness and put both her children through college. Papa Jack was like Johnny Appleseed, but instead of planting apple trees, he cut a goodwill path through the entire country. I no longer doubt it. He did amazing things for a lot of people who will never forget him. It's because of his generosity that I'm treated like royalty wherever I go. Now I have to reconcile why he was so different with his family and especially with me.

The very first thing that Olive Sheridan did after she hugged me was to tell me that she knew I had a fifth-place finish in the Boston Marathon, and that I was invited to the Olympic trials. She is also a runner and a physical fitness nut. Her kids and husband made a grand fuss, and after knowing each other for only one hour, we were already having a good time. I missed Caroline and Sara Ann and wished they could share these moments with me.

Missoula is a delight. I've decided that Montana is indeed a special place. The Sheridans took me, Seth, and Jennifer to a farmer's market. There were all sorts of interesting things for sale, including home-crafted banjos, woven shawls, picnic tables and free-standing swings, jewelry, and crafts. I brought my Blackberry and showed the family back in Indiana all the goodies, and Sara Ann immediately demanded I buy her a cute little canvas tote bag. The craftspeople monogrammed it with her name on one side and the name of her Labrador retriever, Bonkers, on the other side. There was also a hand-embroidered retriever-like dog on either side.

Here's what I learned about Seth and Jennifer. I called Jonathan and asked him if he told them my itinerary. He said he did not because he didn't know it himself, but they had been merciless in their relentless questioning. He suggested that they probably learned where I was going from Caroline. I called her, and she did indeed tell them where I would be headed next. She is very trusting and saw no reason why they shouldn't know. I agreed that she did the right thing.

My brother and sister were all hugs and insisted that they be brought up to date on my travels. They listened to my stories with patience and fixed smiles on their faces. I suspected a hidden agenda that was plain and simple. They want to stay close to me in case I unearth family riches they can get a piece of. Since I suspected this is their agenda, I talked to them privately an hour ago.

I told them that Jonathan suggested that the trip was not about money, but people in need at the end of my journey. I also told them that if money was involved, that it would be apportioned fairly to all members of the family. They didn't like my guarantees; they sure didn't share any of their inheritance with me and doubted that I would include them. They have no reason not to trust me. They don't trust anyone, including each other, and it shows in everything they do.

Now it's getting heavy. Olive told me she was questioned by them before I arrived to learn what my next destination was. She didn't tell them and said they would have to ask me. That is why they are being so doting and patient with their younger brother's tales of wandering. Adele Dobbs calls Caroline and me frequently. Caroline told Adele she gave my contact information to Seth and Jennifer, and Adele advised her not to do it again. She said they would probably go ahead of me from contact to contact and try to beat me to Aberdeen.

I'm lying here in bed listening to my shortwave radio. I just got a call from Jonathan, and he thinks dear brother and sister are working with a private detective agency in Seattle. They told Mom what they were up to, and my mother was upset enough to tell Jonathan. Naturally, she didn't tell me. What they hope to accomplish is beyond my grasp.

Family money, what a travesty. There's someone I haven't yet told you about. As you know, Jonathan is my younger brother, Seth is my older brother, and Jennifer is my older sister, the eldest of us at thirty-four. I also have a younger sister. Her name is Margo, and she's the baby of the family at twenty-six. She just got her MBA and plans to take over product development at...guess where? Right you are, Hall Digital Networks. Tom Cleary, who now runs the company, has already cleared a path for her. They get along rather well, and according to Jonathan, they are seeing each other off work. Margo is not cuddly, but she is honorable and honest. So far I don't know where she and Tom fit into all this, but I'm sure I'll find out from Jonathan. Shit, I'll call her myself and find out.

"You have a duty to keep us informed of your movements. Where does your next contact live?" Jennifer finally said with annoyance, as I was preparing to resume my walk.

I smiled politely, and flashed the same insincere grin she used when I was telling her stories of my trip. I patiently told her and Seth that they should walk along with me, so when I get there, they will also. I suggested it would be good for them, mile after mile, day after day, week after week. I said they would never again take simple lodging and food for granted. I advised them to be careful when two trucks were passing in opposite directions, and also to watch out for snakes. I explained conditioning would be necessary and they would only be able to do about eighteen miles per day at first. I offered them that fine invitation because I was getting really pissed. Then Jennifer said, "We've come all the way to God-forsaken Missoula to see you and you treat us like this?"

We were within earshot of Olive Sheridan when she said that. Olive was ready for battle. I knew that my rebuke would be gentler than hers would have been, so I answered Jennifer right away. I told her that it was impolite to insult someone's home after they have extended you hospitality and given you several meals, and it would be best if they left. Seth and Jennifer stormed out of the house into their rental car and took off, probably for the airport.

The Sheridan family made me promise that we would visit them when this was all over. Olive had talked with Caroline and they got along really well. We've made some wonderful friends. Seth and Jennifer sadden me.

The next person I'm to see is Abraham Hardin in Coeur d'Alene, Idaho. I'm headed for Superior, Montana, and in three days I should cross the Idaho state line. It's about 165 miles from Missoula to Coeur d'Alene. Caroline and I agreed that my brother and sister would not be told my whereabouts. Sara Ann is now strong enough to travel, and Caroline is putting pressure on me to let them join me.

I'm up before dawn on most mornings. The morning temperature is actually chilly, and at this altitude, 2,500 feet or so, it dips into the high forties. Some mornings I wear my wool cap. By midday, however, the temperature climbs to almost ninety. I really power out early, and bite off most of my mileage before it gets hot. The countryside is gorgeous. There are numerous streams, and the land is extremely inviting. The East is very different. In Vermont there are trees everywhere. All the mountains are covered with green carpet, and there are very few rock outcroppings on the hills. In Montana there are stands of trees, and the hills are much more open. The air is so clear, I can see animals on the sides of the mountains ten miles away. I've only been averaging 20 miles per day because I'm getting tired.

Tonight I'm camping on the front porch of an unoccupied ranch house. I got lucky last night. I was stopping for the day and noticed the For Sale sign, just as the real estate broker was driving out of the property. I asked him if I could just pitch my tent for the night, and he said it would be fine as long as I left the place as I found it. The ranch was a small one, only five hundred acres. Gasp! Five hundred acres. In Japan they have to live 500 people to a room. If I had the money, I would have bought the place right then and there. He said it had been vacant for about a month, but someone was going to look at it in two days, so he was making sure everything was in good shape. I thanked him, and told him what I was doing. I took his picture, and he said it would be all right if I slept on the front porch.

It's morning, and there is a creature lying next to me on the porch. It's a black dog, about the size of a retriever, with a white spot on its side, a white spot on top of its head, and a white tip on its tail. He's a funny, floppy-eared animal with a natural rake. His front legs seem two inches too short. He looks more like a spotted hyena than a dog. I said, "Hello, doggy," and he looked straight up as if he were baying at the moon and said, woo, woo, woo, woo, woo. He then half grinned. So help me, that's what it looked like. You've seen dogs curl their mouths when they growl. This dog wasn't growling, he was grinning.

He's a medium-sized animal with no collar and seems to be in good shape except that his fur is somewhat matted. He was obviously hungry and was sniffing around my backpack. I asked him if he wanted food. He cocked his head to the side and said woo, woo, woo, woo, woo. I shared my breakfast with him. He had half an English muffin, some turkey coldcuts, and some coffee cake. I asked him if he liked the food, and he again said woo, woo, woo, woo, woo. His vocabulary isn't very large, but he is consistent. My cellphone was working -- I was still close enough to Missoula

-- so I called Caroline and Sara Ann and showed them the dog. He did his classic five woos. Sara Ann named him Woo Woo. This is only fitting, since it was I who named her dog. Her puppy grabbed my slipper and was shaking it as if she were trying to kill it. I said, "She's going bonkers with my slipper." The name stuck. Sara Ann called the dog Bonkers from that day forward.

I broke camp, or should I say *we* broke camp, and headed back along the highway. I was hoping he had a home and would disappear as fast as he appeared, but that was not the case. He matched me stride for stride for a few miles. I passed a beautiful log home and asked the owners if they had ever seen this dog or knew who it belonged to. They said no, but they were very kind and gave Woo Woo a bowl of dog food and water, and me a chocolate ice cream pop. I thought he would hang where the eating was good, but he followed me right out the gate, and we walked together for the rest of the afternoon.

At the end of my day we finally arrived in Superior. I was looking forward to a shower and tried to register at the Mountain Top Motel on Mullan Road. They said they were sorry, but they didn't allow pets. Here I was at the desk, tired and hungry, and this black and white dog is sitting next to me grinning and wagging its tail. I thanked the clerk and spent the night with Woo Woo camped in the field next to the motel. They did let me recharge my batteries in the motel office. I've got a very furry problem on my hands.

Superior is a fine little town in magnificent country, but they don't have an animal shelter and I could find no one to adopt Woo Woo. As we approached the Bitterroot Mountain Range, I was now carrying food for two.

We crossed into Idaho yesterday, and tonight we're stopped in the town of Kellogg. I found a motel on Jacob's Gulch Road that allows pets. I bought a twelve-foot leash and a collar. He hated the collar at first and tried to slip it off with his paws, but now he's used to it. This dog is a comedian. He is always doing something funny. After we checked into the motel, I filled the ice bucket and put in two bottles of grapefruit juice. I dropped an ice cube on the floor, and he picked it up and flung it across the room, not once but four times, until it melted. He was upset that it turned to water so he did his five woos. I tossed him another ice cube and he repeated the game. Five ice cubes later he finally got bored and jumped on the bed. He snores when he sleeps, very loudly.

Today is a big day for me and I'm especially sad that Caroline, actually no one that I love, is with me. Today is September 11 and I turned 30. Thankfully Woo Woo is here. I'm trying hard not to feel sorry for myself, but I do feel older, more like sixty. Caroline and Sara Ann sang Happy Birthday, and I smiled while I was on camera, but fell apart after I hung up. I don't want to talk about it.

It's time for the Shorty Jones show.

"Good evening, America. I'm Shorty Jones, and we're going to get right to it. Before we have the former Vice President of the United States join us, I'm going to tell you thirteen ways to slime your brother and sister."

Here's number one. *Yes ma'am, she's a beauty. The engine, transmission, and brakes look fine. I know the lady who owned this car, yes ma'am, I do. She used it to go to church on Sundays and to the supermarket.*

Number two. *I'm sorry sir, the price has gone up again. No, Prozac is not expensive to make, but how do you think the drug companies finance all that research it takes to introduce a new product into our economy?*

Here's numbers three, four, five, and six. *I am not a crook. Read my lips, no new taxes. I did not have sex with that woman. We found weapons of mass destruction in Iraq.*

Number seven. *We Republicans believe in the trickledown theory. If you have a healthy economy and relax restrictions against corporations, exciting new positions will be created. Eventually janitors, maids, dishwashers, burger-flippers, apple-pickers, and a whole host of important jobs will be produced by the private sector.*

"Oh baby, I love *that* one. Something trickles down all right. Down their legs."

Number eight. *Those aren't termites sir, those are flying ants. This house and foundation are as sound as a dollar.*

Number nine. *Let me see your license and registration. Step out of the car and keep your hands where I can see them. You're charged with speeding, 34 in a 30 mph zone. What is your name ma'am, would you step out of the car too, please. It is a bit unusual in these parts for a black man to have a white wife. Our speed laws are for everybody. The magistrate is in town on Friday. We'll give you your license back after the fine is paid. What'd you say, boy?*

Number ten. *Mrs. Fontabulla, you have just won a free trip to Bermuda. Congratulations! Now let me tell you what you have to do to claim your prize.*

Number eleven. *I'm sorry hon, I have to take another business trip this weekend.*

Number twelve. *Come to where the flavor is, come to Marlboro country.*

Number thirteen. *I want to privatize Social Security so our retirees will have more options.*

"Fine and dandy, so much for sliming your brother and sister. I'd like to hear from any of you out there in Shorty Jones' land if you had any money trickle down into your bank account this week. I left a pail outside in front of my driveway in case anything trickled down from any of those passing Lexus SUVs or Mercedes convertibles, but when I examined it this morning all I saw was pigeon doo.

"For this next segment of our show, I'm going to need your help. Oh yes, I am. I'm going to give you a situation. After I read what is happening, we are all going to say, in unison, 'Hard, hard, life is so hard.' Okay, has everybody got that? 'Hard, hard, life is so hard.' Here we go."

You are on a mountain top writing a sonnet to your sweetie because she's falling in love with someone else, and your pen runs out of ink.
Hard, hard, life is so hard.

You are traveling far from home at night on an unknown, quiet back road during a thunderstorm, with no house lights to be seen anywhere, and your car runs out of gas.
Hard, hard, life is so hard.

You arrive at the outdoor summer party two hours late. It's hot and you're dying of thirst. You walk over to the beer keg that is sitting in a tub of ice and press the handle. All you get is foam.
Hard, hard, life is so hard.

You have to change a rear tire at night during a blinding snowstorm. You turn on your flashlight, but the light turns yellow and fades away.
Hard, hard, life is so hard.

You are about to make love to a beautiful partner that you have been trying to date for half a year. Knock, knock, your gregarious cousins from Smugsburg, Ohio are just passing through and pay a surprise visit.
Hard, hard, life is so hard.

You are spending the weekend at your in-laws. They serve scallops with mustard and garlic for dinner. They believe in being really close, and they laugh a lot in your face. Big hearty laughs.

Hard, hard, life is so hard.

A strange woman rings your doorbell. She's with her daughter who is selling Girl Scout cookies. You are rude, don't buy any, and tell them to go away. You don't meet this woman again until the company picnic. She's your boss's wife.

Hard, hard, life is so hard.

It's one hundred and three in the shade. You have just spent over an hour shopping for a week's food for the family. You've loaded the car with frozen food and ice cream. You return the cart to the store and notice that you locked the car doors and your keys are in the ignition.

Hard, hard, life is so hard.

You pay two hundred and fifty dollars for front row seats to see the Stones in concert. You drive for five hours, park the car, and realize that you left the tickets at home on your kitchen table.

Hard, hard, life is so hard.

"I've just received a message from the former Vice President. He will not join us this evening after all. He sends his regrets. It's early September, and for old times' sake, as a remembrance of 9/11, he again hides in a bunker under Roundback Mountain along the Maryland-Pennsylvania border. There was much criticism of his administration, so perhaps he decided to disappear earlier. He's a good man who doesn't believe in going to war. He would never go and fight, and during the Vietnam War he had other priorities. He would have, however, sent you or your kid to Iran, Belgium, or Vatican City, if his Lincoln ran low on gas. Long live Halliburton."

Listening to Shorty Jones always makes me laugh, and it always makes me angry. We're camping again after an interesting day and morning. I overtook a man who was walking his bicycle. He had a flat tire and didn't have a patch kit. It was very early, so no pickups had yet gone by. A passenger car would not have been able to handle his bicycle. His name is Michael Wyatt and he was riding to work. I told him what I was doing and did not try to record him on the sneak. He let me tape our conversation.

"Actually, I enjoy riding. It's twenty-five miles from my house to my work, and it only takes me an hour and fifteen minutes. I work for a fence manufacturing company outside of Cataldo. I can't afford gas anymore. My F250 truck only gets fifteen miles to the gallon, so by riding this bike I save about 60 bucks a week. My wife will have to come get me tonight because of this flat tire. As soon as we can afford it, we're going to get one of those hybrid cars."

"Michael, do you have health insurance at the fence company?"

"We used to, but the owner had to drop it because it cost too much. He said we would have to contribute half, and we did, but that was last year. This year they stopped it altogether and said it was up to the employees to find their own group rate. We don't have retirement either. This is a small company that employs nine. Most people around here are in the same boat as we are."

We came to a house, and he knew the people who live there. He left his bike, and his friend drove him to work. They offered to give me a ride, but I thanked them and kept going.

As I walk through the small communities, I'm aware that most people do not have very much in reserve. They live from day to day and do the best they can. Millions of people are three or more months behind in their house payments. I have a feeling of foreboding that really hard times are ahead. Everything is cyclical; sometimes the good guys are ahead, and sometimes the bad guys are winning. It's really not any more complicated than that. I get the feeling we are about to hit bottom, and it will take quite a while for this country to climb out of the hole that has been dug by greedy people. I really don't understand politics, but I can see the results of evil actions. All it may take is another stock market crash or a terrorist attack. I don't know if America will survive intact.

There is one word that I really dislike. It's the word *naïve*. My father used it constantly when I talked about the world as I saw it. He must have told me I was naïve dozens of times. He walked across the country during the Vietnam War, but he never told me what he thought about it. He was withholding, and he hid behind those non-committals. I'm walking across the country during two wars, one in Iraq, and one in Afghanistan. I don't like it. I'll tell Sara Ann I don't like it. I'll tell any cowboy I meet that I don't like it.

These are your retirement benefits after the privatization of Social Security.

This is the air you are now breathing after the Republican-weakened EPA.

This has trickled down to you from the Walton family and Rupert Murdoch.

This is what fell out of the V.P.'s ear when he tilted his head to the side.

This is what we will all become after we are dead.

This is what the rich Republicans look like when they are still alive.

Woo Woo is a big baby and won't sleep outside the tent. My mountain tent is small and it's a tight fit for two. He loves it when I turn on the computer. He lies there, watches the screen, and tilts his head to the side. When we stayed at the Mountain Top Motel in Superior, I downloaded a short video of dogs barking. I played it for him, and he got excited and gave me five woos.

He may have saved my life this morning. I was sleeping soundly just at dawn, and he started barking and growling right next to my head. There's only thin mosquito netting at the end of the tent, and our heads were about a foot from the edge. Outside the tent, probably drawn by the warm bodies inside, was a rattlesnake. His head was only a foot on the other side of the netting, and I could actually hear his tongue moving in and out. I grabbed Woo Woo and pulled him back, and then got my mace. I squirted the rattlesnake in the face and made him very unhappy. He rolled along the ground and disappeared into the grass.

This is probably the first time in Idaho history that anyone shot a snake with mace. I can just hear the cowboys at Cleary's ranch in Montana if I told them that story. Haw, haw, haw, the snake wasn't trying to rape you, should have shot it with a forty-five, har har.

I will see Abraham Hardin in Coeur d'Alene this afternoon. My time walking across the Idaho panhandle has been relatively short. In a few days I will cross into Washington. We are going to celebrate. This city is larger than I expected, and much more beautiful. There are several lakes and quite a bit of culture.

I got very lucky. Abraham Hardin's home is right on Coeur d'Alene lake. We have a small guest cabin all to ourselves that includes a kitchen. It's located next to the main house. Abraham Hardin didn't tell me how old he was, but I'm guessing somewhere in his late seventies. He goes for a swim every day, and believe me, that water is cold. He lives alone, but his daughter visits him every other day since she lives just up the road. He has an engaging smile and is very friendly and welcoming. He also has a dog named Barnacle that's at least part Labrador. He loves to jump in the water as Mr. Hardin is swimming. Woo Woo tried to follow Barnacle, but when he got ten feet off shore he realized that he hated the water, turned around, and came back. He shook himself off and gave five loud woos. He was trying to tell me he was a mountain dog, not a lake dog. Mr. Hardin suggested we bring him to the vet tomorrow for a checkup. That's a great idea.

I am amazed at the wonderful senior citizens I've met on this journey. I wish I could have been around more people like them when I was growing up. I've always had a fear of growing old, but not any more. I re-read a fine poem by Edward Randall.

Old People

Let me tell you about the most wondrous of creatures.

They don't hear very well;
sometimes you really have to shout to get their attention.
This is because they want your words to be sparse,

important and worth listening to.

They walk bent forward, stooped down
from carrying the weight of their families.

They have seen so much, weary eyes can
now just define shapes,
but experience fills in the features
and wisdom sharpens the details.

Their voices quaver in a soft vibrato.
They know the reasons for the seasons
so there's no need for long loud speeches.

They move slowly because they know
that the journey is more important
than the destination.

They carefully examine the little things
because they know that time is too precious
for hurried explanations.

They are so happy to see you today;
they tell you of their yesterday
and ask you about your tomorrow.

They repeat all the medical facts,
describe all the pain and trouble,
not because they want sympathy,
but because they want to display

their campaign medals.

They have purple hearts from living
and need to be told,
good job.

Let me tell you about the most wondrous of creatures.

About long lines on their foreheads
from straining to know.

About hair of silver,
soon to go home,
they will be first to the other side.

Grandmother, Grandfather,
grand ambassadors next in our life cycle.

Can you prepare us?
Can we comfort you?

CHAPTER TWELVE
Coeur d'Alene, Idaho to Spokane, Washington

Abraham Hardin, his daughter Pamela, her husband John, and I had breakfast on the picnic table alongside my cabin. I bought a bathing suit and swam in the lake. Pamela, who is on a diet, asked me how much weight I lost on my trip. Mr. Hardin has a scale so I weighed in at 176 pounds. I've lost nine pounds. I'm at a very important part of my journey. I can smell and taste the end of it. I honestly believe I'm going to make it.

Caroline and Sara Ann are going to fly into Spokane, Washington, which is only a day's walk for me from Coeur d'Alene. We will rent a camper, and they will again travel with me. The camper will be a self-contained unit, not a car or truck pulling anything. We need a larger one because we now have two dogs. I'm going to insist that they sleep with Sara Ann. Perhaps they will keep the little terror occupied so Caroline and I can have some privacy. Do you have any idea how much I'm looking forward to seeing them? This time I got her. The accident is very fresh in all our minds, and I only agreed to let her come here if we get married right away after we get to Aberdeen. She agreed, but said that was her idea in the first place.

Abraham Hardin spoke well of Papa Jack but didn't give away any details. I had to know what miracles the man worked here in Idaho, so I was very truthful with Abraham and told him what I had learned about Papa Jack from my trip. All my father did was find Mr. Hardin's wallet on the

216

side of the road. It had five hundred dollars in it, and he walked to Hardin's house to deliver it. He stayed for two days.

"Those were hard times for everybody. Not so much economically, we've always been prosperous, but the country was being torn apart. Your father and I agreed that the Vietnam War was wrong. The older generation, including both our parents, had a different view. They believed the war reports and trusted in our country's mission."

Mr. Hardin told me that the person I am to see next is Julia Vickers in Ephrata, Washington. She's in her eighties and has lived there all her life. He said we may not like Ephrata because it isn't lush and green. His words went right over my head; all I could think about was meeting Caroline and Sara Ann at the Spokane airport. I will take a cab and resume my walk from where I left off. I said goodbye to Abraham Hardin and his family and walked out of town. We have two days to walk thirty miles. Woo Woo got his shots and was thoroughly checked out by the vet. He said Woo Woo is about two years old. He cautioned me about glass alongside the highway. He has a good point, and as soon as we get the camper this dog will ride instead of walk.

I've really been thinking about the legacy we leave behind us. Papa Jack left a wonderful road legacy, but he gets mixed reviews from his family. I would rather be remembered as kind than powerful or brilliant.

There has been a terrible tragedy. I'm writing this from my motel, only five miles from my starting point. At seven a.m. a motorcyclist went by me at over one hundred miles an hour. About half a mile ahead, he crossed the yellow line and hit a semi head on. I ran as fast as I could and was the first person on the scene. The truck driver wasn't hurt, but there was considerable damage to his rig. The poor cyclist died instantly. We could do nothing for him but say a prayer. He was right in the middle of the other lane, and the driver saw him cross himself just before he hit. It was obviously a suicide. The driver, Joe, was badly shaken. He kept saying, "There was nothing I could do, there was nothing I could do." There was blood all over the road, and we moved the body out of the gasoline that spilled from the demolished cycle. I had to put Woo Woo in the truck's sleeper cab because he was very upset and barked non-stop. The police found the man's wallet and a crowd gathered. One of the passersby knew him. There was no suicide note on his person, but he had lost his job recently, and he and his wife were bickering.

How can anyone judge whether or not he had good reason to kill himself? His despondency was severe. Many of the people he left behind are going to be asking themselves questions. How could they have helped, why didn't they see it coming? I'll never forget the sound of that impact. There were no screeching tires or horns, just a... I can't write about this anymore. What's the point of giving you the details? We all have to live with unspeakable sights and sounds etched into our consciousness.

It's amazing how a death of a loved one, or the death I witnessed, causes you to think about your own life. On the most basic level, are you happy or sad? True happiness is one of the hardest jewels to find. You can't find it if you are

218

out of balance, no matter what you buy or how much power you can wield. On the other hand, you can find happiness in the midst of hardship if you are at peace.

I'm thinking of all the misfits, all the people who are stressed and strained to the breaking point.

I looked up *misfits* in the dictionary:
MIS FIT', n.
(MIS' FIT), a person not suited to his position, status, etc.;
            a maladjusted person.

I wonder what the motorcyclist did for a living. By the way, I'm not going to tell you his name because he and his family deserve privacy. I'll just call him the Honda Man. There was a Honda emblem in the wreckage. He was obviously a misfit.

As you know, I sing the James Taylor song where he says, "The secret of life is enjoying the passing of time." Not time spent on vacation, or once or twice a month for a few measly hours when everyone decides to leave you alone and give you some peace.

You *should* "enjoy the passing of time" every day. But your time during the day belongs to whoever is paying you a wage, or to the customer who insists you provide a perfect product or service. They own you. So here's to all the repressed, hangdog misfits of the industrialized world. We must have shelter, we must have food, so we work. But what is the real product of all this? In order to eat, we are also eaten, steady repetitive little bites of demeanment. The saddest of us, like the Honda Man, kill ourselves.

I'm not generally prone to grabbing a microphone and making pronouncements, but I have something important to say. Anyone who is a caring, loving person who respects the natural world and the dignity of all living beings, anyone who wants to leave a legacy of kindness and wishes to create something wondrous where before there was nothing, when this person is forced to go to work for a corporation in the modern world, he or she will be a misfit.

Let me introduce you to the misfit army:

It's the English teacher who is working behind the counter in a hardware store.

It's the Doctor of Philosophy who drives a taxi cab in downtown Boston.

It's the musician who must work in a noisy gas station.

It's the geologist in Oklahoma who must flip hamburgers.

It's the housewife who returns to the workforce only to be pounded by a switchboard.

It's the Impressionist painter who must saw and hammer.

It's the carpenter who must paint houses.

It's the shy man who must collect money.

It's the lively, gregarious woman who isn't allowed to talk on the job.

It's the tired, contemplative person who has to work sixty-four hours a week.

It's the boilermaker and steamfitter who must wait on tables.

It's the clinical psychologist who must wait on tables.

It's the out of work actor who must wait on tables.

It's the retired couple who must clean motel rooms in New Jersey.

It's the retired couple who are greeters at WalMart.

It's the honest solicitor who must defend a sleazebag.

It's the poet who must run the family construction business.

It's the payables clerk whose cubicle is too small.

It's the typist whose hands and wrists hurt.

It's the jackhammer operator who just felt a sharp pain in his lower back.

It's the writer of avant-garde plays who must enter monthly inventory.

It's the interstate truck driver who can't get enough sleep.

It's the commuter airline pilot who can't get enough sleep.

It's the human resources manager who isn't permitted to hire a qualified woman.

It's me, it's you, it's the Honda Man, forced into alien shapes, pretending to be interested in what we are doing, smiling and nodding our heads when the owner or boss walks by, and getting up morning after morning like zombies in the land of the living dead.

Okay, now that we are all depressed, just what the hell does David Hall offer as an alternative?

Make a list of what makes you happy.

Make a list of what you can merely tolerate.

Make a list of what you despise.

Make a pact with yourself never to do anything you despise. We all know what we really want: Try, try, try, to find something that makes you happy. If you try to be happy doing rotten demeaning work, then you will not survive.

According to the Gospel of Thomas, Jesus said, "If you bring forth what is within you, what you bring forth will save you. If you do not bring forth what is within you, what you do not bring forth will destroy you."

I am not going to ask you to do what I wouldn't do. Here's my put up or shut up. I'm not going to lecture you when I haven't earned the right to. I've made a list of what makes me, me. I don't have all the answers. As the cliché says, it's taken me this long to learn some of the questions.

Here's my list:

1 - What is my favorite: **Least favorite:**

A-Music-	World and jazz	A- Dirty rap
B-Food-	Italian and Chinese	B- Fast food, asparagus
C-Place-	Montana (new for me)	C- Large crowded cities
D-Color-	Green	D- Gray
E-Sport-	Running and rowing	E- Boxing and walking
F-Season-	Autumn	F- Summer (don't like hot and humid)

2 - Name the person or persons who influenced me the most:
A- Bernie Sanders, Senator from Vermont; my track coach, Tom Hoyt
B- Henry David Thoreau, Kurt Cobain, Kurt Vonnegut, many artists

3 - Name the person or persons who did me the most harm:
A- It hurts for me to write this, but Papa Jack made this list.
B- My ex-wife, Joan; I'll tell you why we broke up if I work up my courage.

4 - What is my favorite institution: **Least favorite:**
Any good library   I'm not a government man

222

5 - Name the person or persons who I consider to be my best friend. Why?

   A- My brother Jonathan because he is generous and is a buddy.

   B- Caroline, because she knows more about me than I do about myself.

   C- Adele Dobbs, because she is the warm mother I never had.

6 - Name the person or persons who I consider to be my biggest enemies. Why?

   A- I pray I don't have to list my brother Seth and my sister Jennifer.

   B- Anyone who wants to destroy the planet.

   C- Anyone who wants to destroy the United States and its citizens.

7 - If I had the power to change the qualities of all the people I have met, what would they be?

   A- I would turn liars into truth tellers, selfish people into giving people.

   B- I would turn violent people into gentle people.

8 - If I could change the qualities about myself, what would they be?

   A- I would have more patience and be more tolerant of people with different ideas.

   B- I want to try and understand why I do something, before I do it.

9 - Is my family a source of pleasure or pain to me and why?

   Mixed feelings. It is a source of both.

10 - If I could have any three possessions light enough to carry, what would they be?

   A- A Martin D18 guitar.

   B- My notebook computer (I never thought I would write this).

   C- My navy blue wool cap.

11 - If I could have any three possessions regardless of size, what would they be?

A- A sailboat we could sleep on.

B- A house by the lake to moor the sailboat.

C- An old-fashioned roll-top desk with all those drawers. The biggest I could find.

12 - Name eight material goods that I have absolutely no use for.

A-	Handgun	E- Motorcycle (after seeing that (accident)
B-	SUV	F- Golf clubs
C-	Huge television set	G- Three-piece business suit with tie
D-	Oriental rugs	H- Cocktail bar

13 - What qualities am I attracted to in the opposite (or same) sex?

For me it's the opposite sex. I like Caroline. I would like her if she were tall, short, thin, or round, or if her hair were black, blonde, or red. I'm not a zone man.

14 - What qualities turn me off in the opposite (or same) sex?

It isn't looks, although I am prejudiced against very large people over three hundred pounds. I don't like people who are unkind and materialistic.

15 - What is the one thing in my life, when I look back on it, that I wish I had not done?

There are several. Marrying Joan, using drugs in college, a few violent acts.

16 - What is my biggest regret, that thing I never did, but wish I had done?

I wish I would have tried harder to make the Olympic team.

17 - What do I feel my greatest talents are?

A- Writing

B- Music

C- Art

D- Speaking foreign languages

18 - What do I feel my greatest weaknesses are?

A- Please don't tell me I'm naïve.

B- I have a very quick temper that I must constantly control.

C- I'm very stubborn and intolerant.

19 - Do I believe in a supreme being? What is my spiritual philosophy (if any)?

I don't know. I certainly hope I'm not the highest life-form in the universe.

20 - How do I want to be remembered?

This is my very short epitaph:

I want to be remembered as a man of talent and good will, who left the world a better place. I want to add something, to my friends, to my family. I want people to say, "Oh yeah, David Hall, he helped me start my car one cold January morning." I want to do what my father did on his walk across America.

Okay, I wrote down my feelings, now it's your turn.

1 - What is your favorite: Least favorite:

A-Music_____   A- _____

B-Food_____   B- _____

C-Place_____   C- _____

D-Color_____   D- _____

E-Sport_____   E-_____

F-Season_____   F- _____

2 - Name the person or persons who influenced you the most:

A-

_____

_____

B-

_____

_____

3 - Name the person or persons who did you the most harm:

A-

_____

_____

B-

_____

_____

4 - What are your favorite institutions:

_____

_____

(B) **Least favorite institutions:**

_____

_____

5 - Name the person or persons who you consider to be your best friend. Why?

A-

_____

_____

_____

B-

_____

_____

_____

C-

_____

6 - Name the person or persons who you consider to be your biggest enemies. Why?

A-

_____

_____

B-

_____

_____

C-

_____

_____

7 - If you had the power to change two qualities of all the people you have met, what would they be?

A-

_____

_____

B-

_____

_____

8 - If you could change two qualities about yourself, what would they be?

A-

_____

_____

B-

_____

_____

_____

9 - Is your family a source of pleasure or pain to you and why?

_____

_____

_____

_____

10 - If you could have any three possessions (light enough to carry) what would they be?

A-

_____

_____

B-

_____

_____

C-

_____

_____

11 - If you could have any three possessions regardless of size, what would they be?

A-

_____

_____

B-

_____

_____

C-

_____

_____

12 - Name eight material goods that you have absolutely no use for.

A- _____ E- _____

B- _____ F- _____

C- _____ G- _____

D- _____ H- _____

13 - What qualities are you attracted to in the opposite (or same) sex?

A-

_____

_____

_____

B-

_____

_____

_____

14 - What qualities turn you off in the opposite (or same) sex?

A-

_____

_____

_____

B-

_____

_____

_____

15 - What is the one thing in your life, when you look back on it, that you wish you had not done?

_____

_____

_____

16 - What is your biggest regret, that thing you never did, but wish you had done?

_____

_____

_____

17 - What do you feel your greatest talents are?

A-

_____

_____

B-

_____

_____

C-

_____

_____

_____

18 - What do you feel your greatest weaknesses are?

A-

_____

_____

B-

_____

_____

_____

C-

_____

_____

_____

19 - Do you believe in a supreme being? What is your spiritual philosophy (if any)?

_____

_____

_____

_____

20 - How do you want to be remembered? Write your own short epitaph.

_____

_____

_____

_____

_____

_____

_____

You have to admit, it felt both good and terrible to make that list. Don't leave this book where anyone can find it or your own thoughts may be used against you.

It's almost time for the Shorty Jones show. I talked with Caroline, and they will meet me at the airport the day after tomorrow. I will spend the extra day in Spokane. It's less than twenty-five miles from this motel.

"It's Shorty Circuit night and our gang is ready to entertain you. I'm Shorty Jones and this is my show. Whose show did you think it was? The Shorty Jones show isn't going to have anyone else here say he was Shorty Jones, unless it's me. If someone came on this show who wasn't me and said he was Shorty Jones, he would be lying and it would not be his show. He would have to have another show with *his* name. Do you understand why I named this the Shorty Jones show?

"We got in trouble with the FCC. I will read from their registered letter. 'We find that the obscene language you used during the Split-Screen sequence was unacceptable for family programming. Although no action will be taken, we strongly suggest that you do not exceed the bounds of good taste.'

"Let me see if I have this right. I've done nothing wrong, but the FCC wants me to know that they disapprove of the obscene language I used. Do they give similar warnings to the cable TV stations? I'll tell you right now that they do not. Their theory is that cable TV is a private network, and a person chooses to watch the smut channels. I got news for you, boys and girls in Washington, Desecration of Concubinage. If you don't like what I've got on my show, turn your fucking radio dial.

"On my way to the station yesterday I passed an army convoy. It was quite large and had troop trucks, trucks pulling cannons, and tanks. So in honor of that convoy, and for all our friends in Washington, Descecration of Concubinage, we have an all-military play. If you good folks at the FCC are listening, let us know how we are doing with our obscenities. Are you ready? It's called *Muldoon*."

Muldoon

Ten hut! Okay, you overrated bunch of sissy slimeballs, keep your eyes straight ahead. Your mommies are not here to take care of you now. I'm your mommy. Get that smile off your face, Muldoon, get down and give me thirty.

Thirty what, Sergeant?

Thirty what? Thirty what? Oh, do forgive me for not explaining myself. I would like thirty bonbons with lemon sherbet smeared with Gray Poupon. THIRTY PUSHUPS, YOU ASSHOLE! Do it right now. Okay, open those packs of Alka-Seltzer tablets and swallow them. Wash them down with the Coca-Cola you have been provided with. Drink the complete can gentlemen. Okay, tighten those sphincters. The first man I hear farting or burping is going to spend the rest of the day down the outhouse hole with everybody else pissing on him. Do I make myself clear? Okay, open that second pack of Alka-Seltzer and wash it down with the second can of Coke. I want to see puffy stomachs, sissies, it really turns me on. Okay, Slimeball Company, do you know what the meanest animal in the jungle is? It's a crocogator. It has a head at both ends; all it does is eat and it can't shit. I'm going to make you even meaner than a crocogator, what do you think of that? Muldoon? Muldoon, you didn't eat your Alka-Seltzer or drink your Coke. Is there something wrong with your ears or did those pushups rattle the puny brain inside your thick Mick skull?

No, Sir.

Then why aren't you following my orders?

Because of the bumper sticker, Sir.

The bumper sticker, the bumper sticker, what the fuck are you talking about, what bumper sticker?

The one that says "Question Authority," Sir.

Oh God, why me? God, why me? Why do I always get the weirdo? Why do I always get the conscientious philosopher, why do I always get the faggot who wants to be different? Listen to me, Muldoon, and listen very carefully. I'm giving you ten seconds to open both packs of Alka-Seltzer and drink down both cans of Coke. If you don't do that, everybody in Company D will have shit-house duty for the entire time they are in this camp and it will be your fault. I am going to cancel all leaves right NOW and all of you will spend the next four months in this ugly compound, and it will be your fault. You will be very, very unpopular, Muldoon. What are you going to do, Muldoon?

I would prefer semisweet chocolate, and I would like to wash it down with orange juice. Sergeant, did you know that chocolate and oranges are soul-mates? Sir.

Okay, Company dismissed. Go fart outside building 17 and get ready for inspection. Muldoon, stand at attention and stay where you are. You know, Muldoon, as I walk around you I'm reminded of a movie I saw about an ugly alien creature, a stupid, foul-smelling alien creature who didn't love his country, who didn't love himself, and who didn't have the good sense to stay out of trouble. Do you know what they did to this alien, Muldoon? They stuffed his ass in a microwave oven. The sparks jumped until he was done medium-well. That is exactly what I'm going to do to you, metaphorically, of course. OOOO, I see a different look on your face now. Was it the word *metaphorically*? Could it be that maybe you don't know everything? Could it be that I'm possibly even smarter than you are?

Sir, I wasn't trying to.....

Shut up! I didn't tell you to speak. You will shut up until I ask you for an answer. Do you know how smart I am, Muldoon? I'll tell you. I know you weren't drafted because this is the all-volunteer army. I know you aren't stupid or insane because you passed all your tests with high scores. Therefore I see this as combat. You are trying to break my will before I break yours. You know that the Army isn't a democracy and yet you make a dumb-assed comment about chocolate soul-mates. The way I see it, Muldoon, there are two choices here. We can get the entire Army to conform to the way you think, we can order semisweet chocolate and orange juice for everybody, let you wear what you want and go wherever you please, or we can get you to do what everybody else is doing. Muldoon, there are no other choices here. Either you do everything exactly as ordered or you will wind up in the brig and then be thrown out with a dishonorable discharge. Do you understand what I'm saying, Muldoon? Answer yes or no.

Yes.

Yes, what?

Yes, Sir.

Good, now pick up the tablets and swallow them.

No, Sir.

Okay you fuckhead, I'm reporting you for disobeying orders. You'll be in the brig before five o'clock.

That's not a good idea, Sergeant. If you report me for disobeying orders, Sir, they will ask you what the orders were and then you would have to tell them of your sadistic game. They will talk to other platoon members who are by now suffering gastric distress. They may cite you for endangering the health of your Company. I'll do the thirty pushups, Sir, because that is part of the game, but I have a brain and it tells me what to do. I will not swallow those tablets, Sir.

I'm beginning to get the picture, Muldoon. I have to admit that I was wrong. I said that you got high test scores so you must be sane. I was wrong. You are fucking insane. Do you know what you are, Muldoon, you are a masochist. You are deliberately baiting me because you want me to push your face in. Does it turn you on, slimeball alien? Now that's one request I'll be happy to comply with as soon as we are off this drill field. You better quit, go out on a medical, tell them your mama needs you. You better get out of here because I am going to be your second skin. From the moment you wake up until taps, I am going to hound you, ride you, nag you, and when nobody is looking I will elbow you in the gut. I will make sure you miss chow, I'll make sure you get every disgusting work detail there is. Do you know something, Muldoon, I'm going to do this so skillfully nobody will know what's going on except you and me. Try and report me, and they will ship you out for being a paranoid faggot. What do you think of that, Muldoon?

My bumper sticker says "Question Authority," Sir. And I would still rather have semisweet chocolate and orange juice, Sir. Because they are soul-mates, Sir. Sergeant, have you ever read the works of Henry David Thoreau, especially his essay on civil disobedience?

Muldoon, I told you that I was smarter than you are. I read all of Thoreau's work. This isn't a case of civil disobedience, this is the military. When soldiers question their orders, chaos is the result and the Army falls into disarray. We can then be beaten by any traveling band of gooks who affix bayonets, run in a straight line, and follow orders. I have no intention of letting my small portion of the United States Army disintegrate into Muldoonville. You do not set the standards here. I do.

What about the taxi drivers, Sergeant?

Muldoon, I'm beginning to feel sorry for you. You really are a nut case. What fucking taxi drivers?

The taxi drivers who drove all the French troops to the front and stopped the Germans from entering Paris during World War One. They weren't ordered to do that. They knew that their country was in peril so they all acted as one. We would do the same thing if some enemy put America in peril, Sir.

Who would that enemy be, Muldoon?

I don't know, Sergeant, whoever was attacking us.

What if you were ordered to attack some other country, say Korea or Iran, to defend American interests, what would you do, Muldoon?

Good question, Sergeant. First I would evaluate the righteousness of our cause and determine whether or not I thought the war was justified, then I would study the course of action as planned by our Congress and the military to see if I agreed with our policy. Then, if I agreed with everything, I would go as requested, Sir.

If you disagreed with U.S. policy, would you go?

I would not go, Sergeant.

Okay, we have a different situation here. I'm going to throw you out for being a conscientious objector. The military needs people who will act as one, not a splinter group of free-thinkers who sit and discuss what they are about to do. This isn't the Unitarian Universalist Society, Muldoon. You don't fit in here, and the longer you stay in the worse it's going to get for you and for the U.S. Army. At ease, Muldoon.

Thank you, Sergeant. I have no intention of quitting. The Army needs me, Sir. I'm going to be the Conscience Officer. Since everyone else around me is being whipped up into a frenzied lather, wound up like a tight spring under pressure, ready to blow, it will be up to guys like me to see that the direction they are pointed in is just, and will promote world peace, Sir.

Okay, I've heard enough. Muldoon, fall out and follow me. I'm taking you to the C.O. and I'm recommending a discharge. We have a new C.O., and I hate to make this my first order of business with him, but you leave me no choice, let's go.

Yes, Sir.

Where is the new Commanding Officer, Corporal, is he in his office?

No, Sir, he is....

No problem, we will sit and wait for him. Okay, Muldoon, inside. Let's go. When he gets here, you just tell him what you told me. If you change your story I will kill you, do I make myself clear? What's the new C.O.'s name? Let me look at his desk plate..... Clarence J. Muldoon?

Yes Sergeant, Colonel Clarence J. Muldoon at your service. Let's talk some more about Henry David Thoreau, shall we?

Another good play by Shorty Jones. The sergeant reminded me of the sergeant in Biloxi Blues, by Neil Simon. I saw the movie and Christopher Walken was incredible in that role. Shorty owes Neil Simon for that one.

CHAPTER THIRTEEN
Spokane, Washington to Ephrata, Washington

Caroline and Sara Ann had a very difficult trip. Bonkers was whimpering, Sara Ann was upset, and Caroline was uneasy because she hates airports to begin with. I don't know what kind of country we are becoming. There are new Transportation Security people with the title of Behavior Detection Officers. One of these assholes walks over to her and asks her who she is and where she's going. She knew right away who this guy was, and she calmly told him she was going to board the plane with her daughter to go to the destination that is printed on her ticket. The moron, who was no more than twenty years old, just said thank you and walked away. Caroline then had to pass through a new x-ray device that replaced the metal detectors and can see right through clothing. She said the technicians smirked and leered at her as she walked through. The airport security people are developing machines with automated sensors that will read your vital signs. Your voice, movement, speech, gait, pulse, perspiration, and body odor will be monitored. So far they have stopped over 50,000 people and not caught so much as one terrorist. This country is turning into an Orwellian nightmare.

Caroline finally boarded the plane. She had to pay extra to transport Bonkers in a special carry-on cage. He whined through the whole trip, and the other passengers were complaining. She also brought the Martin guitar she got for me as a present. She refused to check it through because it's so fragile, and carried it onto the plane. The flight attendants had to store it in a special compartment, and they gave her a hard time. Sara Ann cried because she could tell that her mother was unhappy, and the trip was so long. They were delayed at O'Hare Airport in Chicago for two hours, and the trip took seven.

I swooped Sara Ann off the ground and stood there with my arms around both of them for an eternity. I never want to be parted for this long again, ever. Woo Woo sniffed Bonkers through the carrier, and gave her his famous grin. Caroline and Sara Ann couldn't stop laughing. I had combed Woo Woo's fur, and he looked good with his new collar. I bought some paisley bandanas in different colors, and today he had a green one wrapped around his collar. I guessed right that Caroline would be wearing green. She had on blue jeans and a green blouse with white lace trim. Oh God, is she a knockout.

I used yesterday to find us an almost-new camper. I decided to rent one in Spokane, even though I have to return it here. Caroline can drive it to Aberdeen while I walk, and we will all drive back here together. We can fly back to Indiana from Spokane. The best part of this camper is that there are two sleeping areas separated by a door, a lovely aluminum door. The engine is six cylinders and doesn't get bad gas mileage, plus we won't be driving it for very long. We decided to use the camper right away instead of spending the night in a motel. We bought food and water. The propane tank is full, and this camper also has a small air conditioner and a great sound system. Sara Ann wants us to buy some rock music.

Bonkers is driving Woo Woo crazy. She grabs his tail or bites his leg and then runs away, wanting him to chase her. He looked at me and then, so help me, he looked straight up in the air. He wasn't grinning; he just spoke his usual five woos. These woos were different, they were how-could-you-do-this-to-me woos. After romping through the campground, Sara Ann and her two friends settled down. It's so very cozy inside the camper. There's an awning that extends out from the side, and we found two lightweight lounge chairs in the back compartment. Tomorrow morning I resume my walk to Ephrata. I couldn't wait to play my new Martin, and it is a beauty. Sara Ann said I have to name the guitar. I have to think about that. Sara Ann brought her cowgirl hat, the one with the rose. When I saw her with it on, all I could think about was the broken glass on the road, and the hat in a ditch. They, whoever they are, say that what doesn't kill us makes us stronger. I guess it's true.

The first day was wonderful. I was in my light traveling mode with no tent, sleeping bag, or dog food in my backpack. I'm glad Woo Woo is in the camper; it was a lot of work making sure he was okay on the road. Tonight we are stopped about five miles from Davenport. We're now on Route 2 and at Davenport we pick up Route 28 to Ephrata. My goal is to meet Caroline in the town of Harrington tomorrow night.

I got a call from my younger sister, Margo. She and Tom Cleary are getting married later this year, and they want us to come to the wedding. I discussed Seth and Jennifer with her, and she is very upset by their behavior. She said she hopes Papa Jack left everything to me. It would serve them right. I reassured her that if that was the case, the money would be split equally among all family members. She was very warm and loving, and said she didn't need any more money. She and Tom have everything they could possibly want now that they have each other. I invited them to Aberdeen to spend a few days as soon as I find out what's going on, and she agreed to come. We will probably run into Seth and Jennifer. This could be quite a family reunion. She laughed and told me to bring my mace.

I felt very good after talking with Margo. I called Colin Cleary to discuss the wedding, and we had a great conversation. He said Caroline had guts to come back with Sara Ann and ride in the camper. He said he knows a great ranch for sale near the Circle CK. Oh brother, here we go. I didn't yet mention it to Caroline. We both have a fondness for the place. There is magic in Montana. For the next week, that's all we talked about, my family and Montana.

I brought them up again this morning at breakfast. She is all excited about going to Margo and Tom's wedding. When I talk about the ranch, she positively glows. Then she had news for me. When we were shopping yesterday, we went to the drugstore and got sunscreen and a first-aid kit. She also bought something secretly, a testing kit. She sat on my lap, threw her arms around me and said that she is pregnant. I couldn't speak, I just cried. I didn't walk today. So many thoughts are running through my mind, it will take me days to sort them all. This is one of the happiest days of my life.

When this all started, I remember saying that, who knows, I might even find a wife, like Papa Jack did. I'll be going home, wherever that turns out to be, with a wife, daughter, child on the way, and two dogs. I've found my fortune. The old bastard was right. The road was my redemption. I don't care what's in Aberdeen, except that Jonathan says there is someone in need.

Today is unusually warm. I'll need both canteens. We decided not to have an ultrasound and learn what sex the baby is. I can't help but think that if it's a boy, will that poor child have to walk across the country when he matures? I'll be pushing sixty. If my kid says he wants to walk across the United States, I'll hit him in the head with a large wooden spoon until he abandons the notion. I want to be the last Hall to do this. In thirty years, who knows what the country will be like?

I just passed the Davenport city limits sign. Wait, just a minute, oh fuck! Fuck! Fuck! It says Davenport 1974. Whoa! Here we go again. I've got this down to a science. First I check my wallet and my pants pockets; everything is the same. Now I'll turn on the radio and see what the news is. Good, I've found an all-news station.

President Nixon has resigned. Yup, it's 1974. Patricia Hearst has been abducted. A Federal district court overturned the conviction of Lieutenant Calley for the My Lai incident. Incident hell, it was a massacre. I forgot that the conviction was overturned. The first black model is on the cover of a major fashion magazine: Beverly Johnson in *Vogue*. Way to go, Beverly.

Hank Aaron beat Babe Ruth's home run record. Way to go, Hank, and you didn't need steroids to do it. The Freedom of Information Act was passed over President Ford's veto. India tested its first nuclear bomb.

Here's a great news item the world has forgotten. The Kootenai Nation declares war on the United States. The Kootenai Nation, a small tribe of 67 Indians living in Bonners Ferry, Idaho, declared war on the U.S. Government. Among the many grievances listed in the document is the fact that the Tribe never signed an agreement with the U.S., and lands were being taken away without representation of their tribal leadership.

President Ford grants limited amnesty to draft dodgers, and for the first time, girls are allowed to play Little League baseball.

They just reviewed *Jaws*, a new book. I know they made a movie of it the following year. I switched the station to music. No hip-hop. Here's what's on:

"Rikki Don't Lose That Number," Steely Dan

"Time In A Bottle," Jim Croce

"Sundown," Gordon Lightfoot

"Until You Come Back To Me (That's What I'm Gonna Do)," Aretha Franklin

"Billy Don't Be A Hero," Bo Donaldson and The Heywoods

The talk show I'm now listening to has a discussion about Viet Nam and Richard Nixon. Actually, it's not a discussion, it's a shouting match. I'm in a town with absolutely no black people. There are no Hispanics or Native Americans either. Why is God doing this to me? There are American flags everywhere, especially on the cars and trucks. I'm out of place again, but not outrageously so.

The flag on the post office and the city hall are at half-staff. I asked the mail clerk why, and he told me it was for Billie Dawkins, who was killed last week in Viet Nam. I told him I was passing through from Chicago. He asked me if I was a hippie, and I said no. He asked me if I supported the troops, and I said yes. I told him that if you are an American, you have to support the people who give their lives for our freedom. That's what he wanted to hear, and it wasn't a lie. I do support the troops in Iraq, even though I think the war itself is disgusting. I'm just glad he didn't ask me what I thought of the war. I would have tried to switch the subject and instead talk about our brave fighting men. I guess you were either a flag waver or a flag burner in 1974.

Look what I found alongside the road.

The sunglasses are very large and tinted light yellow. I found the dice just like that. It's a seven, and I hope it brings us luck. I put them in my pocket, but they will probably disappear when I cross the city limits. The three shells say "W-W 45 auto." There are lots of holes in the highway signs. Some of the locals must be bored. There must have been some anti-war people through town. The two buttons are rusted on the backs, so they were sitting for quite a while. On the bottom of the "War Solves Everthing – even people" button there are the initials S. P. U.

I wonder why there aren't more protests against these wars in the Middle East. I never protested anything in my life. I never carried a banner, or stood outside to listen to someone making speeches. Activism is something that completely escaped my generation. I guess if we were in danger of being drafted and sent off, it would be very different. I've heard more than one person say that if you volunteer to be in the military, don't complain if they ask you to go to war. Me, me, me, I need gas for my SUV.

I used to be a violent person. Not a criminal by any means, but I did some things I'm not proud of. I was in my art class when I saw a fellow student take my textbook and drawing book. I went into a rage and tried to punch him. He held up a table easel to protect himself, and I punched right through the one-by-three board and split his lip. It turned out that he mistakenly grabbed my book, thinking it was his. His desk was next to mine. He eventually forgave me, and I immediately went into therapy to understand the source of my anger. I had a great doctor who asked me to look at the common element whenever I was about to lose my temper.

It took me a while, but I finally figured it out. The common element was fear. Whenever I was afraid, I became angry.

One day, about five years ago, someone cut me off and I had to jam on my brakes. I leaned on the horn, and he turned around and gave me the finger. I chased that person until he had to stop at a traffic light, and boxed him in. I got out of my car, and all I could see was a look of terror on the man's face. He was also handicapped and had special controls to operate his car. I was about to rip the door handle off. It took an instant for me to see that he was really helpless. I looked at him and said, "You have got to stop cutting people off. You could cause an accident." I then went back to my car and asked God to calm me down. That is the last time I flew into a rage. I've gotten angry and even challenged people to a fight once or twice, but in my heart of hearts I knew that nothing would come of it.

I can't expect to see the world at peace if I can't find the peace within myself. Walking into Davenport in 1974 has really brought home the ugly continuum of war and violence as national policy. Will there always be someone we have to attack? My favorite anti-war poem is by Edward Randall, who is my favorite poet. It's called appropriately enough, "The Anti-Warrior." I'm going to record it in this memoir.

The Anti-Warrior

...1
In the beginning,
when Niagara Falls was
truly a perfect horseshoe shape,

and the very biggest
tyrannosaur was king supreme
of all the earth,
in some lowland cave
lizards and hairy beasts
commenced to walk
straighter and straighter,
to become you and I.

The most sensitive of us,
who they called the Anti-Warrior,
was nearly at the
end of his existence.
He kneeled at the edge
of his prehistoric tar pit,
and prophesized two creatures
named Cain and Abel,
the Second World War,
Palestine, and the M16 rifle.

He said that to rise,
man had to suffer,
eat of rotten fruit and fall.
With every fraction
of an inch he grew,
thousands of his own cells
would be destroyed.
He wept for us
who must ride rafts of truth
through a narrowing delta.

...2

After the World War bombs fell,
stone and steel cities
were rebuilt
back into the form
of their original structure.
We study the craters
of these wars before,
and observe the previous
mistakes which have
proven such a price for
our ignorance.

We desperately try to understand,
but several thousand people
have died today,
blood spilled by other men,
and they will again attack
those same places
where the bombs fell before.
They have made the same
footsteps in the sand
for thousands of years.

With guns in hand,
their primitive nature
forces them to wander again on their
twenty-first century caravan macabre.
To appease their gods of death,

tomorrow they will maim or die
for the same non-reasons.

But there is a new Anti-Warrior
in the land,
breathing breaths
of what is,
was, of what will be,
knowing that each time
man crosses his desert,
he must return like the camel
to the oasis of peace.

...3
Ready to endure the hot desert sand,
the Anti-Warrior fearlessly begins
his journey to end all suffering.

He ascends from rubbled catacombs,
reaches out to overcome darkness,
and bathes it in absolute white.

He fails to completely enfold it,
but he creates a lighter grey.

The Anti-Warrior knows,
he will speak,
he will sing,
he will save us all.

I really am getting some dirty looks as I walk along Route 2. I was thinking of the Shorty Jones show when he answered my question by saying I should wear foreign clothes and ask to cook couscous at every gas station I pass. If I were Asian, walking along this same road, I would be in real trouble. There's a car that's passed me twice; they've turned around and are approaching me again. I do smell trouble, but there's nowhere to run.

"Go back where you came from, spook."

I knew they were trouble. The car has Texas license plates, and there are three of them inside. The passenger who shouted at me has a Southern accent. I don't know what game God is playing with me. Am I supposed to just observe? Since this isn't my time, does what I do or say have any effect on the future? I'm frightened now and hope this is over soon. Oh shit, now they have stopped ahead of me and are getting out of the car.

"Looks like you're still here, spook, I told you to go back where you came from."

They were in their early twenties, and I tried to walk around them. The ringleader attempted to grab my arm, but I squirted him with my can of mace. I slipped off my backpack and shoved the next person who lunged at me into the ditch. The third guy was smaller than the other two, and he could see that I wasn't going to back down. He grabbed the other guy in the ditch and said, "Let's go!" The guy who I squirted was wiping his eyes and cursing at me. He called me all those names that my ancestors have had to listen to. You know what they are. They drove off.

What's the point of all this? Why was this confrontation necessary? Is it to show me that the twenty-first century is better? You know something, it is. I wouldn't trade Davenport, Washington today for 1974, not a chance. I tried to avoid the violence, but I can't just let myself get beat up. I inflicted minimum harm. I'm glad they didn't have any guns, or if they did, that their hatred didn't cut deep enough to use them. I'll be glad when I get on the other side of the city limits sign. I can see it a quarter of a mile ahead.

I'm dazed as I speak into my tape recorder. There's a broken bottle of beer next to me, and I heard a rebel-yell as the car drove away. That Texas car came by again, and someone must have thrown the bottle at me. It was full; there's beer all over my shirt. My head is bleeding, and I'm very wobbly on my feet. I can feel the gash on the back of my head, and I think I'm going to black out. I've got only a hundred yards to go. I know I'm staggering, but I have to keep walking. Now there's a police car behind me, but I dare not stop. The cop ordered me to halt and sounded his siren. Now he's in front of me blocking my path.

"Officer, there's a car with Texas license plates. The passenger threw a beer bottle and hit me in the head. My brother is in the Marine Corps, and I'm walking through Washington to show support for our troops."

"We need to get you to a hospital."

He went inside his patrol car to radio for an ambulance, and I ran as fast as I could toward the city-limits sign. I collapsed before I got to it and crawled along the ground until I reached the other side. My wound disappeared, as did the blood and beer on my shirt. The dice in my pocket also vanished. On the other side of the sign, I could see the policeman looking for me, but I had obviously disappeared from his world.

I walked ahead for a few minutes before I used the Blackberry to call Caroline. I told her to drive to Davenport and meet me. I don't want to walk anymore. Alongside the road, the same Chevrolet that had the Texas license plates was stopped with a flat tire. It now has Washington license plates and is rusty and sand-blown. There are two men in their sixties trying to change the tire. They are quite obviously impaired; *drunk* would be a better word.

"Hey, mister, could you give us a hand changing this tire? I'm a little under the weather, ain't that right, Clyde? Do I know you from someplace?"

I helped him change the tire. They both had a Southern drawl. I asked them where their buddy was, the ringleader who threw the bottle. They were so out of it, they didn't even question how I could have possibly known about that guy.

"Oh, you mean old Virgil. He died ten years ago. Thanks for helping with the tire. Can we give you a ride someplace?"

"No thanks, my wife is meeting me in a few minutes. You shouldn't be driving, you're going to kill yourselves or somebody else." I thought, *You're in my world now.* I grabbed the car keys out of the ignition. All I could think of was those drunken old fools running into Caroline. They were shouting at me to bring the keys back, but I kept on walking. About ten minutes before Caroline showed up with the camper, I flung them into a field.

I showed her the photographs of Davenport 1974. She assured me that I would never have to go through that again.

She was still rubbing my head, although the pain was gone. I'm suffering severe traumatic stress. Violence is so ugly. It is so unnecessary and demeaning to the human spirit. I don't think I will ever lose my temper again. When you dismiss violence as an option, you can creatively reach a solution. Yes, I admit there are those times when you have no choice, but they are very rare. Most violence is preventable.

It's taken me three days to gather myself. I continued my walk this morning after an incredible breakfast of French toast with real Vermont maple syrup. Caroline found some dark-roast coffee that is very strong. The aroma is so wonderful that it actually attracted company for breakfast. This land belongs to a man that owns a construction company. He let us camp on the edge of his property. He and his wife were driving down their long driveway, and they must have smelled what Caroline was cooking. They stopped to say hello and wound up having breakfast with us.

They tried to get us interested in moving to Washington. I've noticed that about people who really like you. They want to be your neighbors. There is no greater compliment than to hear that. Caroline and I are both sensitive to such an invitation. We've talked about it before. We always tell our new friends that we promise to think very hard about it, because their home is a wonderful place. The truth is, we could probably be happy living in any one of the states we've traveled through. Indiana will always be special for me because that's where Caroline was born. Old Forge, New York, where the Dobbs family lives, is the warmest cold place I've ever visited. Montana, yes, then there's Montana.

Two days of peaceful walking has brought us to our second to last destination. Woo Woo made such a fuss this morning when I was leaving that he's walking with me today. He has on an orange bandana for the sake of visibility. Caroline found me a great walking stick. I like to stride without a stick, but this is a special one with a carved handle wrapped with rawhide. Walking has helped me deal with the horrible nightmare of 1974.

We have reached the town of Ephrata, and we are going to visit Julia Vickers. She lives on Hilltop Drive off Dobson Road N.W. Caroline has gone ahead to make contact, and I will arrive at the end of the day today.

"David, we have a problem. Poor Julia Vickers died two weeks ago. Her house was locked, and when I drove up with the camper and knocked on the door, her neighbor told me what happened. She gave me the name of her son and her daughter, but they won't be back in Ephrata for several weeks. I did get the name of the family attorney. Perhaps we can get his help to learn what we should do next."

CHAPTER FOURTEEN
Ephrata, Washington to Aberdeen, Washington

Have you ever noticed that all people have an aura about them? I have friends who have a positive aura. As soon as they come into a room, they bring everybody up. They don't even have to speak; people are glad to see them. Jonathan is like that. Caroline and the Dobbs family are like that. Others are neutral. They don't add and they don't detract, and you are not particularly glad or sorry to see them.

Mr. Wallace G. Mumbley, Esquire, the lawyer we just met, is from a third group. He is such a miserably ugly son of a bitch that he could curdle milk with one sarcastic look. He is one of the negative-aura people. The minute we saw him, we knew. His handshake is the diametric opposite of Colin Cleary's. Shaking Mumbley's hand is like grabbing congealed Jell-O from the bottom shelf of the fridge. His secretary is from the same school of downers. Her name is Concavia. They could turn any joyous gathering of merry people into a wake.

Like it or not, we are in the office of Mumbley and Mumbley and are talking with Wallace G. Mumbley, Esquire, lawyer, tax specialist, and undoubtedly a staunch, upstanding Republican. He is probably very upright and moral when he's being watched. I'll bet when he goes home he does all sorts of kinky things in his broom closet with his household staff. I asked him if we could examine Julia Vickers' desk to look for information on our next contact in Aberdeen. I told him the whole story, but instead of finding it interesting, he used the first available opening in our conversation to cut me off. The dourpuss didn't know that I had my tape recorder on. Here's our conversation. This is the last part, after I explained our journey.

"All Mrs. Vickers' personal effects have been sealed by order of the court pending review by her son and daughter. The son is in Spain, and the daughter is in New Zealand. They are both scheduled to be in this office in three weeks."

"We're not asking for permission to examine the contents of her estate. There is just one bit of vital information pertaining to someone in trouble in Aberdeen, and we desperately need to know who we should contact. The information is probably accessible in a conspicuous place, such as a desk drawer."

"I cannot permit you to examine the contents of her estate."

"I am not asking for permission to examine the contents of her estate. I will be happy to contract you to do it. We will pay you at your usual fee to walk into her house, open her desk drawer, and let us know who we are to see in Aberdeen."

"That would be impossible. It is a conflict of interest."

"How is it a conflict of interest?"

"If you wish to make a claim on the estate, you will need an attorney to file the papers. I cannot permit you to have access to any assets because you have not been named as an heir in her will."

"We're not making a claim. If a neighbor left her cookbook on Mrs. Vickers' kitchen table, would she need an attorney to retrieve it?"

"Not necessarily. If the neighbor could describe the book, and could prove it belonged to her, we might be able to avoid a protracted transaction."

"Excellent, that is exactly what we are asking. There is the name and address of a person in Aberdeen, Washington who we are supposed to see to offer help. Mrs. Vickers was last in a long line of contacts that stretched across the United States. This journey has taken many months. All we need is that name and address."

"You are not a neighbor, and we have no proof that you have ever known Mrs. Vickers."

It went on like this for another ten minutes before I lost my temper. I called him a moron and said he would be hearing from me very soon. I felt so impotent because I knew that in reality we could do nothing but wait until her son or daughter arrived in Ephrata. Caroline had an idea to call the daughter in New Zealand and get her permission.

We contacted the daughter in Auckland, and she was totally supportive. She called Mumbley for us. He still refused to honor our request, even though the daughter was agreeable. He said once the date of estate examination is fixed, it cannot be altered unless all heirs are present.

THE MUSEUM OF NATURAL HISTORY

BRONTOSAURUS
ALLOSAURUS
STEGOSAURUS

Lived together in Western North America
during the Upper Jurassic Period
about 140 million years ago.

Little did they know
that they would
evolve into Siamese cats
for Hollywood movie stars.

All that is remembered of their lives
is a bag of bones
from a community fossil quarry.

REPUBLICAN
LAWYER
TAX SPECIALIST

Lived together in Western North A.....

The very bottom of the evolutionary scale.

We decided to drive to the American Star Camp Ground and Driving Range and figure out what to do next. It was just a place to sleep, with absolutely no redeeming qualities. Caroline made an incredible meal with chopped steak and green peppers. I had no idea she was such a wonderful cook. I am again reminded of a poem by Edward Randall.

What is Greater than a Green Pepper?

I settle wearily into a chair
just before supper,
place my feet
on the living room floor,
and start to read a magazine
article about Marianne Moore,
while peppers and onions
start to simmer.

Chopped meat is added,
Worcestershire sauce is added,
I inhale as their essences blend.
I can no longer read words,
she stirs the pan gently,
pouring tomato sauce slowly,
I flip pages wildly.

I race into the kitchen
shouting,
when! when!

She sighs, and points to
the red and white timer,
35 more minutes
ticking, ticking, ticking.

I called Jonathan and told him what had happened in Mumbley's office.

Do you know what he did? He found out the name of the detective agency in Seattle that Seth and Jennifer are using. It's the Atlas Security Agency. He discovered what they are doing. He pretended to be Seth and asked them if they had learned anything yet from shadowing me. They told him that they knew I was stopped in Ephrata and would try to get to my contact.

I thanked Jonathan for the information and for sticking his neck out. I got a call a few hours later. The detective agency must have spoken with either Seth or Jennifer, and they all realized that they'd been had. Jennifer didn't know that Jonathan made the call, and she had the absolute nerve to yell at me for calling their agency claiming to be Seth. I laughed at her. She's having me followed and is yelling at *me*? I told her there had been a change in plans. If and when Papa Jack's fortune is discovered, and if I'm lucky enough to be named executor, neither she nor Seth would get one dime. She was all boo hoo, boo hoo, and then screamed that I was not her brother.

I am unquiet. As I lie here typing into my notebook computer, I'm trying to think of cars that have passed me more than once, trying to remember if I saw the same car in different states, but everything is a blur. Whoever is tailing me is obviously a professional who knows our routine. Now that we have been tipped off by Jonathan, we're going to be on the lookout for any vehicles following us.

I don't have much trouble controlling my anger. When I called that lawyer a moron, I wasn't shouting. All I said, very deliberately in a low tone of voice, was "You are a moron, and you will be hearing from us shortly." When I was in therapy, I remember my doctor saying that when you lose your temper, you lose your power. Caroline said I shouldn't have called him a moron.

Sara Ann waited with the two dogs in the waiting room on a sofa near the secretary. I am constantly amazed at what Sara Ann knows. As we were leaving Mumbley's office, she asked us if we can get the map now. I said the lawyer won't let us. Sara Ann called him a poop head and Woo Woo growled. To reverse W.C. Fields, any man who's hated by little children and dogs has got to be bad. We had another disagreement, Caroline is angry at Sara Ann's behavior and I'm delighted.

So much for the day's events. It's time for the Shorty Jones show. It's Thursday night, and Shorty morphs into the infamous Doctor Prozak. I tuned in a little late and missed the intro. I tried to call in, but I've been put on hold.

"This is Doctor Prozak, how may I be of assistance?"

263

"Doctor Prozak, my father, a lifelong Republican, said if I don't vote Republican I have no right to complain. Should I get involved in politics? I'm a Proud American in Arizona."

When I was a boy I was told that anybody could become President; I'm beginning to believe it.
Clarence Darrow

"Hello, American. Everything the President, senators, and congressmen do is for you and me. They do not base their decisions on popularity. They care more for us than their own wallets or getting re-elected. They have no egos and will labor anonymously for years for the public good. They do not waste the taxpayers' money or cater to the special interests of their rich and influential friends. They are morally upright and would never think of compromising their ethics for any reason. Since all of the above is true, of course you should get involved in politics."

Your Germ of the Day:
This afternoon I will visit my Republican party headquarters and pledge my money and loyalty to the candidate with the most sincere face and the best blow-dried hairstyle. I'll learn about all the things he or she will do for me.

"Doctor Prozak, I don't know what to think about today's youth. No one respects the flag anymore. Professors refuse to take loyalty oaths. If our military continues to get smaller and weaker, any half-assed South American nation will take

264

us on. How can we convince Americans that we must remain strong? I am Bullish in Boise."

Patriotism is the willingness to kill and be killed for trivial reasons.
Bertrand Russell

"Hello, Mr. Esteemed Bullish. Just when we were about to build sleek new radar-evading delta wing bombers and perfect our Star Wars laser satellite technology, the Cold War ended. What about defense jobs? Our American way of life is threatened! Retooling to manufacture recycling equipment is just not the same as building an M1 Abrams tank. Even if we do keep on manufacturing to sell overseas, it's just not as satisfying as real-life testing by our own armed forces. We need to remind people of history. Every new generation needs a big conflict to exercise its testosterone. Young men can only watch so much boxing and football, and even their wives are beginning to fight back. We need the Religious Right to trump up a good cause. Let's bring back the old glory days!"

Your Germ of the Day:
I am not a citizen of the world. If I suck in my gut, my uniform still fits. My assault rifle is loaded and I'm ready. I notice a lot of Asian-looking immigrants in California, and there's thousands of Arabs in Michigan. Now there are some good testing grounds!

"Hello Doctor, I'm a sophomore at Michigan State. I'm not sure whether to marry a man who is honest and sensitive or one who is rich and powerful. Do you know of any men who are honest, sensitive, rich, and powerful? I'm A Searching Spartan."

Woman was God's second mistake.
Friedrich Nietzsche

"Hi, Searching. No, I don't know of any."

Your Germ of the Day:
I will continue to look under every rock, down every alley, and across every ocean. Up every mountain, in the city, and in the country I will look. At college football games, at the library and at church, I will search high and low until I find a man who is good enough for me. It will probably take me the rest of my life, but why should I lower my standards?

"Hello Doctor, I maxed out my credit card, so I applied for another one with a higher limit. Soon it will also be maxed out. Do the interest payments increase each month, or can I pay them a minimum amount? I'm having so much fun, I think I'll apply for a third Gold card. Is this wrong? I'm A Credit to my Family."

The richer your friends, the more they will cost you.
Elizabeth Marbury

"My dear Credit, what is your telephone number? I admire your spirit so much that I thought we'd go shopping together and then invite a bunch of our street friends over for a catered party. There are two kinds of people in the world: the 'now' people and the 'later' people. It's refreshing to meet another 'now' person. All those bank and collection folk (later people) don't know how to have a good time like we do. Besides, they're ingrates. It's people like you who keep them in business. They owe their JOBS to you. Have you ever been to Martinique? I know a wonderful hotel there."

Your Germ of the Day:
Today I will reach for the plastic. My eyes will be bigger than my wallet. Why shouldn't I have everything I want? I have no spiritual life or culture, so it's the only way I can find true happiness. Stereos, cars, vacations, new clothes, expensive restaurants: Stand back, Mr. Gucci, here I come!

"Doctor Prozak, what would you do if you found out that your father left you fifty million dollars in a special trust fund? It's The Walking Man again."

I've been rich and I've been poor, rich is better.
Sophie Tucker

"Hello again, Walking Man. That would be impossible because my father already left me a trust fund. He didn't trust me so I ran out of funds. Why do you think I sit by this damn microphone talking to unrealistic dreamers like you?"

Your Germ of the Day, Walking Man:
If your father leaves you fifty million dollars, you will find
friends you never knew you had. Financial opportunities
will present themselves at three in the morning, if you don't
get an unlisted number. Everyone will tell you how
wonderful you are, how handsome, every woman will offer
you sex, some men will offer you sex, you will be able to buy
anything you want except for health care. If I were you I'd
give it all to charity. Try the Shorty Jones Fund, Box 118, in
care of this station.

We are having a good time in spite of our recent misfortune. Sara Ann wants to call Shorty Jones and ask if it's wrong to call a lawyer a poop head. I laughed so hard, but Caroline got mad at me again for encouraging her. There is more than a germ of truth in Shorty's Germ of the Day. He's probably right, big money equals big problems. We will never be as happy as we are now, here in this camper. We just talked about it and made a pact that we would always carry this feeling with us.

I had nightmares last night. In spite of our party atmosphere yesterday evening, I couldn't sleep because I keep dreaming about our lost contact. Caroline said we should just drive to Aberdeen and see if we can find out something from the old photographs in my computer. She said if we aren't tense and leave ourselves open to really seeing, we may be able to find our person. I decided that it beats sitting around here for three weeks. I can't see the point of walking when I don't know where I'm going.

When we left American Star campground I was especially conscious of spotting any cars that could be following us. I did notice a blonde woman in a gray Jeep Cherokee pull out just after we did. I can't see her in my rearview mirror. The camper mirrors are large but they vibrate. I have absolutely no visibility directly behind me, like I would in a car. I decided to pull off Highway 283 and stop at a small restaurant. We had only a light breakfast in the campground, and we could all use some more food. The Jeep Cherokee also pulled into the restaurant parking lot. The woman just sat there studying a map. This could be coincidence. I told Caroline not to look at her, to totally ignore her. I decided to go back to Ephrata and see if she followed us.

Ten miles later, we pulled into an AutoStop combination gas station and convenience store, and she followed us into the parking lot. She hid discreetly behind a UPS truck, got out of her car, and followed Caroline and Sara Ann into the store. I hid in the camper and then crouched low to the ground and got between her car and the truck. I took a serrated-blade bread knife and cut the two tire valve stems on that side. We quickly left the AutoStop with a couple of bags of potato chips and sped away in the camper. She was watching us as we left, and then she looked at her jeep. The last thing I saw her do was use her cellphone. Blondie will be out of action for quite a while, unless she has two spare tires in that Jeep. Even then, she won't catch us. We're on the way to Route 90, and I'm in no mood to deal with her detective agency, or certain members of my family.

In all the time we have been together on the road, this is the first long trip we have taken. Usually it's just a couple of miles to pick me up or go to a motel. Finally we are on the open road. It's 260 miles to Aberdeen. We passed another walker, an older guy with a long white beard. We waved and he waved back. I always liked it when people waved to me. It was mostly children. I got a lot of waves when Woo Woo was walking with me. Some people took our picture. His orange bandana really attracted attention.

When we get to Aberdeen we will check into a motel. I'll try to park this camper out of sight, but Aberdeen isn't very big and eventually we will be found. They can't do anything to us, and I don't care if they watch us. Our movements and plans will be based on our photos, and a very private itinerary. They can't possibly know what is going on. As a matter of fact, it will drive them crazy following us around. I called Jonathan and he said I should tell the police about being tailed. He said I could claim harassment. I don't think it's actionable. The private detective agency is full of ex-cops, and they could tell the police any number of lies. I did call dear sweet Jennifer. Here is our conversation. I used the code to block the call identifier so she doesn't know our number.

"Jennifer, you have now created a state of war between us. You had us shadowed by a blonde in a Cherokee. She is out of action for the moment. Did your detective agency tell you that? The Atlas Security Network is the wrong name for them. They should be called the Lilliput Agency. You have lost the goodwill of your sister Margo, your brother Jonathan, my soon-to-be-wife Caroline, and myself. I also know that our mother is very upset with you and Seth. You've made your choices, and now the two of you have to live with them. If you do get your ultimate prize of millions of dollars, which by the way I care nothing about, it will corrode you like acid. You better wake the fuck up before it's too late."

"Oh, you are so self-righteous! You don't care about the money, all you care about is helping someone in need. That's bullshit. You want control of Dad's company."

"What the hell are you talking about?"

"You know damn well what I'm talking about. Before Dad left the company, he made the employees who were buying him out agree that he would have the majority vote on all matters of policy and company direction. When he died, that temporarily fell to Tom Cleary. When Dad's estate is ultimately found, it will include the information on who is to have that vote. Don't play dumb with me, you and Jonathan know all about it."

"Jennifer, you really are a nut case. I have no idea what you are talking about. Who told you this stuff?"

"Mom told me. Tom Cleary said that since she was Papa Jack's wife, the vote should fall to her, but she declined and gave her vote to Tom."

"So, that should be the end of it. Are you so power hungry that you want to have the vote to override Tom and Margo, who forgot more about the business than you Seth or I will ever know? If I get the vote, as you call it, I'll pass it right back to them, just like I would have shared the money with you and Seth before I learned that you are both vipers. I will give you one warning. If you, Seth, or your associates ever harm my family, you will have grief that is unimaginable. Do I make myself clear?"

"I don't want to harm anybody, all I want is my share."

"This is our last conversation. If I ever see you again, you better give me a wide berth. You are a rotten woman. Tell Seth he's a piece of shit also."

An hour after our conversation, I got a call from Jennifer. She was very upset, called Jonathan, and persuaded him to give her my number. She did her patented boo hoo, boo hoo, and said that she was sorry for everything. I honestly don't know if her apology is sincere or if she's hedging her bets in case we come out on top. Sometimes the complications of life are too much for me. I'd rather camp by a lake and throw rocks in the water.

Speaking of throwing rocks in the water, listen to this. Adele Dobbs called and told us to go to the Quinault Beach Resort on Route 115 in Gray's Harbor. She booked us for two weeks. This is a delightful upscale oceanfront resort and is very expensive, at least for us. Our room cost $150 per night. This is the best hotel we have stayed at. She said it would be good for us to stay out of Aberdeen. The resort is only ten miles from the city. I could not conceal my sadness when I spoke with her. She assured me that all manner of things would be well. I told her we could afford it, but she had already paid for our stay. I insisted that we pay her back, but she just said to pass it on.

We finally reached the Pacific. The sunset was fantastic. I'm really unhappy that we can't take advantage of such a beautiful place. We must get to work immediately. Caroline said we need to schedule one enjoyable outing every day, no exceptions or we will both burn out. I really hate it when she is smarter than I am, which is most of the time.

I showed her many photographs, including some of women who were rather scantily clad. They looked to be hookers, or whores, or prostitutes, or working girls, or whatever name people use for women who sell sex. The photos were old and were taken by my grandfather or my great-grandfather. Caroline noticed hoop earrings in one of the photos. She said they were from the fifties and not the thirties. She pointed out some other fashion elements that put the photos solidly in the fifties. Good, we now can confirm that my grandfather snapped them. There's a better chance of uncovering information from the fifties than the thirties.

We visited the Pacific County Historical Society and Museum in South Bend to see if we could place any of the photos. I told the resident historian that my grandfather had taken them and I was interested in learning who, what, why, when, where, and how. I told her about his walk across America. She was very interested in the photos, including the older ones taken by Great-Grandfather Sam Hall. I told her I would be happy to donate them to the museum. She spent the entire day helping us look through old records, newspapers, and magazines to get some clues.

We finally turned up a lead. There was a photo of a woman who looked to be Native American, standing in front of a post office and a school. We found a photograph of the buildings in an October 9, 1955 edition of *The Centralia Daily Chronicle*. It's in Taholah, on the Quinault Indian

Reservation, which is twenty miles north of our hotel. I don't know what we will learn by visiting there, but it's a start.

CHAPTER FIFTEEN
Aberdeen, Washington to Burlington, Vermont

We are very weary. After five days of false starts and dead ends, we are no closer to learning who our contact is than the day we arrived. We're walking along the water, in front of our hotel. Bonkers is showing her retriever heritage by chasing sticks that Sara Ann throws in the water. I guess that's what dogs love to do, chase sticks. People chase money. Woo Woo just grins when Bonkers darts into the surf. He's not going to get *his* bandana wet. The October air is chilly and a low-hanging fog surrounds everything.

Yesterday we went into Aberdeen and looked through the morgue of the *Aberdeen Daily World*. We read issue after issue, trying to find any of the people in the photographs, or perhaps a news story that had some resonance. We came up with nothing. We thought about putting an ad in the paper, but the people who are working against us would also know what we're doing and could intercept our contact. Even a box number would be vulnerable. That's when I had my idea.

I told Caroline that we were going about this quest backwards. We are not going to be able to find them, we have to let our contact find us. It's time for me to do what was originally intended. I am going fifty miles out of town and am going to walk into Aberdeen. With a little bit of luck, I'll be noticed by the person or persons who we are supposed to see. Caroline would not be meeting me after the first day. She wanted to drive the camper, but I said no. I want to camp alongside the road in the most conspicuous spot I can find. She reluctantly agreed but was uneasy about my being on my own. I told her I would be fine. I had my mace, in place, in case I needed to squirt someone in the face. She didn't laugh at my quip. It was a dumb thing to say and probably made her even more nervous.

Here I am again, walking. I've got the walking stick; I've really grown attached to it. I'm also somewhat paranoid and like having this long hardwood staff at the ready. Only a gun is superior. I really chomped off some miles yesterday before I camped. I'm very rested, and I swear I must have walked close to forty miles. This was probably a stupid idea. I was passed by car after car, and for a second I thought it had paid off. Someone stopped and backed up. It was two young women. One of them said I was cute, and they both giggled and drove off. Glad I'm cute. I've got an orange bandana tied around my neck. We forgot to wash it, and it smells like dog. I put it on my walking stick and stuck it outside my tent. I guess it's my flag. See the walking man, inquire within. Breakfast is finished, and I'm ready to do the last ten miles. The sky is very dark, and we are going to get some rain. It was in the forecast yesterday.

It's really pouring and the air is cold. I've got my wool cap on again.

Once again walking has freed up my thoughts. This has been such a long journey. For me it's just the beginning of seeking wisdom. My sneakers have become a portable Bodhi tree as I walk the Buddha path. I now know enough about this nation to share my thoughts.

As you know, the President of the United States gives a State of the Union address. This doesn't happen nearly often enough: Americans are lucky if they hear from the Major Commander once every two years. I know more than he does, because I've just walked across the country. I've learned things first hand that the President's limp-dick advisors are only guessing at after they talk to their overpaid aides. Their policies are formed, not from first-hand knowledge, but from warmed-over second and third-hand gossip. I can hear the briefing now, "I believe there's a homeless person or two living under a bridge in Michigan, a couple of foreclosures in Nevada have been noted, and a few seniors in Mississippi have to eat dog food, or so my Chief of Staff's friend's cousin remarked."

So, since the Major Commander, the junior Commander, the Majorettes and their cousins are all going to stay cooped up in their D.C. cages, this is my opportunity to tell you what's really going on.

David Hall's State of the Union Address

Good evening, my fellow Americans. I would like to get right to the facts and cut out all the bullshit. I've had the privilege of seeing this country in four different time periods. I can tell you here and now that conditions are no better today than they were in the Great Depression.

I don't have any lobbyists who are paying me to approve bad policies that favor insurance companies or Wall Street executives. I will not be a chameleon like President Obama and tell you what you want to hear. I will not say that those banking executives really deserve their bonuses because they're good hard-working people. I will tell you that they deserve to have their insides ripped out by rusty chainsaws for what they have done to Americans and to the world. Congress is not your friend. Collectively they can only be counted on to enrich themselves and their power base. They stuff the pork-barrel full of special-interest money that will serve them long after they leave office.

I have seen rapid deterioration taking place in every corner of this land. Proud people who once made products that were the envy of the world are now working for fifty cents on the dollar, if they are lucky. They are forced into jobs at Wal-Mart, working for minimum wage, stacking shelves full of products from Asia that they used to make here at home. They are without health insurance and they are losing their homes.

It doesn't matter who you elect. The Republicrats are all the same. The country is run by the multi-billionaires, the Walton family, et al, who have bought, sold, and subjugated the lawmakers who are supposed to be making sure you, your mother, or your father can afford that operation.

I'm going to cut this Address short because I'm about to lose my temper and curse. I have a duty to remain calm and in control, and to practice forgiveness no matter what the stimulus to the contrary.....

Go straight to mother-fucking hell, you disgusting boil-sucking bunch of putrefied leeches. You have ruined our country, and we will never get it back!

Sorry, I lost it.

Since I'm incapable of talking rationally about the State of the Union, perhaps you should try. I think it is every citizen's duty to write down what she/he thinks about the direction the United States is headed. This will force us away from watching *Dancing with the Stars* into some needed action. Perhaps we can all compare notes. What if several million of us got together and learned that we all have a hatred of Wall Street and bail-outs? Those executives who got millions in bonuses had better duck and cover because the next step isn't going to be passive resistance. No one ever gives up money or power. You have to take it back by legislation or by force. Legislation has failed.

Helmet on, powder dry.

"Hello, David Hall?"

"How did you know my name?" I did a classic double-take. I should have recognized the car. It was the gray Cherokee, and the blonde woman who was tailing us from Ephrata was driving.

"I'm not who you think I am. My name is Susan Campbell, and I'm going to take you to your contact in Aberdeen. The investigator from Atlas followed you to Mumbley's office in Ephrata. They bribed him and learned the name of your contact, and somehow learned the name of the institution where your father has his estate money. Please get in the car."

"Exactly who are you, and why should I trust you? You look like a college kid who's in way over her head."

"Very good, I am going to the University of Washington, majoring in English literature. First I want you to know that your brother and sister tried to talk to your contact without success. They did go to Pacific Fidelity Funds, where your father has his account. We don't think they will have any success in getting them to release the funds, but we can't be sure."

"Listen Susan, or whatever your real name is, why should I believe you, and what do you mean by *we*?"

"Your contact in Aberdeen is Ramona Campbell. She's my mother. When we lost contact with Mrs. Vickers in Ephrata, we checked up and learned of her death. We knew you would be coming through. The instructions were very clear that you had to finish your journey. My mother wanted me to stay with you until you got here, but unfortunately you changed those plans with your knife when you cut my tires. I'm very glad I found you. That was a great idea to get back on the road. I've got four friends helping me search around the county. I'm going to call one of them now, and tell her to call the others. 'Hello Becky, I found him. Please tell the others. Oh yeah! Way to go!'

"Your brother and sister visited my mother and tried to find out what was going on. She insisted they tell her how they found out she was the contact. That's when they admitted getting the info from Mumbley. She told them nothing."

On the back seat of her Jeep were textbooks and several books of poetry. I noticed a book by Wallace Stevens. I asked Susan Campbell what Wallace Stevens did for a living.

"Is this a test? He was an executive for an insurance company. I believe it was the Hartford Insurance Company.

Do you know what the symbolism is in his poem 'Thirteen Ways of Looking at a Blackbird'?"

"Yes I do, it's death. I'm so sorry I cut your tires, but I thought you were sent by the Atlas Agency to shadow us. I owe you some new valve stems. Actually, I owe you much more than that, my God, what am I saying, valve stems."

I called Caroline, told her the news, and asked her to grab the gang and meet us at Ramona Campbell's house in Aberdeen.

Susan and I are about the same distance from the house as Caroline, but Caroline has an amazing sense of direction and got there first. The Campbells live in a new house on Harborview Road in Aberdeen Highlands. There was a lot of hugging and kissing going on. Caroline and I both felt our blood pressure drop about two hundred points. Two balloons that were about to pop suddenly got all their air released. We collapsed into each other's arms, oblivious of our hosts. We finally sat down in their living room and learned what was going on. I'm now writing this from our hotel room, so I will recap the day's events.

Susan organized a search party for me. She belongs to a drama club at the University of Washington, and some of her friends traveled hundreds of miles to help. Ramona Campbell, Susan's mother, told us of her family's connection to my ancestors' journeys.

Bill Hall stayed in Aberdeen for two months before he returned home to Vermont. During that time he had a relationship with the Native American woman whose photo is on our computer. We tried unsuccessfully to find information about her, although we did learn that the post office and school in the photograph was in Taholah, on the Quinault Indian Reservation.

Ramona had all the details. Her name was Raven John. She and my grandfather, Bill Hall, had a son named Kurtis. Bill found out about it twenty years later when Kurtis located him in Vermont. At first Bill refused to believe he was his son, and even after Kurtis proved it to him, my grandfather was unwilling to accept it. He never did acknowledge his existence, or do anything to help the man. My father was only a teenager, but he remembered Kurtis John's visit. The young man from Washington was just slightly older than he was. He had found a brother he didn't know he had.

Papa Jack stayed with the Campbell family when he visited Aberdeen. He tried unsuccessfully to locate Kurtis and was told that he had moved away to parts unknown. Five years ago, Ramona discovered what had happened to him. It took some excellent detective work on her part. He married an Asian-American woman, and they had a son. Kurtis died three years ago and his wife, whose name was Shin, had died two years before Kurtis. Shin and Kurtis had a child named Elizabeth. Three years ago, Elizabeth became a single mother, and shortly thereafter died of a drug overdose in Los Angeles. Her child was put in a foster home. The little girl is now three years old and her name is Fawn.

Ramona left the living room and reappeared holding a little girl's hand as she walked beside her. I was sitting next to Caroline on the couch, and they walked up to me. The child had jet black hair, bright eyes, and a mischievous expression on her face. She was wearing a turquoise and silver pendant that was a gift from Papa Jack.

"David, it was your father's wish that you care for Fawn John."

She handed me an envelope with Fawn's birth certificate, medical records, and a very short note from my father. It said, "David, your cousin needs you to take care of her."

I thought to myself, the old bastard has really done it this time. He couldn't tell me there was a child who needed a home. If he had mentioned, her I would have said no. Caroline saw the look of hesitation on my face, and her answer was to run to Fawn, lift her off the ground, and spin her around and around. Ramona and Susan sat on the couch smiling.

I was thinking, let me get this straight, I walk across the country, a single man with a city apartment, a library, some acoustic and electric guitars, and I return home with a wife, *two* children, two dogs, and a child on the way. Good thing I'm not *walking* back to Burlington, I'd probably have to buy the Sheraton Hotel to house my immediate family.

Fawn is an exotic and beautiful child. She and Sara Ann were already fighting. Bonkers likes Fawn and was kissing her hand. Sara Ann was jealous, and said "*My* dog!" Fawn stuck out her tongue at Sara Ann.

We talked with Ramona about other details. Did Papa Jack give her any money to care for Fawn? The answer was no. He said I would take care of everything. I examined the contents of the envelope, and there is no mention of any funds, accounts, or any means of finding or providing support. Ramona did not know what arrangements, if any, Papa Jack would have made. This is just like him. I was really pissed, but Caroline said that my father was really my greatest teacher. She asked me what was more important, for Fawn to have a loving home, or for us to have a new blue Lexus SUV?

Caroline knows how to put things in perspective. She instantly accepted Fawn into the family. She did this without thinking. It was almost a reflex action. I can't be as accepting as she is.

The child is a blessing, but I wanted some closure to all my questions about why Papa Jack did what he did and acted the way he acted. Why did he choose me for the assignment of raising a three-year-old, when I have two siblings who are females? I'll probably never know what he was thinking.

There is still one piece of the puzzle remaining. What's at Pacific Fidelity Funds? Tomorrow morning we will find out. I called their office and set up an appointment for eleven a.m. Tonight we are getting to know Fawn. She is just like Sara Ann, smart and savvy. She is the same height as Sara Ann and slightly pudgy. The two are now getting along fine. As a matter of fact, Sara Ann is teaching Fawn about dirty tricks. We found seaweed and some clamshells in our bed, and the two of them laughed. Great, we will be raising a kiddie Mafia. The two of them are going to be impossible to handle. Poor Woo Woo looked at me again and then looked straight up in the air. Two sets of five woos later he made his point. He was trying to tell me he would do the best he could.

Caroline has more in reserve tonight than I do. She's playing with the girls and the dogs while I'm crashing in bed. My God, the girls and the dogs. I don't feel like listening to Shorty Jones. I'm not in the mood. I'm so tired I know that if I try to read a book, I will fall asleep after the first few pages. I'll read a short essay or poem and call it a night.

I found one that's apropos. In my journey across America I've noticed the extremes of people's behavior. I've walked through snow and on burning hot asphalt. My own feelings have likewise run the gamut from joy to anger and back. This Edward Randall essay nails it.

Children of Fire and Ice

July is trapped by June and August. You are hot, baby. You are hot going in and you are hot coming out. The only relief we can hope for is a Northern breeze from Canada or a couple of rain showers.

January is trapped by December and February. You are cold, baby. You are cold going in and you are cold coming out. The only relief we can hope for is a Southern breeze from Carolina or an early one-day thaw.

We are walking through both extremes at once. We have one foot in July and one foot in January. It is necessary for us to do this for the rest of our bodies to be at the right temperature. We long for those rare and wondrous days where it is cool in the shade and warm in the sun, dry with a blue sky, and too early or late in the season for mosquitoes to bite. The joy produced within us on those days is so high because we know where our feet are placed.

The same is true for our season of humanity.

Hate is trapped by evil, avarice, and its own continuation in time. Nothing can break the spell, not even a stray ray of light that is merely absorbed by dark surfaces.

Good is captured by love and happiness and its own continuation in time. Nothing can break the spell, not even a dark corner that is merely bathed in sunlight.

We always have one foot in each place. Smooth would not be smooth without rough. Cold would not be cold without hot to define it. Hate would not hurt so much if we had never been loved.

All things quiet or set in motion and existing in time are the children of fire and ice. Heaven and hell are the ultimate repositories where life creates death and death creates life. There is a final sorting out.

Heaven is our reward. Heaven is the I-told-you-so of our moral statements, and for changing that flat tire on the senior citizen's car even though it made us late for work. Heaven is our life-spirit held to its highest. There is no more up than heaven. This is as high as we can go. But we can look down. Ultimately we have to look down and follow the path of the fallen angels.

There, we rot in hell made by all the horrible things we have done in our lives. But our evil will fertilize the soil on the Plains of Abraham. The fire and brimstone that will perpetually cleanse our spirits is the sun that will provide joy, and the wrong turns we have taken in our lives will be the corpses that will nurture infant flowers to propagate the universe.

The cycle is repeated. These flowers are innocent and grow until we see and understand evil. Then it is experienced and we wither and die.

Then, on a rare and wondrous day, we rise again.

We got a call ten minutes ago from Jonathan. He is now standing in our hotel room and has just met my family. He didn't tell me he was coming to Aberdeen, and we're totally delighted to see him. We introduced him to Fawn, and told him all about her history. He's as perplexed as we are. He said somehow Papa Jack knew that I would find a woman like Caroline. None of the five of us are married yet, although Margo and Tom are officially engaged.

He had dozens of questions about the trip. He said I had lost weight but looked very fit and strong. We told him Caroline is pregnant, so in a very loud voice that could probably be heard by everyone in the hotel he asks, "Well, are you or aren't you getting married?" Sara Ann and Fawn chimed in like a Greek chorus and echoed Jonathan, "Are you or aren't you getting married?" Then Sara Ann said she needed a new daddy. Fawn said, "Me too." You can see how this relationship is going to go. He took me aside and said I was the luckiest person he's ever known. He was so happy for us.

He got a room just down the hall from us. Now it's ten o'clock. We debated whether or not to bring the children with us to see the lawyer, because our experience tells us that these solicitors can be extremely stuffy at best.

I'm going to be a pushover of a father. I took one look at Sara Ann; she must have heard our conversation. I could tell she was ready for me to say that Jonathan and I would go. I swear she had her response all planned. I couldn't say, stay here. The words wouldn't come out. That means that two children and two dogs will descend on Pacific Fidelity Funds. Perhaps we can leave the dogs in the camper. Sara Ann and Fawn won't like that, they will whine and get their way, so I'm resigned to being like a mother duck. As you know, a mother duck doesn't swim anywhere unless all her chicks are riding on her back. After a while, when they get old enough, they swim right behind her. Everywhere she goes, they go, until they are finally on their own. In human terms, that can be a very long time.

You are not going to believe who we met at Pacific Fidelity. My mother, Margo, and Tom Cleary. We all arrived at the same time. Explanations and greetings were being exchanged rapid fire from us to them to us. We sounded like those announcers who speed-read the commercials. When we all walked into the office of George Bramwell, Solicitor, guess who was sitting there waiting for us. You got it: Seth and Jennifer.

This reminded me of an Agatha Christie novel where all the major suspects are brought together at the end of the story, in the parlor of some mansion, awaiting the verdict of the detective. I was waiting for an apology from those two troublemakers and received none. I glared at both of them and was about to speak when Caroline grabbed my hand and said one word, "Later."

Bramwell was so typical. He wore a navy-blue pinstriped suit with a white handkerchief folded neatly in his pocket. I didn't bring my tape recorder, so I'm remembering this as best as I can. He asked me if I had any information for him. I responded that I thought he would have information for us on Papa Jack's accounts, estate, or whatever was in question here. He said his information was conditional on my giving *him* a vital piece of information. I nearly lost it. Here we go again with another double-talking lawyer who is playing verbal games with me. I kept my cool, and I'm glad I did.

He asked our newly adopted daughter if her name was Fawn, and she said yes. Then he said, "Good, she is the key." By this time I was going more bonkers than our dog. Bramwell was cool. He asked if there was anything in the material that Papa Jack left with Ramona Campbell that would reference this account. I said no, and he asked if Papa Jack gave anything else to Fawn. I said no again, but Fawn held up her pendant. He asked to see the pendant and then smiled. He showed me the back. Engraved there was a serial number: 5748-9683-2471. He said this was the number he needed to access the funds. Papa Jack constructed such a convoluted estate deposition that not even the attorney of record, George Bramwell, could access the information without this number. He put it into the Pacific Fidelity's master computer and it instantly gave him the codes he needed to process the account.

I said out loud, "George, you're a genius. Holy shit, what if she had lost the pendant?"

There was a letter from Papa Jack to me. Bramwell printed it out, and I folded it and put it in my pocket to be read later. He then read from my father's disbursement instructions. I got a copy of it, so I've reproduced it exactly. Jennifer was right; there was mention of a vote. He gave his vote for Hall Digital Networks to me. Margo threw her arms around me, and said, "Thank God!" My mother was crying, Caroline was crying, and because Caroline was crying, Sara Ann was crying, and since Sara Ann was crying, Fawn was crying.

The total value of his estate after taxes is one hundred and twenty-five million dollars. Papa Jack suggested that twenty-five million of it be put back into his old company for future research and development. He said the decision would be mine. I immediately said it was a go. Tom Cleary pumped his fist and said a loud yes. Papa Jack left Jonathan, Margo, Seth, and Jennifer eight million dollars each in cash. He left me ten million dollars to make up for the two million he already gave to the others. He left my mother an additional twenty-five million over and above the trust funds she already has. The remaining twenty-four million will be shared by all the people who our ancestors met on their journeys.

George Bramwell said this was so highly unusual because when a will or estate settlement is read, all those who have inherited something are usually present or have been notified by mail. He couldn't do that in this case, since he couldn't confirm the people involved until this moment. One thing is for sure, the Dobbs family, the Campbells, the Jeffersons, and all the other wonderful people I met are now millionaires. The Campbell family got three million dollars, and they deserve every penny.

Papa Jack left me something else. It was in a separate document and again Bramwell was reading it. The heading was, "Since you are a very special person, with qualities and talents that few people could ever hope to have, I bequeath to you the following property. I know you better than you think I do. I know the state that you probably liked the best in your travels, and bought you this property there. If I'm wrong, you can always sell it."

Bramwell read that he had left me a five-thousand acre ranch, not unlike Colin Cleary's, in Montana. When he read that, I started crying.

I still don't know why he was so rough on me.

EPILOGUE

There are many websites that review products. There is a musicians' site that I often access called Harmony Central. They have user reviews of guitars and amplifiers. I always check the site before I buy an instrument, and I've written some reviews myself. If you want to buy a vacuum cleaner, a car, a new sound system, or a lawn mower, there are user reviews available online that are very honest and helpful. Most reviewers wait until they have tried the product for a long enough time before they pass judgment.

I'm writing this exactly one year after my marriage to Caroline, which occurred on December 11. We got married in a joint ceremony with Margo and Tom. Don't get me wrong, I'm not implying that Caroline is a product who has been tested for a year. I just wanted to let some time go by before I tied up loose ends for you, my reader. After all, you paid good money for this book, and you deserve to know how things got sorted out. Did you notice that I've already used two clichés: *tied up loose ends*, and *things got sorted out*. I haven't written for a while since I finished my memoir.

I gave total control of my father's company to Tom and Margo. I put this in writing. They will do the right thing. I have made a CD of new music that I wrote and produced it in my recording studio. My neighbor called me up to complain about the noise, and I apologized. Now I have to soundproof the room. He's two miles away as the crow flies (third cliché), but it's so quiet here that I can hear his dogs barking, so I know how he feels. We kept the sprawling ranch in

Montana and live there for months at a time. We bought the same camper we rented in Spokane and use it to drive back and forth between Vermont and Montana.

Caroline sold the house in Nappanee to her housemates. Actually, she practically gave it to them. She loves Lake Champlain. We bought a house on North Hero Island on the lake, and Jonathan bought the three-story house where I used to have the apartment. He uses the first two floors and the top floor is now a library and meditation center that we share.

We have a baby girl. Her name is Adele. No, I didn't pick the name, Caroline did. When we travel back and forth from Montana to Vermont, we always stay with the Dobbs family. Adele can work her magic on any caring person. I have a house full of females, except for Woo Woo. Although we live on the lake, he still won't go in the water. He grins and looks up in the air when the girls torment him.

Fawn and Sara Ann are, well, sisters. They are great together, and they love to play tricks on us. They continue the putting-things-in-our-bed trick that Sara Ann started with the snake. Every night before we go to sleep, we have to examine under the covers. You'd never believe what they put in our bed last week. They gathered pine cones, pine needles, and twigs and threw them under the sheets. There were little red bugs hiding in the pine cones, and we had to strip the entire bed and vacuum the mattress. I became a strict disciplinarian. I told them that from now on, they could only play the trick on Wednesday. On Friday there was another surprise under the sheet. They made drawings for each of us with their crayons that said "I love you." I couldn't yell at them. I'm outmatched and outwitted.

I don't see Jennifer or Seth. They got what they wanted. The next time I'll have contact with them is when my mother dies. They will no doubt be maneuvering to get as much from her as possible. There are two sets of family gatherings. When Margo, Tom, Jonathan, Caroline, and I are at my mother's mansion, Jennifer and Seth are not, and visa-versa. You could officially call this a family feud. In time it may change, but I'll have to be the one who tries for rapprochement.

We are starting a treatment center for autistic children. Jonathan is majoring in Pediatrics and is acting as a consultant. Caroline already is a specialist in speech therapy, and is going to run the center. We've found a great building in Essex, with convenient parking. We're going to hire the best staff available. Our goal is to have the highest-rated treatment center in New England. We agreed to put millions of dollars into the project. My mother liked the idea and hinted that she would also back us. That's only just happened, so I can't tell you the outcome.

A big change in my life is that I no longer have to worry about where the money for next month's rent is coming from. So far I haven't gotten my books published, although last month I found a good literary agent.

I said that I would tell you why I split up with Joan. It was nothing really dramatic, such as one of us was caught having sex with a stranger, or she really was a lesbian and ran off with the meter maid. Joan loved the *idea* of marriage. You should have seen the size of our wedding. The preparations took months and involved every member of two complete families. She had one hundred and forty-nine bridesmaids, and seven hundred and thirteen ladies in attendance. Well, it seemed like that many. Her gown cost more than a new Lexus, and the train was so long it stretched out the church, all the way to Miami, you get the idea.

Before we were married, she purred, and was very sexy. Our families were loving and gave us everything. We made love four times before we were married and she acted like a wild woman. She drove me crazy. About a week after we were married, she totally withdrew. She ran home to visit her mother at every opportunity, slept on our fold-out couch, and five times a week attended yoga classes. I asked her what was wrong and, with a look of total disgust she said, "I didn't realize that you would be around all the time, and I hate having sex with you."

I will admit that these were the single most devastating words anyone has ever spoken to me. We had sex only twice in the time we were married, I felt like she was performing an unwanted act at great sacrifice. I still don't know why she changed so completely. I cried for a week afterward. It was a long time before I could get close to another female. Not until I met Caroline. I couldn't talk about it until now. It took years of therapy before I realized that there was really nothing wrong with me.

Joan had an incredible body, and it was lust at first sight for me. The families were like the top of a huge funnel swirling us around and directing us toward the narrow opening of marriage. I should have examined more closely whether or not she was sincere. I took everything for

295

granted. I thought she would be my mate and adjust to married life. Then she started finding fault with everything I did, and on a snowy Tuesday evening, I got a call from her mother saying that Joan wanted a divorce. I could hear her in the background crying. It was that forced crying that babies do when they don't get their way. My bad. If I may paraphrase Helen Keller, none are so blind as those who should have seen.

So what else can I report to you? We bought a new Nissan Leaf, a completely electric car that will go 100 miles without recharging. I love to sit on our deck and look out at the water. I'm writing poetry and am working on a play. I'll tell you right now that none of the projects I'm involved in will satisfy me for long. Caroline has the autistic treatment center, and I'm helping to get that started. The ghost of Albert Schweitzer has visited me. Living from day to day, doing anything that I want, will ultimately not work for me. I need to have a calling, but I just don't know what it will be.

My walk across America left me a rich man, and money is the least of it. I have some information to share with you. When the family was gathered before George Bramwell, the attorney in Aberdeen, he read from my father's will. He also handed me a letter that I stuffed in my shirt pocket. Before I comment on it, I'll print the entire, unedited contents.

"Congratulations, David. If you are reading this letter, you must have successfully crossed the United States. Before you read any further, you must promise not to share what I have written with anyone else in the family. If that is not acceptable, tear this letter up now and don't continue. At various times in my life I have given similar letters to your brothers and sisters. They all have different messages, but I did not request that they keep secret the contents of their letters. A family is as sick as its secrets, but I have always had an approach-avoidance mechanism alive in me that vacillated between the two extremes of disclosure and self-protection. Most of the time, I admit that I was closed and withholding. You may or may not like my request that my letter to you not be shared, but since you are reading these words you've agreed to our bargain. If you back out of it, I will haunt you forevermore.

"I have always had trouble displaying emotions. Shit, I even have trouble writing down my feelings. This is the kind of man I am, or should I say, I was, because when you read this, I'm off in never-never land.

"I went into a restaurant, alone on one of my business trips, and I was served by a young woman who was very pleasant, but new on the job. She was a very good waitress, but I gave her a hard time. I sent the food back twice, complained about the dessert, and how long it took the cashier to bring me the check. She kept her composure. The meal cost me thirty-seven dollars and I left her a two-hundred dollar tip. You can go ahead and check with that lame-brained psychiatrist you used to see, and ask him what my behavior means. I really don't give a shit. Whenever I thought a person was doing a good job, I was afraid to tell them, because I thought they would stop doing a good job.

"Do you remember when I hit you with my pastry at the family dinner? You told me you wanted to write books after I tried to get you interested in Hall Digital Networks. Do you know that I was actually delighted that you were answering your own call? You might want to mention that to your psychiatrist as well. He will probably tell you I was a sadist, or a masochist, or even worse, a closet Republican.

"Your mother used to volunteer for the Flynn Center for the Performing Arts. She was on all the committees like the fund-raisers, production, publicity, that sort of thing. Did you ever hear of the jazz musician Thaddeus Wilson? He was a trumpet player. He played every year at the Discover Jazz Festival, and one year your mother was in charge of making all the arrangements for his band's visit to Burlington. It turned out that she and Thaddeus Wilson had a brief affair. He was in town for a week. Your mother used to be a very attractive woman, still is I suppose, and she is human. Nine months later, you were born. She didn't tell me until after your birth, because you could have been mine.

"There isn't any mixed blood in her family. That is a myth we created to protect her from anyone knowing of her indiscretion. Your father, Thaddeus Wilson, was about fifty when he met your mother. He died four years ago. His band is still together and still uses his name. I would always leave town during the Jazz Festival because I didn't want to be reminded. You can't blame me for that. I tried not to take it out on you. I guess that's why I was equally surly to all my kids. Number one, that is, or should I say was, my nature. I'm sour, and I don't relate to people, up close and personal, the way that you do.

Don't mention this to your mother. She may suspect that I wrote the truth of your birth to you, but if she hints around,

I suggest that you deny it. She will handle your knowing very badly. This is a lot to ask, but give it a try.

"If any of the other four were not really my children, I never would have told them. They couldn't have handled it either. You are going to feel many emotions. The first thing you will do is curse at the top of your lungs and blame me for not telling you earlier, especially when your father was still alive. Then, when you calm down, you will see, as I do, that the only time you should have known, or could have been told, is now. When you were younger, your own very fiery nature would have caused problems, and you probably would have damaged yourself. Please don't think badly of your mother. She's always done the best she could. One mistake doesn't condemn a person, not that you are a mistake. I forgave her long ago.

"I'm proud of you, Jonathan, and Margo. I'll bet that Tom Cleary and Margo get together. I saw the way he was looking at her at our last company Christmas party. You now have enough money to do whatever you want, but I suggest that you keep writing. Perhaps you could revisit all the people on your journey. It's okay not to walk this time. Make the book about them and not about you.

"Seth and Jennifer need work. It's hard to raise kids when you and they have so much money. You and Margo are both very stubborn. Jonathan has a kind nature. He will make a wonderful doctor. You would also make a great physician. Give that some thought. But if you ever decide to become a corporate lawyer, I will find a way to come back to earth, and I'll make sure that you are miserable.

"I haven't done much praying in my life. I have a feeling that my time is getting close. Shit, at my age, any time is getting close. I have tailored my prayers for each one of you. I do not have one generic prayer for my entire family. For you, I asked God to show you America the way it was, to somehow give you a glimpse of what we saw. I wanted you to find some of the same places and people we visited on our journeys. I thought this might help you decide what you want America to look like tomorrow. Someday soon, you will be an instrument for change. You may run for office. I hope so. I feel strongly that you will be an important man in American history. You are blessed with a big-picture view, even if it is somewhat naïve.

"The people I met on my journey across America were treated no differently than I treated most others I've encountered. I wasn't surly, because after all, I was accepting their hospitality. I wasn't Saint Jack either. In the years following my trip, they were shocked when I helped them out of jams, and looked after their families. To tell you the truth, so was I. I guess I found it easier to display emotions to someone in Washington or Montana, than to my own family here at home. Your shrink could probably tell you why.

"What do you think of your grandfather and Raven John? I'll bet you didn't expect to adopt that cute little girl. Don't worry, you'll find the right woman for you, and the child won't prevent a good relationship from forming. I'll bet you go back to school and marry a young graduate student. Have a good life.

Love,
Papa Jack

Whoa! He was certainly wrong about that. I wish he could have met Caroline. So, Papa Jack prayed that I would see America the way he and my ancestors saw it. I didn't know he had such influence with the Almighty. I still don't know how it happened. All the photos I took from my time travels vanished from my camera and my computer. Thank God, Caroline also saw them, or I would seriously question my sanity. Perhaps we're both delusional.

He was also wrong about something else. My next book will not be about the people I met on my journey. It will be called *Papa Jack*. I will write about the old bastard, stuff the manuscript in the bottom drawer of my roll-top desk, and publish it when my mother dies.

Joe Randazzo has traveled extensively and writes about what he sees. He believes in the heroism of the ordinary working person, the transformative power of love, and the rejuvenating effects of a truly fine pizza. He is the author of six previous books. His artwork has been exhibited at many venues throughout New England including Castleton State College, T. W. Wood Art Gallery, and the Helen Day Art Center. He lives with his wife Rita in South Burlington, Vermont.